DAUFUSKIE ISLAND

WHAT ELSE
WOULD THIS
BE? BEST
WISHES!!!
JOHN

DAUFUSKIE ISLAND

JOHN LUEDER

MOUNTAIN ARBOR
PRESS

Alpharetta, GA

This novel is a work of fiction, except for the parts that are real.

Copyright © 2016 by John Lueder

ISBN: 978-1-63183-031-0
Library of Congress Control Number: 2016943498

10 9 8 7 6 5 4 3 2   0 8 1 2 1 6

Printed in the United States of America

♾This paper meets the requirements of ANSI/NISO Z39.48-1992 (Permanence of Paper)

To Lara, Camille, Brigitte, Tom, and Faith.

INTRODUCTION

DAUFUSKIE ISLAND.

Maybe you've heard of it.

If you've been to Hilton Head Island off the South Carolina coast and looked out across the water from Harbour Town, you probably saw Daufuskie a mile away.

Maybe you didn't notice it in the distance. You wouldn't be the first. Most people vacationing on Hilton Head have no idea Daufuskie Island even exists.

Getting there may take some planning.

That's because unlike most other inhabited islands along the Atlantic coast, Daufuskie Island doesn't have a bridge. No airport, either. As a result, the island's deserted beaches, dunes, sea oats, tidal marshes, palm trees, and massive live oaks draped with Spanish moss remain to this day largely unknown to the rest of the world. And truth be told, most of Daufuskie's scant population of only 350 year-round and part-time residents prefer their island to remain an undiscovered treasure.

If you want to visit Daufuskie, you'll need to take a boat. One of the island's few ferries will do. There's a public ferry across the Calibogue Sound to Freeport Marina that the random visitors from Hilton Head usually take. The private ferries to Haig Point and Bloody Point might be an option too if you know the right people in those secluded communities.

However you get there, you'll notice it's a relatively small island at only five miles long from tip to tip and a little over two miles wide. You might see a stray car or truck here and there, but golf carts are the most common form of transportation.

You'll also notice that the majority of the island's few roads are a gritty mix of sand and dirt. There's not a single traffic light on the entire island. This adds to the charm and laid-back living generally known as Daufuskie time, as if all the island's residents collectively agreed long ago that being in a hurry would not be permitted on their Lowcountry paradise.

Some of the residents you find might be Gullah, the descendants of freed slaves who worked the island's pre-Civil War plantations. Gullah communities were once common on the sea islands of South Carolina and Georgia when the geographic isolation of the Lowcountry islands preserved their culture. But nowadays, most of the islands have bridges, and most of the Gullah have moved on.

Daufuskie too has seen its share of Gullah descendants resettle elsewhere on the mainland. Across the water, as they say.

But some of the Gullah families are still there. The old twins, Evelyn and Philomena Mills, turned ninety-two last winter. The faithful at the island's only church, the First

African Baptist Church, can still hear them singing songs of praise most Sunday mornings. There's Michael Burris too. He's getting up in his years like the Mills twins, but on a few Saturday mornings each month, you'll find him down by the public boat launch selling crab cakes—made from his great-granddaddy's recipe, he'll be apt to tell you. He only brings about two dozen these days, and he's usually sold out by noon.

You'll find the island pretty much the same as it's been for quite some time. Eerily quiet and largely forgotten.

If you're on the island when the sun begins to set, you might see a ghost. That sometimes happens. And if you were on Daufuskie at the beginning of last summer, after that big storm, you might even swear you saw a girl flying.

CHAPTER 1

THE STAIRS AT THE BEACH HOUSE STARTED CREAKING A FEW years ago. Evan couldn't remember whether it was the sixth or seventh step that made the sound. The kids had told him after they'd run up and down the stairway one rainy afternoon when there was nothing better to do. They knew the exact spot on the exact board that produced the best result.

Evan climbed the stairs this morning without counting steps, and there it was. Creak.

"Daddy?" Will called from his upstairs bedroom.

Like his father, Will was a morning person. Evan figured his seven-year-old son would likely be awake at this early hour as he went upstairs to check on his three children. Sure enough, Will was on his bed playing with a model of a Coast Guard helicopter.

"Good morning, big man," Evan said. "I'm leaving in a few minutes and wanted to see you before I go. I'll be back on Thursday."

"I don't want you to go."

"I'll be back before you know it. We'll go fishing on Friday. Sound good?"

"Can't you stay the whole week?"

"No, buddy, I have to go to work today. I'll see you on Thursday."

"And we'll go fishing?" Will asked.

"The day after I get back."

"Just you and me?"

"And the girls too if they want to go."

Will wrapped his arms around his daddy's neck. "I love you." He pulled close to his father.

"I love you too." Evan gave him a bear hug and kissed his forehead. "Be good to your sisters. I'll see you in a few days."

He left Will's room and checked on his daughters.

Unlike their brother, Katie and Abby were not morning people. They were both sound asleep in their rooms.

Evan headed down the stairs and into the kitchen, where Caris had a cup of coffee waiting for him.

"Thanks, hun," he said to his wife. "Don't forget the bug man is coming tomorrow morning at nine to spray."

"I have it on my calendar. The girls still asleep?"

"Yeah, they're both out. I didn't want to wake them. Will's awake."

Evan took a sip of his coffee.

"Drive safely. Call me when you get home," Caris said.

"I'm not going right home. I'm heading to the office first. I'll change clothes there. Or maybe I'll wear shorts to work." He gestured with his hand, modeling his olive shorts, faded orange T-shirt, and flip-flops. "Gotta love casual Mondays."

By leaving now, Evan would be in his office in Atlanta by lunch, even taking into account his thirty-minute boat ride to Savannah and the four-hour drive from there. He'd made the same trip countless times. It was their Monday morning, summer routine. The same as it'd been for the past several summers. Caris and the kids would spend most of the summer at their beach house on Daufuskie Island, while Evan would commute back and forth to Atlanta at the beginning and end of each week.

With his coffee in hand, he went into the attached garage and down a short flight of steps to where their two golf carts were parked. One was a lifted, black six-seater with large knobby tires. Evan got onto the smaller, light blue cart next to it, pressed the remote to open the garage door, and drove out into the early morning. The start of another beautiful day.

He was soon at the Haig Point community dock less than a quarter mile away, where he parked in the large wooden cart barn, finished his coffee, and walked onto the dock where his boat was tied. His eighteen-foot boat was perfect for fishing in the Calibogue Sound and Intracoastal Waterway that surrounded most of the island. He looked forward to taking Will fishing on Friday. Katie and Abby, too, if they wanted to go. They probably would.

He untied his boat and pushed off from the dock. The sun was rising over the horizon of the Atlantic, and he squinted while the morning sunshine danced on the glistening Calibogue Sound.

His weekly boat trip took him through the heart of the South Carolina and Georgia Lowcountry. The expansive fields of marsh grass that lined the Intracoastal Waterway were vibrant green, almost neon, and stretched for miles against the contrast of the dark blue water of early morning. Evan thought this must be one of the most peaceful places on the planet.

The sun continued to rise and was shining brightly by the time he reached the marina in Savannah where he rented a boat slip and kept his car. Pulling out of the marina's parking lot ten minutes later and turning onto the expressway to bypass historic downtown Savannah, Evan tuned the radio to the local news.

The first tropical storm of the season was making its way across the Atlantic. Its projected path would bring it through the warm waters of the Caribbean, where it was expected to strengthen before making landfall late Wednesday night near Miami—about five hundred miles south of Daufuskie Island.

Evan knew that storms hitting southern Florida usually caused strong winds and isolated thunderstorms in the Lowcountry. With the storm forecast to hit Miami on Wednesday night, he wondered if he'd be able to take the kids fishing on Friday after all. He'd see how the weather was after getting back on Thursday. He could have no idea that the storm was going to change all of their lives forever.

Thursday came, and Caris was awake well before sunup. She hadn't been able to sleep due to heavy rain and wind throughout the night. The day before had been gusty, which was not uncommon for an island facing the ocean. The rain began shortly before she and the kids had gone to bed and picked up after midnight.

Caris had not checked the weather in days and decided to turn on the morning news, hoping to catch a weather report. Flipping through the channels, she stopped when she saw a reporter standing in the rain on a beach. He was wearing shorts and a yellow rain poncho that blew against his chest. With rain and wind gusting into the microphone, Caris heard him say, "I'm at Palmetto Dunes Beach on Hilton Head Island where the eye of Hurricane Arlene is expected to pass."

Surprised at the news, she watched for another few minutes. Hurricane Arlene was still over two hundred miles offshore, now moving toward the coast at fifteen to twenty miles per hour. It was not expected to make landfall until late in the evening.

She turned off the television.

The western side of Daufuskie faced the open Atlantic, and if a hurricane was on its way, she wanted to leave the island as soon as possible.

Will came down the stairs from his bedroom rubbing sleep from his eyes. He joined his mother in the living room.

"Go wake up Katie and Abby," Caris said.

"I'm already awake," she heard Katie say, as her oldest daughter came down the steps. "The rain kept me up."

"Okay, one of you go back upstairs and get Abby. We need to head to the ferry. There's a big storm coming, and we're going home. We'll come back in a few days."

Caris looked for her purse while Will went upstairs to wake his sister. Caris could hear Abby moaning at Will to leave her alone.

"Abby, we need to go," Caris called up from the bottom of the stairway.

A few minutes later, the four of them wearing rain jackets climbed onto their large, black golf cart and headed toward the Haig Point ferry dock. They had plenty of time to make the 7:40 a.m. departure.

As they made their way, rain blew diagonally and drenched Caris and the kids. The golf cart's cover provided almost no protection, and the fabric valance along the top flapped wildly in the wind, soaking them further.

Caris pulled into the wooden cart barn and parked two spots from where Evan had parked their blue golf cart earlier in the week. His empty coffee cup was on the passenger seat.

They ran out of the cart barn through the downpour to make it to the dock in time for the ferry. Caris was surprised to discover that it was not already tied to the end of the dock waiting for passengers.

"It must be running late," she said.

Instead of standing in the rain to wait, Caris and the kids went into the nearby welcome center. The ferries were almost always on time, but with the current bad weather, Caris could understand the delay.

Inside the welcome center, Caris's friend, Natalie Larkin, sat at a large wooden desk in a corner. Natalie was Gullah and lived full-time on the island. She was about fifty, although Caris would never dream of asking her friend her age.

"Good morning," Natalie said. She spoke with a slight Gullah accent that sounded almost Creole.

"Good morning, Natalie," Caris replied. "Is the ferry almost here?"

"I have some bad news, Caris. The ferries aren't running today."

Well before sunrise, the storm's forward rain bands had stretched ahead for hundreds of miles. By 5:30 a.m., wind gusts had reached over fifty-five miles per hour. Ferries operating in those conditions weren't safe because the strong winds caused them to crash into the docks when they approached to load and unload passengers. All ferry service to and from Daufuskie Island had been suspended before passengers for Haig Point's first scheduled run would otherwise embark at 6:30 a.m.

Caris stood there processing what Natalie had said. *I have some bad news, Caris. The ferries aren't running today.*

"The storm's taken a lot of folks by surprise," Natalie continued. "It was supposed to be down in Florida last night. The public ferry to Freeport Marina isn't running. Neither is the Bloody Point ferry."

"Wait a minute," Caris said. "If the ferries aren't running, then how are we getting off the island?"

"That's what I'm saying to you," Natalie responded. "You're not."

Chapter 2

EVAN WORKED THROUGH THE WEEK AND LOOKED FORWARD to seeing his family. He decided to surprise Caris and the kids by leaving Atlanta early Thursday morning and arriving back at the beach house for lunch. On his way through Macon, a little more than a third of the way to where his boat was docked in Savannah, he encountered the first drops of rain and turned on the windshield wipers. The rain increased to a downpour a few minutes later.

His cell phone rang. It was Caris.

The constant sound of the rain battering the roof of the car made it difficult to hear. His windshield wipers on full speed added to the noise. She was at the welcome center with the kids, and he wasn't sure if he was hearing her correctly.

"Did you say a hurricane?" he asked.

Caris told him the few details she learned from Natalie and the television reporter. Natalie had said that the island's ferries were now anchored miles away in a protected stretch of the May River to ride out the storm. The reporter had said that instead of making landfall near Miami, the storm had spun easterly back out to sea, where it unexpectedly

9

strengthened into a Category 1 hurricane overnight before changing course to the northwest, putting Savannah and Hilton Head directly into its path. That meant Daufuskie Island too.

"I think I should be able to make it over in the boat when I get to Savannah and get you and the kids," Evan said.

"I've been on the ferry dock," Caris responded. "Trust me. That's not a good idea. Some of the waves I've already seen could capsize your boat, and you're still hours away. It's going to get a lot worse by the time you get to Savannah."

"If I can make it, I will."

"Honey, the waves are crazy big. I don't want the kids in the boat. I don't want you in the boat either."

"Is it really that bad?"

"Evan, are you not listening to me? It's a hurricane. Yeah, the waves are that bad."

"But I thought you said the hurricane's not supposed to arrive until later this evening."

"That's what the reporter said. I don't know how bad it's going to get, but it's already bad. Promise me that you won't try to come over in the boat."

He could hear the growing anxiety in her voice. He wouldn't risk the safety of the kids. "I promise," he assured her.

"I love you," Caris said. "I'm going to get the kids back to the house."

"Okay, I love you too. I'll call you when I get to Savannah."

He ended the call and flipped through radio stations until he found news of the hurricane. Why hadn't he followed the news of the storm after he'd left Savannah earlier in the week? He was not with his family, and it bothered him deeply. He felt he had let them down. He cautiously increased his speed toward Savannah trying to come up with a way to get his family off the island.

Natalie had been through a lifetime of storms on Daufuskie. They didn't drive her from her home or from the island. She planned to stay at the welcome center for the next few hours to let other would-be passengers know that the ferries weren't running.

"You'll be *fine*," she said to Caris and the kids. The way Natalie had pronounced *fine* with her Gullah accent was strangely comforting to Caris. They wished each other well before Caris and the children ran back through the rain to the cart barn.

They were soon at the beach house hanging their soaking rain jackets on hooks in the garage. The rain had increased steadily during the short time they'd been gone.

"Why's the hurricane named Arlene?" Will asked.

"I don't know," Caris answered.

"Does Daddy know?"

"I don't know. He might."

"I know," Katie said. "We learned about hurricanes last year. They start out as tropical storms and have people names. They're named in alphabetical order. This one's named Arlene because it's the first big storm of the year. It has to start with an A. The next one will start with a B and might be called Brigitte or something like that."

"And the one after that could be Cinderella or Camille and the next one Dracula," Abby interrupted.

Abby had turned nine two months ago. She was the true middle child—two years younger than Katie and two years older than Will.

"Dracula," Will repeated. "Would there really be a hurricane named Dracula?"

"Of course there would," Abby insisted, "and it'd only come at night when you're sleeping and suck your blood."

Caris knew that Will was terrified of vampires after he had asked his Uncle Mike if they were real, and his uncle had said they were. Evan's brother had been joking, of course, but seven-year-old children do not always understand when adults are teasing.

"Mom, is that true? Can a storm suck my blood?"

"No, it won't," Caris said. "There aren't any storms named Dracula either, and there are no vampires. Abby, quit trying to scare your brother."

Caris had enough fear of her own. She did not want to be stranded on the island with a hurricane on its way. A bolt of lightning lit up the living room. The instant thunderclap made all three kids jump.

"I'm scared," Will mumbled. He began to cry.

"Me too," Katie and Abby said in unison.

"We'll be okay," Caris assured them.

She pulled Will to her and ran her fingers through his blond hair. The early June sun had already lightened his hair considerably. She looked at her two daughters and smiled. Caris needed to be calm and maintain a positive appearance for her children, but on the inside, she thought, me too. I'm as scared as you.

She held Will in her arms, wiped away his tears, and put a comforting hand onto Abby's shoulder. "Guys, we'll be okay. We've been through storms before in this house. Everything's going to be *fine*. Just like Natalie said."

"But never a hurricane before," Katie said. "What if Miss Natalie's wrong? How do you know we'll be okay?"

"Because of the lighthouse," Caris answered thoughtfully.

"The lighthouse?" Katie asked.

"Yeah, the lighthouse. It's been standing for about a hundred and fifty years right at the water. It's been through countless storms."

The lighthouse was at the far end of a large field about two hundred yards down the road from their beach house.

"If that little lighthouse can survive storms for a century and a half, we'll be okay too." Caris added.

"Then can we spend the night in the lighthouse?" Abby asked.

"I don't want to go to the lighthouse," Will protested. "It's haunted."

"We're staying put right here," Caris said. "We'll be *fine*."

Throughout the day, the storm grew worse. Much worse than Caris had anticipated. The ever-increasing howl of the wind announced the hurricane's steady approach.

She had spoken with Evan a few minutes earlier. He'd made it to Savannah before the Georgia State Patrol closed the interstate and had discovered that the marina was closed. Although he had hoped to find a boat large enough to get Caris and the kids off the island, he had no success. Evan was talking to her after checking into one of the few hotels still open when Caris's cell phone went dead.

She couldn't get a signal after that. Caris was wondering if the storm had damaged a cell tower when a branch smacked into one of the windows. The thud echoed throughout the house.

"What if the windows break?" Katie questioned. "Will glass fly in and hit us?"

"The windows are impact resistant," Caris answered. "The county requires that for houses built on the islands. They won't shatter."

"What if a tree lands on the roof?" Abby asked.

"Can a tree crush our house?" Will quickly followed.

"Kids, stop asking what if this and what if that? Whatever happens, happens. We'll deal with it together. This is where we're going to be. This is a strong house. We'll be safe."

Natalie's accented *fine* from that morning was no longer comforting. Caris had never heard the wind like this. The moaning sound was constant, filling her with fear.

The beach house was usually well lit in the afternoons with windows on all sides. The same windows were now taking a beating to prevent the unwelcome entry of the storm. Caris could see that the wind had bent some palm trees almost parallel to the ground. The rain was no longer falling diagonally. It too was sideways. The sky grew increasingly darker.

Earlier in the day, their closest neighbor, Jerry Culpepper, had checked on Caris and the kids. Jerry and his wife, Emily, were retired and lived year-round on the island. They too had been to the ferry dock this morning and received the same unwelcome news from Natalie that the ferries weren't running. And they too were not looking forward to riding out the hurricane.

The dilemma that Caris had discussed with Jerry Culpepper was where in the house would be the safest place for her and the kids to sleep, if sleep would at all be possible. The windows were indeed impact resistant with an exceptionally strong polymer between two planes of glass designed to withstand the impact of a two-by-four traveling at ninety miles per hour. Broken windows and flying glass in the house were not Caris's biggest concerns.

Instead, what if the wind tore off the roof, or knocked over one of their tall trees into the upper part of the house? Caris didn't want the kids upstairs. On the other hand, a storm surge from the Calibogue Sound could flood the first floor of the house.

Caris ultimately decided to put all of their bath towels and beach towels onto the hardwood floor in the hall at the bottom of the stairway for cushioning and put sleeping bags on top of the towels. That way, they'd be near the front door and could make it out quickly to the Culpeppers' house if they needed to, or up the stairs to the second floor.

And if the unthinkable happened — both a storm surge that flooded the house and a fallen tree or wind that destroyed the roof — well, she didn't want to think about that. But that exact scenario kept playing itself out in her head, and she became more and more panicked that she'd not be able to protect her children.

"Stay calm," she repeated to herself. "Stay calm. We'll get through this."

As the hours passed, Caris and the kids had a perfect view from the hallway to the living room windows and an almost black sky. A lightning strike hit a nearby tree. The foundation of the house vibrated with the instant boom of the thunder. The lights flickered and went out.

All three kids screamed.

"I'm scared," Abby cried out.

"It's okay. We have flashlights," Caris said with as much assurance as she could muster.

She wanted to close her eyes and have the storm be over. She instead kept her eyes fixed on the wall of windows along the back of the living room hoping they were as impact resistant as their builder had told them years ago.

Cracks of lightning lit up the sky followed instantly by thunder that shook the house. Wind-hurled branches bounced off the windows. They could hear trees cracking and falling outside. The pounding from the rain increased.

"Stay calm. Stay calm," Caris whispered. "Please, Jesus," she prayed, "help us get through this."

CHAPTER 3

AT SOME POINT DURING THE NIGHT, SITTING IN THE HALL-way huddled together, exhaustion and sleep had finally overtaken them. Will was the first awake.

"A helicopter!" he called out. "Do you hear it? It's a helicopter!"

Will was right. It was a helicopter.

The thumping blades of the helicopter soon had them all awake.

Caris stood, stretched, and headed the few feet to the front door, not knowing what to expect when she opened it.

Sunshine flooded into the house.

The large front porch was covered with leaves, pine needles, twigs, branches, and Spanish moss. She walked outside. The children came pouring out to join her.

"Wow," Abby remarked.

It took everyone a few moments to take in the destruction that surrounded them. They all had the same reaction as Abby. "Wow."

Trees were toppled in all directions. Unrecognizable debris covered the front lawn. Dwarf palm trees Evan had planted years earlier that lined the driveway had been stripped of their palm branches. Bare trunks now stood as silent witnesses to the storm.

The helicopter landed about two hundred yards away in the field. It was bright orange. A Coast Guard helicopter.

Caris wondered for a moment what the helicopter was doing there. Two men jumped out. Caris looked ahead to where they were running. The Culpeppers' house. She gasped.

The entire front of the Culpeppers' house was gone. It looked like a two-story dollhouse, the kind with a missing front wall so all of the rooms were exposed. Two large trees had also crashed through the roof.

Caris's immediate concern was for the safety of Jerry and Emily. She wanted to rush to their house, but at the same time, with the destruction she saw, she wanted to shield her children from what she feared she'd find.

"Kids, I want you to stay here. I'll be back in a few minutes."

Caris headed down the few steps of the front porch and was soon in the field. As she approached the Culpeppers' house, she stopped. She didn't make a conscious decision to stop. The devastation and thought that Jerry and Emily could be in there were overwhelming. She willed herself to continue.

As Caris came nearer, she saw a man from the helicopter on the other side of the house helping Emily. Emily had a large bandage wrapped around her head. Caris ran to her.

"Emily, are you okay?"

Her question was met with a dazed look from Emily.

"Where's Jerry?" Caris asked.

"She's going to need several stiches," the man said. "They're lucky to be alive. Her husband is around back. We need to get them to Hilton Head Regional." He walked Emily toward the helicopter.

Caris found Jerry on the ground behind the house with another man from the helicopter. Jerry was wearing shorts, and Caris could see that his leg was broken.

"How are you and the kids?" Jerry managed to say.

"Don't worry about us. We made it through okay. What happened? I just saw Emily."

She knelt beside him.

"We were in the kitchen," Jerry said. "We heard trees coming down into the roof and thought the whole house was going to come down on us, so we hightailed it out the back door. We were headed to your house when that branch came down and hit both of us." Jerry motioned to a large branch a few feet away. "The small end hit Emily in the head and knocked her down. The rest of it landed on my leg. I couldn't move it."

Caris recoiled at the thought of the massive limb hitting her friends.

"I've never been so scared." Jerry started to choke up. "I thought it killed her." He wiped away a tear. "I kept calling to Emily and trying to reach her. She finally came to a little bit ago. She got up and was about to head to your house when we heard the helicopter and started waving our arms like mad."

The pilot had been flying close to the island's northern shore and had seen the couple frantically signaling for help. The helicopter's rescue swimmer, who was also an EMT, and the flight mechanic were able to move the branch off Jerry.

One of them, the man who'd been helping Emily, returned with a collapsible stretcher in his arms. After unfolding it, the two men carefully placed Jerry onto the stretcher.

Caris walked beside Jerry to the waiting aircraft and could see the agony in his face. Jerry was soon aboard with Emily, and the helicopter lifted into the blue sky on its way to Hilton Head Regional Hospital above the now calm waters of the Calibogue Sound.

The kids ran to their mother standing in the field, and the four of them stood in amazement at the site of the Culpeppers' house. Caris wanted to speak with Evan and tried her cell phone. Still no signal.

Katie turned toward the other end of the field. "Look at the lighthouse," she said. "It doesn't look damaged at all."

"Can we go see it?" Abby asked.

"Sure," Caris answered.

"I don't want to go inside," Will said. "It's haunted."

"Oh, honey, it's not haunted," Caris replied.

The lighthouse didn't look like traditional lighthouses with a round tower, nor was it constructed of stone or brick. The St. John family had seen lighthouses like those on their family trips to New England to visit Evan's brother, who had moved to Duxbury, Massachusetts. The Haig Point lighthouse was instead a small, two-story, clapboard-siding house with wooden shingles. A tall rectangular tower for the light was perched on top, and the exterior of the house and tower was painted white with black shutters.

The front of the lighthouse with its covered porch faced the Calibogue Sound. About ten feet from the front porch was a tall flagpole. From where Caris was standing in the field, she was surprised to see that the American flag had survived the storm and was still fastened to its line at the top of the pole, fluttering in the light morning breeze.

Katie and Abby were the first across the field and up the lighthouse's front porch steps. They looked inside.

"It's in perfect shape," Abby yelled back to Caris and Will. "I think the lighthouse is protected by Maggie's ghost. Can we go in? The front door is unlocked."

"We're not going inside, are we?" Will asked his mother, as he gripped her hand.

"No, we're not," Caris said. "And there's no ghost."

As Caris and Will approached the front porch, they passed a historic marker stating that the lighthouse had been operational for nearly half a century from 1873 to 1924. A sentence at the end included that Maggie Comer, the daughter of the first lighthouse keeper, had fallen more than sixty feet to her death from the tower's observation platform.

Maggie's ghost was rumored to still haunt the lighthouse. And Katie and Abby sometimes scared Will with made-up ghost stories.

A few years earlier, when Caris, Evan, and the kids had been inside, one of the doors upstairs had shut by itself.

The air conditioning had kicked on right at that time, causing a rush of air, which explained why the door had shut, but Will was convinced Maggie's ghost had closed the door. He refused to go into the lighthouse after that.

Caris could feel Will's grip on her hand getting tighter as they came closer to the front porch. The storm last night had been enough of a scare for Will. It had been enough of a scare for her too.

"Hey, I have an idea," Caris called to Katie and Abby. "Let's see if the storm washed up anything interesting."

"Oh, yeah, good idea," Will said.

Not far away, there was a stretch of beach where the Calibogue Sound met the Atlantic Ocean. A short walk on the beach was exactly what they needed to unwind. After that, they'd get their golf cart from the house and go to the welcome center to use a phone with a landline to try to reach Evan.

Katie and Abby ran off the porch. Caris and Will caught up, and the four of them were soon passing a row of tabby ruins on the other side of the field. The ruins had been slave quarters built centuries earlier when Haig Point had been a substantial plantation that grew Sea Island cotton. The lighthouse itself had been built on the site of the old plantation mansion.

A few minutes later, and they were on the beach. To Caris's surprise, however, they didn't find much of anything. Instead of the storm washing deposits from the ocean onto the beach, it had washed the beach clean, except for two fresh palm trees with their root balls still attached.

"Why don't they have coconuts on them?" Will asked.

"Maybe the coconuts fell off," Abby said.

"Not all palm trees have coconuts," Katie informed her brother and sister. "None of them on Daufuskie do. Palm trees in the Caribbean and Hawaii have coconuts."

"When can we go to Hawaii?" Will asked his mother. "We've never been there."

"I want to learn how to hula dance," Abby added.

"We'll go someday," Caris said. "Maybe when you're in high school, Abby. I wouldn't plan on that happening before then."

They continued along the beach for a few more minutes hoping to find anything interesting until they reached a narrow sandy trail that led through the dunes and sea oats to a wide path that everyone called the beach road. It was loosely paved with crushed oyster shells and paralleled the beach on one side and tidal salt marshes on the other.

"When's Daddy going to be here?" Will asked.

"I don't know," Caris answered. "Depends on whether his boat or the ferries made it through the storm. Speaking of Daddy, I think it's about time we head back. We'll go over to the welcome center and see if the phones are working."

"I'll race you back to the house," Abby said to Katie and ran ahead.

Katie soon overtook her younger sister. Caris and Will followed behind.

A little more than halfway back to the house, Caris noticed a wooden box about ten feet from the beach road in the marsh to her left. It was the size of a small plastic cooler, similar to the one she'd bring to the beach with drinks and sandwiches for the kids. The box was upright in the marsh grass, leaning a bit in the mud to one side. Katie and Abby had run past without noticing it.

The wood looked old and weathered. The box had a rounded top and was plain except for tarnished silver handles on each side and a large, tarnished silver latch on the front.

"It looks like a treasure chest," Will said.

"Yeah, it does," Caris answered. "Girls!" she called ahead to Katie and Abby. "I think we found something interesting."

CHAPTER 4

"WHAT'D YOU FIND?" KATIE SHOUTED BACK TO HER MOM and brother.

"A treasure chest!" Will yelled with excitement. "Come see it!"

"A treasure chest?" Katie replied. "What is it really?"

Abby had already run back to Caris and Will and was standing with them looking at the wooden box. "Katie, it really is a treasure chest!"

Katie jogged back to join them. The wooden box in the marsh did indeed look like a treasure chest.

"Oh, cool. Let's get it," Katie offered.

"I don't know about that," Caris said. She didn't like snakes that she knew lived in the marsh. She didn't like alligators either.

The chest wasn't that far from them. The tide was out, and the water between Caris and the marsh grass where the chest sat looked only a few inches deep. Yet, she didn't like the idea of crossing into the marsh to get it.

"Guys, I don't want us going over there."

"Please?" Abby begged. "We're not going to leave a treasure chest sitting there, are we? What if it's filled with gold?"

"I highly doubt that," Caris said, thinking the wooden box resembled some of the treasure chests from the *Black Dagger*.

The *Black Dagger* was a boat out of Harbour Town on Hilton Head Island that had been outfitted to look like a pirate ship. With water cannons, skulls and crossbones, toy swords, and a crew dressed as pirates who threatened to make young passengers walk the plank, the *Black Dagger* was great summer fun that the St. John family had enjoyed two summers ago. Caris assumed the chest had been washed overboard during the storm and had made it the mile across the Calibogue Sound before being deposited into the marsh on Daufuskie Island.

"And besides, there could be snakes," Caris pointed out.

"What if we make a bridge?" Katie asked, already walking toward nearby driftwood.

"I don't think so."

"Come on, Mom," Will pleaded, "it could be full of treasure. Let's get it."

Abby joined Katie, and together they returned dragging two pieces of driftwood that looked long enough to span the water to the chest. One piece of driftwood was a board about four inches wide, and the second was a long branch a little thicker than a baseball bat.

Also nearby, they noticed several chunks of wood that had been painted blue. Large sections of torn metal the same blue color were in the marsh near the wooden chest. "Great places for snakes to hide," Caris remarked.

"These'll work great to make a bridge," Katie said, holding the board and branch that Abby and she had found.

Whether the wooden chest had come from the *Black Dagger* or not, it wasn't every day they discovered a treasure chest. "Okay," Caris reluctantly agreed. "Let's see if we can make a bridge."

They placed one end of the board onto the ground at the edge of the water and lifted the other end into the air. They carefully pushed the end in the air over so it landed next to the wooden chest. Half of the bridge was complete.

Caris and Katie then slid the branch along the board toward the chest, and when the far end of the branch reached the far end of the board, Katie adjusted the branch so it was laying parallel to the board about a foot apart.

"Step with your left foot on the board and your right on the branch," Katie said to her mom.

"I can walk over and get it," Abby volunteered.

"No, I'll get it," Caris said, surveying for anything that slithered.

Caris began walking across the bridge, assuming the board and branch would support her. She was wrong.

On her fourth step with her left foot on the board, it sagged into the water and cracked. She fell back, slipped off the branch with her other foot, and landed in the water. The khaki shorts and purple top she'd been wearing since the day before were soaked.

"Mom, you're all wet," Will laughed.

The water was only a few inches deep, as Caris had thought, and sandy on the bottom. With the commotion they had made while constructing the bridge, plus Caris's fall into the water, any snake or alligator in the area had surely been scared away by now.

Caris stood, smiled playfully at the kids, and sloshed the few remaining steps to the chest. "It really does look like a treasure chest," she said to them over her shoulder, as she bent forward to examine it.

She took the handle on the right side and lifted it out of the muck. It made a squishy suction noise, like getting a shoe stuck in mud and pulling it out. With both hands, she lifted the chest from its resting place. It wasn't heavy.

"I think it might be empty," she called back to the kids.

Turning with the chest to return to the beach road, she stumbled a bit and felt an object slide across the inside of the chest.

"Well, there's definitely something in it," she said.

Keeping an eye out for snakes and gators, she was soon on the beach road and set the chest onto the crushed oyster shells where her children were waiting.

"Let's open it!" Will shouted. "I know it's treasure. We're rich!"

"Yeah, let's open it," Abby excitedly agreed.

Caris knelt and examined the chest. The wood looked old but wasn't weathered like the driftwood. It must not have spent much time in the water, she thought. "I think it came across the Calibogue Sound from the *Black Dagger* last night in the storm," Caris said.

She examined the large silver latch in the front and the two silver hinges on the back. All of the silver was badly tarnished. There was no lock on the chest. Caris carefully unclasped the latch.

"Go ahead and open it, Mom," Katie said.

Caris pulled up on the top and discovered it wouldn't budge. She looked again at the large latch and hinges. There was no other latch keeping the top shut.

"The hinges must be stuck," she said.

"I wish we had an oil can like Dorothy used for the tin woodsman," Will said. "That would work."

"We're fresh out of oil cans," Caris replied smiling.

She pulled hard to try to free the rounded top of the chest. It opened about an inch. She tugged a few more times, but the top would not move any farther.

"Katie, hand me that piece of wood," Caris said.

"This one?" Katie asked, pointing to one of the larger pieces of blue painted wood.

"Yeah, that one. I can't get it open, but maybe I can pry it up with that."

Katie handed her mother the wood, and Caris fitted it into the slight opening and pushed. She felt the hinges pop free and opened the top the rest of the way. There was an old, musty smell that reminded Caris of books in her grandparents' basement in Michigan.

The four of them looked into the chest.

They saw a red cloth that looked like silk. It was bundled and tied together with a few strands of twine. Something was wrapped inside the cloth.

"What is it?" Katie asked.

"I don't know." Caris felt the cloth. It felt like silk.

"It sure is red," Will said.

"Like a raspberry," Abby agreed.

"Can I feel it?" Katie asked. "Something's inside it. I hope it's not a snake."

Caris pulled her hands quickly from the chest and gave Katie a look.

"Oh, I'm sorry, Mom," Katie laughed. "I'm sure it's not a snake. Nobody would wrap up a snake and put it in a treasure chest."

Caris took the wood she'd used to pry open the chest and poked at whatever was inside the cloth. It was solid. Not a snake. Something solid was wrapped and tied in the red cloth. She poked it again, wondering what it was. Even if it had come from the *Black Dagger*, Caris had to admit she was a little curious about what they'd found. "I don't know what's wrapped inside," she said. "Let me get it out of the chest."

Will moved closer. "I hope it's treasure. Please let it be treasure," he whispered.

"Will," Caris said, "step back a bit, honey."

Caris felt the edges of whatever was wrapped inside. It was round and cylindrical. She lifted the bundle out of the chest, placed it on the beach road, and untied the twine. She pulled back the red silk. "It's a jar."

It looked old.

Through the dingy glass, Caris could see more red cloth wadded inside.

"What's in it?" Will asked and pressed closer.

"It looks like more silk. Honey, you need to step back a bit and not crowd me."

"Will, back up and let Mom open it," Abby said. "You can be so annoying sometimes."

"Mom, Abby called me annoying."

"Get back so Mom can open it," Abby insisted.

"Guys, knock it off. Both of you. Do you want me to open it or not?"

"Oh, I definitely want you to open it," Katie said. "Abby and Will, grow up and stop bickering. Let's see what's inside the jar."

"Let me see if I can get it open," Caris said. She tried to unscrew the lid. It was stuck. She tightened her grip and tried again. "I can't get it open."

"Let me try," Abby said, quickly wrenching the jar from her mother's hands.

Will lurched to his feet. "No, me! I can do it."

He grabbed at the jar. Abby jerked back and lifted it above her head. "Go away!" she shouted at him.

Will jumped toward the jar and knocked into Abby's outstretched arm. The jar slipped from her grasp and fell to the ground, shattering on the oyster shells of the beach road.

"You dropped it!" Will yelled.

Caris looked at both of them and at the broken glass. "Stop the bickering. I cannot believe you two."

"It was Will's fault! He knocked it out of my hand!"

"Abby," Caris said sternly, "had you not taken it from me, it wouldn't have been in your hand for Will to knock out. And Will, what were you thinking trying to grab it from Abby? This doesn't belong to us, and the two of you broke it. I think we need to head back to the house now. I've had enough of your arguing."

"Wait!" Katie implored. "Can't we at least get out whatever's inside the jar? I want to see what's in it. It's not my fault those two can't behave. They shouldn't spoil it for the rest of us."

"Who's the rest of us?" Caris asked.

"Well, I guess that's just me," Katie answered, "and you. Don't you want to see what's inside?"

Caris was not happy with Abby and Will's behavior. She started to lift the largest piece of the broken jar to put it back into the wooden chest, and when she did, the wadded red silk slid out onto the beach road.

She looked at her three kids, the open chest, and the wad of cloth on the ground.

"Okay," she said, "we'll take a look to see what's wrapped inside, but Abby and Will, we're going to talk about this later. I'm disappointed in both of you."

She picked up the wadded silk and unwrapped it. All three of the kids leaned forward.

There was a key inside, silver, about five inches long, resembling a skeleton key. It was bright and shiny in the morning sun. There was no tarnish like the latch and hinges on the chest. In fact, it might have been the brightest silver Caris had ever seen.

The numbers 1529 were engraved along the length of the key. One end had an oval loop with a cross in it, and on the other end where the teeth should have been was a grooved S-shape.

Caris felt something else wrapped in the silk. She continued to unwrap it and found a piece of paper that had been folded once in half. The paper was about the size of a postcard. It was old and had the same musty smell as the inside of the chest.

"Maybe it's a treasure map," Will said.

Caris unfolded the paper. It was a handwritten note.

"I don't have my reading glasses," she said. "I'm not sure if I can read it."

"I won't touch it," Abby promised.

"Me neither," said Will. "I'm sorry that Abby broke the jar."

"You broke the jar," Abby snapped. "You grabbed it from me."

Hurricane or no hurricane, Caris had enough of the bickering. "Knock it off," she warned.

"I'm sorry," Abby and Will both said at the same time.

"What does it say?" Katie asked.

Caris looked closely at the note and managed to read the handwritten words:

The holder of the key of Schottenklein Abbey, created in the Year of Our Lord 1529 by Abbott Friedrich Kragh and blessed by God for the defense of the City of Vienna against the onslaught of the Ottoman Empire, may be granted one wish made in private known only to God. Beware to enter with care and vigilance through the Schottenklein door.

William Graffin
March 25, 1875
Daufuskie Island, SC

Caris read it aloud a second time, ending with the signature, date, and location. "William Graffin, March 25, 1875. Daufuskie Island. South Carolina."

Katie looked at the paper in her mom's hand. "Do you think it's from 1875?"

"When was 1875?" Will asked.

"About a hundred and fifty years ago," Caris answered. "But, guys, the chest looks like it's from the *Black Dagger*. I think it was just made to look old."

"We never saw a treasure chest like that on the pirate ship, or the note, or the key," Katie said. "What if it's really from 1875?"

Caris was certain the so-called treasure chest and its contents had come from the *Black Dagger*. They were surely the props for make-believe adventures on the high seas that the tourists enjoyed. There were no real treasure chests.

Caris then thought of the anxiety from last night. If the kids wanted to believe they'd found a treasure chest, Caris would not ruin their morning adventure.

"I don't know," she said. "It might be real. I mean, you're right. I don't remember seeing a chest like this on the *Black Dagger*. This might actually be from 1875."

She looked up to see all three of her children smiling. They were smiling like children who had discovered a treasure chest.

"Mom, I don't follow what the notes says. Can you explain it?" Abby asked.

Caris read it again.

"Okay, the first part says the key was created in 1529. If you look at the key, you can see 1529 on one side of it. See, look here."

Katie, Abby, and Will looked at the numbers engraved into the silver key.

"I wonder what it unlocks," Will said.

"Apparently some door in an abbey, which is like a big, old church," Caris said. "The key seems to have something to do with defending Vienna against the Ottoman Empire. I have no idea how the key or door plays into that. Vienna's a city in Austria. But I'm afraid I don't know much about the history of that part of the world. I don't know anything about that abbey or the person named in the note, or anything about this William Graffin who signed it. I think the second part of the note says the holder of the key may make one wish—"

"—I wish for treasure," Will interrupted.

"Will, stop being annoying and let Mom finish," Abby said.

"Mom, she called me annoying again. Make her stop."

Katie shot a look at her brother and sister. "Will you two stop before Mom makes us go back. Mom, please finish explaining it."

Caris continued. "It says that one wish may be made in private and known only to God. That probably means your wish has to be secret. Maybe it means you can't tell anyone your wish."

"So if Will says his wish, it won't come true?" Abby asked.

"I don't know, but that might be what it means. It also says 'the holder of the key.' Maybe you have to be actually holding the key when you make your wish."

"Can I have it and make a wish?" Will asked.

"You can't wish for treasure," Abby said, "because you already said that, and now we know what your wish is going to be. It's not a secret. You have to wish for something else. Don't tell us what it is."

Will looked at Abby. "I don't think that's right, but if one of you can wish for treasure, I'll make a different wish. Can I have the key, Mom?"

Caris gave the key to Will. He closed his eyes and quietly made a wish, making sure nobody heard him.

"Will, don't say what it is," Katie said, "or it might not come true."

"I won't," he answered.

Abby turned toward her brother. "My turn. Give me the key."

"Say please," Will said.

"Just give me the key."

He put the key behind his back. "Say please."

"Will, give your sister the key," Caris said. "And, Abby, say please."

"Will, may I *please* have the key?" Abby said irritated.

Will gave her the key. Abby took it, and looking at Will, she made her wish. Abby then gave the key to Katie.

"Oh, I have a good wish," Katie said. "I hope it comes true." Katie closed her eyes and made her wish.

"Mom, do you think the wishes will come true?" Will asked.

"Maybe."

"I think they'll come true," he said. "You should make a wish too, Mom. You should wish for treasure."

"You three are all the treasure I could wish for."

"Go ahead and make a wish anyway," Katie said, as she handed the key to her mother.

"Yeah, make a wish," Abby added.

"Okay, I have a wish." Caris took the key and closed her eyes, making her secret wish. "And now we really do need to head back."

They carefully picked up the broken pieces of the glass jar and put them into the wooden chest. Caris then placed the red silk, twine, note, and silver key into the chest and closed the rounded top.

"We'll bring these with us just in case the chest does belong on the *Black Dagger*. I'm not saying it does, but if it does, I'm sure they'll be happy to get all this stuff back."

And with that, the four of them headed back to the beach house. It was not yet nine o'clock on the morning following the night of the hurricane—a hurricane that had washed out to sea and then back to shore a wooden chest from Daufuskie Island that had last been opened on March 25, 1875.

CHAPTER 5

WILL WAS THE FIRST TO SEE HIM. DESPITE THE DISTANCE, Will spotted his father's familiar orange T-shirt, the one with Duxbury, Massachusetts, printed in large white letters across the front.

"Daddy!" Will yelled.

Evan was in the road in front of the beach house surveying the debris from the hurricane when he heard his son. He turned and saw Katie and Abby in the field run toward him past Will. He could see Caris farther behind setting a wooden chest onto the grass.

"Oh, did I miss you," he said, as he closed his eyes and hugged his daughters.

Will reached them, and Evan lifted him into the air.

"I missed you too, big man. I was so worried about all of you."

"It was so scary," Will said, throwing his arms around his daddy's neck.

"Will cried," Abby said.

Caris reached them. "We all cried." She put out her arms to Evan, and the two embraced, holding a long hug.

"You look great," he said.

She smoothed her brown hair behind her ear. "I need a shower."

"I'm sorry I wasn't here."

"It *was* scary," Caris said. "I never want to go through that again."

"I still can't believe I didn't know a hurricane was coming and that you were here by yourselves. I feel horrible. I'm really sorry."

"I forgive you. We didn't know it was coming either, and we were here on the island. How'd you get here? Don't tell me the boat made it through the storm."

"It did. The boat was completely fine this morning. In fact, it was the only one that wasn't damaged. Kind of a miracle. I would have been here sooner, but it took me a while to drive to the marina this morning with all of the fallen trees and limbs in Savannah. I can't imagine what you went through here."

He looked at the Culpeppers' house. It looked like a scene from a war.

"They're at the hospital on Hilton Head," Caris said. "Jerry's leg was pretty badly broken."

"A helicopter took Mr. and Mrs. Culpepper," Will said. "Like the one we saw last year at the Coast Guard station. It was probably the same one. Do you think it was the same one?"

"I don't know," Evan said to Will. "Are they going to be okay?" he asked Caris.

"I'm not sure, but I think so. I'd like to go over and check on them a little later today."

"You were my wish, Daddy," Will interrupted. "I wished you'd be here when we got back from our walk, and here you are. My wish came true. Maybe that's why the boat was okay. I'm so glad you're back."

"That was your wish?" Abby asked. "You wished for Daddy?"

"Yeah, and now he's here," Will said. "My wish came true."

"That was a very sweet wish," Caris said and rubbed Will's blond head.

"Katie, what'd you wish for?" Abby asked.

"I'm not going to say it," Katie answered. "It won't come true if I say it."

"I'm hungry," Will said. "I haven't had breakfast yet. Can I have something to eat?"

"Sure," Evan said.

"Honey, head inside," Caris added. "I'll be inside in a minute to make breakfast."

Will ran up the drive and into the house, forgetting to close the front door behind him. Abby and Katie remained in the road with their mom and dad. And then the most peculiar thing happened. Katie lifted off the ground.

Evan was looking at her when it happened. At first, her heels rose up as if she were going to stand on her toes. Then both of her feet left the ground. At first, Evan thought Katie must be jumping.

But it wasn't a jump. A jump is quick. Quick up and quick down. This was different. Much different. She wasn't coming down.

She was slowly lifting into the air. When she was about three feet off the ground, Evan's mind couldn't process what his eyes were seeing. Katie was rising. It didn't make sense. She was a few feet in front of him and continuing to rise.

She screamed.

Evan instinctively reached to help his daughter and grasped her around the waist. He held her suspended in the air. It must have been less than five seconds, but it seemed like an eternity.

"I think I can get down now," Katie said apprehensively.

With her father still holding her, she descended back to the ground. Evan looked at her in stunned silence. Not knowing what else to do, he put his hands onto her shoulders to hold her feet to the ground.

"Katie, what just happened?" Evan managed to say.

"I was thinking of my wish," Katie said. "And I lifted into the air. Daddy, I think I'm okay. You can let go of me."

Evan had no idea what to think and hesitantly moved his hands from Katie's shoulders. "What just happened?" he asked again, this time to his wife and both of his daughters.

Katie closed her eyes. "I'm going to think about my wish again."

She opened her eyes and again lifted into the air. She stopped a foot off the ground and stayed there. Evan began moving toward her, but she raised her hand gesturing for him to stop.

"Wait, Daddy, please."

He hesitantly stopped.

Katie raised about three more feet into the air and stayed at that height for a few seconds. She then rose again to about ten feet above the ground and paused.

Her parents and sister stared up at her with disbelief and bewilderment. Katie rose another ten feet and flew in a wide circle before coming back down and landing on her feet in front of them.

"You wished you could fly?" Abby yelled.

"I can't say my wish," Katie said. "It might not continue to come true."

"You wished you could fly!" Abby shouted again. "Will said his wish! He told us he wished for Daddy to be back. You can say your wish."

"Yeah, and Daddy's back now. Will's wish is complete. He wished for Daddy to be here, and Daddy's here. I'm not saying my wish because I don't want my wish to stop."

"You wished you could fly?" Caris asked. "That was your wish?" She looked behind her at the wooden chest she'd placed in the field.

"Mom, I don't want to say my wish. It might not continue to come true if I say it."

"Somebody tell me what's going on," Evan insisted.

Will came to the open front door holding a clear plastic pitcher of orange juice. "What's going on?" he called. "Are you coming in? I'm starving."

Abby looked at Will standing in the open doorway. "So, if I say my wish, it won't come true?"

"I'm not sure," Katie answered, "but I don't want to risk saying mine. I'm only going on what Mom read in the note."

"What Mom read?" Evan asked, having no idea what his daughters were talking about. "Caris, what's going on?"

"But if I say *my* wish it won't come true," Abby said again quickly looking at Will with noticeable anxiety. "Okay, I wished that—"

But before she could finish her sentence, Will disappeared. Poof. Hocus-pocus. Gone.

The plastic pitcher of orange juice Will was holding fell onto the front porch. It landed with a thud.

"Will!" Abby screamed.

They'd all been looking at Will when he vanished. One moment he was there. The next he was gone.

Evan couldn't comprehend what he'd seen. Will must have gone back into the house. That must've been what he saw. Will had dropped the orange juice and ran into the house. But Evan knew that wasn't what he'd just witnessed.

He would never have believed Katie had flown had he not seen it himself. Had something similar happened to Will? He looked up, half believing Will would be in the air flying above him. But Will wasn't there. He wasn't anywhere.

"Will!" Evan called out, as he ran up the driveway and onto the porch. He looked into the house through the open doorway. "Where are you?" He went inside calling for his son.

Abby was crying and ran to the porch. Caris and Katie were close behind her.

Evan came out. "I couldn't find him inside. I'll see if he's around back. Will, where are you?" he yelled.

"Where's Will?" Katie demanded of Abby. "Where is he?"

"I don't know," Abby said between growing tears. "I don't know."

"What do you mean you don't know?" Katie glared. "What was your wish?"

Caris knelt in front of Abby and put her hands onto Abby's arms. They were face-to-face. Abby was crying uncontrollably.

"Honey, calm down. Calm down. You have to calm down."

Abby put her arms around Caris and buried her tear-streaked face into her mom's shoulder. "I'm sorry," she managed to say. "I'm so sorry."

"Abby," Caris said with growing fear, "what happened? What was your wish? What happened to your brother?"

She had seen her son disappear. Like Evan, she didn't want to believe what she saw. But Katie had flown. The wishes were coming true. It didn't make sense.

"Where's Will?" she demanded.

"I don't know."

"Abby, look at me. What was your wish? You need to tell me."

"Oh, Mom," Abby said between deep sobs, "I thought the treasure chest came from the *Black Dagger* like you said. I didn't think it was real. I didn't mean it," Abby cried. "I didn't mean it."

"You didn't mean what?"

"I'm so sorry."

"You need to tell me your wish! What was it?"

Abby was crying harder than before. "I wished he'd go away."

"Go away? Go away where?"

"Just go away," Abby cried. "I didn't mean it. Will was being annoying. I was playing. I was going to tell him later today that my wish was that he'd go away. I didn't think it was going to come true. I promise. I didn't."

"That was your wish?" Caris said. "You wished your brother would go away?"

"I didn't think it was real."

"It doesn't matter if you didn't think it was real. Why would you wish that? That's ugly. That's not how we taught you to treat each other. Where did you wish Will to go? Tell me."

"I was joking. I didn't mean it."

"It doesn't matter if you were joking. That's not how you treat your brother. You know that. Where is he? Tell me where he is."

"I don't know. I just wished he'd go away."

"What do you mean you don't know?"

"That's what I mean. I don't know. I didn't wish for him to go anywhere. Just that he'd go away."

Caris suddenly felt numb. "Just go away?"

"Yes," Abby hesitantly said. "That he'd just go away." She wiped her tears with her palm and pulled herself into her mother's arms.

Caris gently pushed Abby back so she could see her. "Where was the last place you were thinking about before you made your wish?"

The only thing that Caris wanted yesterday was the protection of her children from the hurricane, and now, Will was gone.

"Honey, you have to think. You have to remember. Where was the last place you thought of before your wish?"

"I was thinking of learning to hula dance."

"Hula dance?"

"Yes," Abby answered. "I was thinking of Hawaii."

Evan joined them on the porch.

"I can't find him anywhere," he said. "What's going on? Caris, tell me. What's happening?"

"I'm trying to figure that out. All I know is that Will's gone."

"What do you mean, he's gone? He didn't just vanish into thin air."

"That's exactly what happened," Caris said. "I don't want to believe any of this, but it's real. You saw Katie fly, and you saw Will disappear."

"Please tell me what's going on." He needed to know what was happening to his family.

"Mom found a treasure chest," Katie said.

"A what?"

"Let me tell it," Caris said.

Caris explained that they'd walked on the beach looking for something interesting after the storm and that they'd found the wooden chest in the marsh. She told Evan about the jar with the silver key and note and about the holder of the key being able to make a secret wish.

"I thought it was from that pirate ship over at Harbour Town. You know the one. The *Black Dagger*. I was playing along with the kids. We were all terrified last night because of the hurricane. The treasure chest and key took their minds off that. I had no idea it could be real. Who would think it could be real?"

"I thought it was real," Katie said.

"I thought it was from the *Black Dagger* like Mom," Abby said. "If I'd known it was real, I would have never wished for Will to go away."

"You wished for Will to go away?" Evan stared at Abby. "Go away to where?"

Abby looked at him blankly, tears welling up again in her eyes.

"We don't know," Caris said.

"What?" Evan responded. "Will's gone, and we don't know where he is?"

"No, we don't." Caris wiped away her own tear.

Evan didn't want to believe any of it. He was an attorney who lived in a world of facts and reasonable analysis. This situation was neither factual nor reasonable. There was no such thing as wishes coming true. Yet he had seen his daughter fly. He had seen his son disappear.

"Caris, where are the treasure chest and key now? Is that the chest I saw you holding in the field?"

She nodded.

"I'm having a hard time accepting this," Evan said. "I'm gone for a few days, and the place turns into a freak show."

He could tell that Caris did not like his comment or his tone. She walked down the steps from the porch and into the road, heading toward the field.

Evan caught up with her.

"I'm sorry," he said, as he walked with her. "Let's figure this out together."

"I don't know what I'll do if we can't find him," Caris said. She was shaking.

"We'll find him."

"What if we can't?"

"We will. We'll figure it out."

Katie and Abby caught up.

"Okay," Evan said. He still looked dazed. "If I understand it, you make a wish while you hold the silver key. But the wish has to be secret."

"That's right," Caris said. "At least that's how I think it works. I don't know for sure."

"Abby made the wish for Will to go away. We know her wish. She said it. Now that we know Abby's wish, do you think her wish will stop, and he'll come back?"

"I have no idea," Caris responded. Tears were welling in her eyes. "Will's wish was that you'd be here when we came back from our walk, and no matter how you got here, his wish technically came true. The boat was fine, and you were here when we got back. He told us his wish. But his wish hasn't been undone, even though it's no longer a secret."

"That's right. I'm still here," Evan said.

"Do you think Daddy might disappear too?" Abby asked.

"I don't know," Caris said. "I don't know how any of this works."

"But I can use the key to make a wish too," Evan said. "If Will doesn't come back, couldn't I make a wish to bring him back? Wouldn't that work?"

"Daddy, you just said what you'd wish for. It has to be a secret," Katie said.

"I could make my wish in secret," Evan responded. "I could change it up a bit, so you wouldn't know the full wish. Maybe that Will would reappear holding a pogo stick or something."

"I just want him back," Caris said.

"Hold on," Evan said. "Did the note say anything about wishes being undone if they're no longer a secret? Maybe they won't come true if they're not secret, but once they're made, maybe it doesn't matter if the wish isn't secret anymore. Katie, you won't say your wish, but it's pretty obvious that your wish was that you can fly."

"Maybe I can't fly anymore," she said. "I didn't say my wish, but you figured it out, so you're right, it's not a secret anymore."

"You know my wish too," Abby added. "I'm hoping that once a wish is known, it becomes reversed. That way Will would come back. I want my wish to be undone."

"But Will's wish that Daddy is here could also be undone because we know Will's wish," Katie said. "Will's wish isn't a secret. What if Daddy disappears too? I mean, Will wished for Daddy to be here. What if his wish gets undone? Does Daddy go back to Savannah? To Atlanta? Does he disappear like Will?"

"Maybe Daddy would end up back in Savannah or at home," Caris said. "I don't know. But I'm pretty certain that he'd be safe. Will's somewhere safe."

"Will's safe?" Evan asked. "How do you know that? How do you know I'd be safe?"

She looked at him without responding.

"Wait a minute," Evan said. "Did you make a wish too? You did, didn't you? What'd you wish for? We know the wishes for Katie, Abby, and Will. You made a wish too, didn't you?"

"Yeah," Katie said. "Mom, you were the last one to make a wish."

"We're not talking about my wish," Caris said.

"Oh yes we are," Evan responded. "I don't believe in magic, or ghosts, or things that go bump in the night, but you're right. This is real. I don't know how, and I don't know why. But this is really happening. Caris, if you made a wish, you need to say what it is so it won't come true."

"Maybe we need my wish to come true," Caris answered.

She walked quicker toward the field and wooden chest. Evan and Abby caught up with her.

Katie stopped walking.

"I'm going to try to fly again," she announced. "I want to make sure my wish hasn't ended now that everyone knows it."

Before her parents could object, Katie stretched her arms like a child pretending to be an airplane and took a step forward. She was immediately in the air.

She flew over their heads and made a large circle like

before. She then made two larger circles about twenty feet higher, increasing her speed each time. She straightened and flew ahead to the wooden chest, landing in the field in front of her parents and sister.

"Don't do that again," Evan said sternly.

"Daddy, it's really fun," Katie responded.

"How are you able to do that?" Abby asked.

"I don't know. I just am."

"Well, you're not anymore," Evan said.

"Why?" Katie asked.

"For starters, it's dangerous."

"Oh, man, I should have wished to fly," Abby said. "Or maybe for three more wishes."

"And Abby, I can't believe you wished for Will to go away," Evan said to her. "Why would you do that?"

Abby started to cry again.

"I think there's a general rule against wishing for more wishes," Katie said. "At least that's how it works on television."

"Well, this isn't television," Evan said. "This is real."

He looked at the treasure chest in front of them.

Caris put her hand on his shoulder.

"Let's get the chest and key back to the house," she said. "Maybe Abby's wish will be undone. If not, you need to use that key to bring him back from wherever he is."

"By making a secret wish?" Evan said.

"That's right," Caris answered. "Whatever we need to do to get him back."

CHAPTER 6

ABOUT A HUNDRED YARDS AWAY FROM THE ST. JOHN family, Natalie Larkin was riding in the passenger seat of a golf cart on Haig Point Road coming to see Caris and the kids following the hurricane. Her own golf cart had a downed tree limb across its front, so Kenny Shivers, one of the teenage boys who lived on the island, had offered her a ride.

"Did you see that?" Natalie asked him.

"See what?" Kenny said.

His head had been turned toward the side of the road looking at trees that had been uprooted.

"Nothing," Natalie answered. "It was nothing."

But Natalie was certain she'd just seen Katie St. John flying.

"They're up there in the field. You see Caris up there?"

"Yeah, I think that's her," Kenny said.

Kenny drove the golf cart toward the field.

Caris saw them coming and picked up the wooden chest.

"I wanted to make sure you were okay," Natalie said to Caris. "I was sure scared for you and the kids. That was a bad storm. A real bad one. But I knew you'd all be *fine*."

"Thanks for checking on us," Caris said. "I appreciate it. I really do. Evan got here this morning."

Evan gave Natalie a hug. "Thanks for checking on them. Our house made it through without a problem also."

"That one didn't," Kenny Shivers interrupted, pointing to the remains of the Culpeppers' house. "It looks like a bomb hit it."

"Do you know Kenny?" Natalie asked. "He was nice enough to drive me over to check on you. There's a tree across my golf cart."

The St. Johns knew Kenny Shivers. All of Daufuskie Island knew Kenny Shivers. He was about eighteen or nineteen, skinny as a rail, and had the reputation for being the island's resident troublemaker. Evan and Caris had told their kids that when they were out playing, they were to avoid snakes, alligators, and Kenny Shivers.

"That was nice of you, Kenny," Evan said.

Kenny was sunburned and wearing a dark blue baseball cap that covered some of his long blond hair. There was a white patch sewn onto the front of the cap above the brim with a red crab on it. He stepped off the golf cart.

"Were the people in that house killed?" Kenny asked.

"Kenny!" Natalie said and swatted him on the side of his head, causing his cap to tilt forward.

Caris looked at Kenny as he adjusted his cap. "I saw them this morning," she said. "The Coast Guard flew them over to Hilton Head. They were pretty banged up."

"Oh," Kenny said, "I thought they'd be goners from the look of their house." He turned his gaze from the Culpeppers' house to the wooden chest that Caris was holding. "You get that from the *Black Dagger*? You know, the pirate ship over at Harbour Town."

"No," Caris answered flatly. "It's not from the *Black Dagger*."

"Sure," Kenny replied, apparently dismissing her answer.

"Caris, can I have a few moments of your time?" Natalie asked, looking at the wooden chest in Caris's hands. "Kenny, can you stay here if you don't mind? I want to speak alone with Mr. and Mrs. St. John."

"Sure," Kenny responded, "but we only have a few minutes."

"We only have a few minutes too," Evan said. "We're having something of a family crisis."

"I'll be quick," Natalie said, still eying the chest Caris was holding.

Caris turned to Katie and Abby. "Natalie wants to speak with Daddy and me. I want you two to walk back to the house. We'll be there in a few minutes. Katie, I said walk. Got that? Walk."

Natalie watched Katie closely as Katie and Abby headed toward the beach house. She then turned and started walking in the opposite direction. Evan and Caris joined her.

"Kenny's a good boy at heart," Natalie said. "He just makes some bad decisions sometimes."

"I heard he makes a lot of bad decisions most of the time," Evan said.

"I know he does. I sure hope he'll change, but I didn't want to speak to you about Kenny. I want to speak with you about that wooden chest you have there, Caris. I saw you pick it up as soon as you saw us. You know what else I saw?"

Caris didn't answer.

"I saw Miss Katie flying. I know what I saw. Kenny said he didn't see anything, but I saw with my own two eyes Miss Katie flying. You don't see that in Haig Point. You don't see that anywhere. I know it has to do with that chest you have there and what's inside it."

Natalie looked closer at them.

"Inside of that chest is magic," Natalie continued. "I've never seen the chest myself, but I've heard of it. It looks exactly like I heard it would look, even with the silver handles and latch."

"Where'd you hear that?" Evan asked.

"Mary Ellen Hadley told me. She said there was magic in the chest. She used to tell me all kinds of stories. Stories of slaves and those tabby houses over there where the slaves lived." She pointed to the tabby ruins on the other side of the field. "Stories of the Haig Point mansion and a mean overseer who beat the slaves. She used to tell stories of magic too. I don't think she made those stories up. Do you know Mary Ellen?"

"I know the name, but I've never met her," Evan answered.

"Me neither," Caris said. "I've never met her, but I heard she moved from the island. What does she know about the chest?"

"I think she knows a lot about it," Natalie said. "She doesn't live on Daufuskie anymore. She's been gone maybe five, six years now. She's over the water in Bluffton but still keeps her old place here. She's back once or twice a year to check on it."

Kenny came toward them. "Ms. Natalie, we need to get on our way. The ferries are running again, you know. I said I'd drive you and take you back home, but I still have to get to the dock to pick up Mr. Rose. He'll be on the ferry when it gets here and needs my help on a project."

"I'll be right there," Natalie said. "Just another few minutes."

Kenny turned and headed back to his golf cart, reaching under his dark blue baseball cap to scratch his head.

"Natalie," Caris said, "what do you know about the chest? Do you know anything about a silver key inside it?"

"A key? No. Mary Ellen never mentioned a key. It's been at least twenty years since Mary Ellen mentioned the chest. That was a long time ago. She used to tell me that when I find the folks who have the wooden chest with the silver handles and silver latch, like the one you have right there now, I need to tell them to go see her right off."

"She said that? Come on, there are chests like this over on that pirate ship in Harbour Town," Evan said. "I'm sure you can buy chests like this at a bunch of places on Hilton Head or Savannah."

"That might be," Natalie said, "but I see Caris here holding a chest like Mary Ellen described, and I know I saw Miss Katie flying. That was magic. I think that's the chest Mary Ellen was talking about right there in your hands."

"Did she say you?" Caris asked. "Specifically that *you'd* find the people with this wooden chest?"

"Yes, she did. And here you are with the chest that she talked about all those years ago. I never dreamed you'd be the ones to find it."

"Did she tell you why the people who found the chest are supposed to see her?" Evan asked.

"No, I can't say that she did. She always used the words *supposed to*, like she knew I'd find the people with this chest one day and that they needed to see her. If you ask me, I don't think that chest was meant to be opened. But by the looks of Miss Katie flying, I think you opened it. You need to go see Mary Ellen because she said you're supposed to, and that's a fact. She'll know what to tell you. She said something else too."

"What'd she say?" Caris intently asked.

"I don't know what it means, but she said that when I talk to the people who find the chest, I'm to tell them that their son is safe and for them not to worry."

Natalie had never seen anyone have a heart attack before, but she was certain she had said something that was going to cause Caris and Evan to have heart attacks now. And as she thought about it, when she and Kenny arrived in the field, only Katie and Abby were with their parents. She had assumed their son was at the house. What was his name? Will, she remembered.

"Caris," she said, "where's your son? Where's Will?"

"What else did she tell you?" Caris asked. The anxiety came through in her voice. "What else did Mary Ellen say about our son?"

"Oh, Lordy," Natalie said. "Where's your boy?"

"What else did she say?" Caris repeated. "Can you remember anything else?"

"That's it," Natalie said in a panicked voice. "Just that he's okay and for you not to worry. Where is he?"

"We don't know," Evan said.

"You don't know?"

"He's gone," Caris said. She held the chest out toward Natalie. "This thing. You're right. There's magic inside. It's how Katie was able to fly and why Will . . . disappeared."

"Disappeared! Oh, Lord," Natalie said, putting her hand over her mouth. "Mercy me. You need to go speak with Mary Ellen."

"What's her number?" Evan asked.

"She doesn't have a phone," Natalie said, trying to regain her composure. "She swore she'd never own one. She believes folks should talk together in person like they used to before everyone had phones. You need to go to her as soon as you can. I have the address for her house in Bluffton. I can't remember the name of her street right now, but I have it at home. You know where I live."

Kenny Shivers was waving to Natalie from his golf cart.

"Ms. Natalie," he called loudly, "we need to go!"

"Okay, okay," Natalie said. "I'm coming." She turned her attention again to Caris and Evan. "Mary Ellen said he's okay, and I believe her. Come by my house for her address. I'll see you in a bit, and then you go see her. She'll know what to do."

Caris and Evan watched them leave.

"How could she know that Will's okay?" Caris asked, placing the chest onto the ground. "That doesn't make sense."

"We'll find out when we get to Bluffton," Evan said. "She knew Natalie would find us with the chest. I know it doesn't make sense, but she knew it. She knows that Will's okay. She was letting us know not to worry."

"But I am worried."

"Yeah, me too. Let's head back to the house to get the girls and the golf cart. We'll all drive over to Natalie's and get the address. I guess we could have given her a ride home."

"Evan, what have you heard about Mary Ellen Hadley?"

"Not much," he said. "I know she's Gullah. I remember Natalie saying a few years ago that Mary Ellen had taught her a lot of the Gullah traditions. She was something of a folk hero around here. That's pretty much all I know about her. How about you?"

"I heard she's a witch."

"A witch?"

"Yeah."

"I don't believe in witches," Evan said.

"I didn't believe in magic until this morning," Caris replied.

Evan looked at the chest and picked it up. "If Will doesn't return on his own, I know what I'm going to wish for with that key."

"Maybe we should see Mary Ellen first," Caris said. "I don't know how she knows these things, but we need to talk with her before anyone else makes a wish. She might know where Will is. We need to get over to Bluffton and see her."

"I think that's a good idea," Evan agreed. "If I get one wish to get him back, I want to make sure we know what we're doing with this thing."

They walked across the field toward the beach house. On the other side of the field behind them, the Haig Point lighthouse stood with the morning sun reflecting off its windows. If they had turned and looked, they would have sworn the sunlight dancing off the windows looked like someone inside moving.

CHAPTER 7

EVAN AND CARIS JOINED KATIE AND ABBY ON THE FRONT porch of the beach house. Evan carried the chest.

"What'd Miss Natalie want to talk to you about?" Katie asked.

"Well, for starters, you. She saw you flying," Evan said. "And she knew why you were able to fly. The magic in this chest is what she said."

"She knew about the chest? She said magic?"

"She also said she didn't think it was supposed to be opened," Evan continued.

"How'd she know that?" Abby asked.

"There's a woman named Mary Ellen Hadley who lived on the island who told Natalie about the chest," Evan said.

"Mary Ellen Hadley?" Katie replied. "She's a witch."

Evan wondered if everyone except him had heard that Mary Ellen Hadley was a witch. "Where'd you hear that?"

"I just heard it," Katie said. "I don't remember where. That's what the kids say. They say she's a witch. A real witch."

"Well, we're going to see her," Evan said. "About twenty years ago, she described this exact chest to Natalie and told her that she'd one day meet the people who find this chest."

"No way," Katie exclaimed.

"Yeah, and she said that the people are supposed to go see this Mary Ellen. She also told Natalie to tell them their son is safe and not to worry."

"She really said that?" Katie asked. "She knew about Abby's wish? She knew Will was gone?"

"She only said that he's safe and not to worry," Evan answered. "We're driving over to Natalie's house to get Mary Ellen's address. Natalie says she lives in Bluffton, so go in and get something quick to eat first. I don't know when you'll get a chance to have breakfast or lunch, or if anything is even open yet in Bluffton following the storm. I don't want to hear complaining that you're hungry."

Evan went into the house holding the chest and set it onto the kitchen table. Caris and the girls followed him in from the front porch.

Caris could not believe what had happened to her son. She had been strong the night before. She had held it together. She had wanted the hurricane to be over and for her children to be safe. That was all that she wanted. She was their mom, and it was her job to keep them safe. She understood Evan not being with them during the hurricane. It wasn't his fault. None of them knew it was coming.

But with the treasure chest and key, she felt everything was her fault. Why had she dismissed the chest and key as props from the *Black Dagger*? How could anyone have thought they were real? She knew she shouldn't blame herself. But she did.

The initial shock of seeing Will disappear had given way to a feeling of nausea. She felt sick. She needed to go back outside.

She needed her son back. She wanted it more than anything. Yet, at the same time, she knew in her heart that Will was safe. The other wishes had come true. She knew that Will would be protected. She stood at the railing of the front porch looking blankly ahead at nothing, thinking of her own wish.

Evan came out to the porch railing and joined her.

"Listen," he said, "we'll get through this. Will's okay. You heard what Natalie said. We'll get him back."

"I'm a horrible mother."

Caris began to cry.

"What? Are you serious? You're a great mom. You got them through a hurricane. There's no way you could've known this would happen. How could you? I've seen it with my own eyes, and I don't believe this is happening."

"I want him back."

Evan held her.

"Should I make a wish for him to return?" he said. "The key's inside the chest in the kitchen."

"Yes. I don't know. Maybe. I honestly don't know. Part of me thinks that you should go ahead now and make a wish to fix this, but part of me thinks we have one shot with your wish and that we need to speak with that woman first. If you wish for Will to come back, that's not a secret. What if you make your wish, and it doesn't come true? It kills me to wait, but we need to see her first. I know he's safe."

"We'll see her in Bluffton. I hope she's home. I can't believe she doesn't own a phone. Who doesn't have a phone?"

"A witch," Caris said apprehensively.

"So, we're going to knowingly see a witch?"

Caris looked at him. "I don't know if she's a witch, but I'd see the devil himself to get Will back."

Evan and Caris returned into the house, closing the front door behind them. Katie and Abby were working on their bowls of cereal with the chest on the kitchen table next to them.

Caris unclasped the silver latch and opened the rounded top. Evan looked inside.

"So that's the key," he said.

It was at the bottom of the chest next to the broken glass jar and red silk.

"I don't want to touch it and unintentionally have a wish pop into my head," Evan said. "I've had enough surprises for the day. We don't need me to accidently wish for a forty-foot marshmallow man. If I get one wish, I want to use it to wish for—"

"—Daddy," Abby yelled, "don't say your wish! It won't come true if you say it."

"Remember it has to be a secret," Katie quickly added.

"Geez, I know. I'm not going to say it. If I have to make a wish to bring Will back, I'll figure out a way to make it secret."

"Can't you go ahead and make a secret wish now to help Will?" Abby asked.

"Your mom and I were just talking about that. This Mary Ellen Hadley woman knows about the chest. I bet she knows a lot more too. We both think we should speak with her before anyone else in this family makes another wish."

He looked at the key again at the bottom of the chest. He could see the numbers 1529 engraved along one side.

"Here's the note," Caris said, reaching into the chest.

Evan read it silently to himself.

"What do you think this has to do with Vienna?" he asked.

"I thought you might know something about it. You're the history buff."

"I'd look it up online, but with the power out, the computer's down." Evan took his iPhone from his pocket. "I can't get the Internet on my phone either. I'm not picking up a signal at all."

"Go ahead and finish eating so we can go," Caris said to Katie and Abby.

"You know," Evan said, "I never heard of the door in the note called the Schottenklein door, but do you remember a silver door upstairs in the lighthouse? Most of it's bright silver like the key. I remember there's a large cross etched into the silver and some numbers on the door. I think they might be the same numbers, 1529. I remember looking at that door the last time we were in the lighthouse. We were inside when the air conditioning kicked on. A door upstairs slammed, and Will thought it was Maggie's ghost. He didn't want us to go upstairs, but we wanted to show him there wasn't anything spooky up there. Remember that?"

"Yeah, I do," Caris said. "I was actually thinking about that this morning when we walked over to check out the lighthouse before we found the chest."

"There's definitely a silver door upstairs," Evan said. "I remember joking that the numbers etched into the silver looked like the numbers on a door for a hotel room and that we should all check into the lighthouse for a weekend."

"You're thinking the door in the note is the same door upstairs in the lighthouse?" Caris asked.

"I guess not. If there's a door from 1529, that would make it nearly five hundred years old. I can't imagine what it would be doing in the lighthouse."

He read the note again and placed it into a pocket of his shorts, along with his phone. He stepped out of his brown flip-flops, stretched his toes on the kitchen rug, and tried to make sense of everything he'd seen.

Katie and Abby finished their breakfast.

"Let's leave the chest and key here while we speak with Natalie," Caris said. "I'd feel better about that. We can come back and get them on the way to the dock if you want to bring them with us to Mary Ellen's."

"That's fine," Evan agreed. "The key can't do any more harm if we leave it here."

On the way to Natalie's house on the other side of the island, they passed Kenny Shivers headed in the opposite direction with a dust cloud from the road trailing behind him. Evan gave a half-hearted wave, but Kenny didn't wave back.

"Do you know what he's working on for Dan?" Evan asked Caris.

"Excuse me?"

"Dan. Dan Rose. Kenny said he needed to pick up Dan from the dock after he dropped off Natalie. He said Dan needed him for a project. Dan usually has some kind of construction project going on. Looks like Kenny's helping him on one."

"I have no idea," Caris said.

"Well if he is," Evan said, "that's one construction project that's probably going to have some serious problems."

Evan had to navigate the golf cart around several downed trees and limbs along the way. The hurricane had made quite a mess of the island.

Natalie was outside her house when they arrived, standing next to her golf cart with a huge downed limb across it.

Caris stepped from their own golf cart and gave Natalie a hug.

"I have some boys coming over tomorrow with a chainsaw to help me," Natalie said. "I'm sorry we were rushed earlier. I didn't want Kenny to overhear. We can talk now. Tell me everything that's happened."

Caris told her of the walk on the beach, finding the chest, and the wishes with the key that had come true. She told Natalie of the magic that makes girls fly and boys disappear.

"I'm so sorry," Natalie said.

"And Mary Ellen didn't say anything about the key?" Evan asked.

"No, she never said what was in the chest, other than magic." Natalie looked at Evan and Caris and then at the girls. "She's a witch, you know."

There it was again. Another person saying she was a witch.

"A witch," Evan repeated. "Come on, Natalie. How do you know she's a witch?"

"Oh, the stories that old woman would tell. Some of them would make the hair on the back of your neck stand up. Nobody but a witch would know things like that. You know she's been on this island since, well, forever."

"Did she ever tell you she's a witch?" Evan questioned.

"I don't think anyone ever wanted to ask her. I know I didn't. I mean, she's the sweetest old woman you'd ever want to meet. She taught me so many things about being Gullah. Whether she's a witch or not is really none of my concern. We don't meddle in other folks' business around here. You've been coming to this island long enough to know that. Do I think she's a witch? Yes, I do. I definitely do. But so what about it? It doesn't change anything. I love her all the same."

"Do you think I'd be able to make a wish with the key that all of the other wishes would be undone?" Evan asked.

"I have no idea," Natalie said. "I don't know anything about how the magic works. You need to talk to Mary Ellen about that."

"Evan, I don't want my wish undone," Caris said.

"Excuse me? I'm not sure I heard that right. Did you say you don't want your wish undone?"

"That's exactly what I said," Caris replied. "Right now my wish might be all Will has."

"I want to keep my wish too," Katie said, still sitting on the golf cart next to Abby. "I like flying. It's fun."

"I want my wish undone," Abby said. "I'm sorry that I ever made it."

"Wait a minute," Evan said. He looked at Katie. "My daughter is not going to fly."

"Why not?" Caris asked. "I mean, it's her wish. What's the harm that she can fly?"

"Am I hearing you right? You're okay with our flying daughter?"

"I could get a job in the circus," Katie said with excitement.

"Exactly! She's making my point," Evan said.

"Honey, maybe joining the circus is not the angle you want to take to convince your father," Caris said to Katie.

"Are you seriously okay if she can fly?"

"Kind of," Caris answered. "How about we talk about that later. For now, let's get Mary Ellen's address and concentrate on getting Will."

Katie looked at her mother and smiled.

"I have the address right here," Natalie said, taking a slip of paper from a pocket of her summer dress. "She lives at 320 Sycamore Street over in Bluffton."

Evan reached into his shorts pocket and took out the note Caris had found in the chest. He took a pen from the storage compartment of the golf cart and starting writing the address on the back.

"Really?" Caris said. "That note's almost a century and a half old, and you're going to write on it."

"Here, take this," Natalie said, and she put the slip of paper with the address into Evan's hand. She also had a map of Hilton Head that included a part of Bluffton. She handed it to Evan. "When you get to Bluffton, head down Wharf Street. Sycamore is one of the side streets. It's not shown on the map. If you get to the end of Wharf and hit the Bluffton Oyster Company, you've gone too far. Do you know where that is?"

"Yeah, we've been there fishing," Evan answered. "I know where it is."

"Her house has a blue roof," Natalie said. "You'll know Mary Ellen's house in Bluffton by its blue roof. The last time I saw her about a year ago, she was talking about painting her shutters and doors blue too. Have you seen her old house here on the island? That woman loves blue. It wards off evil spirits, you know. When you get to Sycamore Street in Bluffton, look for the blue roof."

"We'll find it," Evan said.

They gave Natalie a hug good-bye.

"Let me know what she tells you," Natalie said. "I've known her my whole life. She'll do what she can to find Will. I promise you that."

"Evan," Caris said a few minutes later on their way back to the beach house, "Mary Ellen lived on Daufuskie for years.

Her old house is on the back side of the island. Natalie showed it to me a couple of years ago. I want to go by."

"Why?"

"We have time before the next ferry. I'll show you where it is."

"Do you think Will might be there?"

"I don't know. He might. He's somewhere. This is all connected in some way to that woman."

"Then that's where we're going. Let me know where it is."

Caris directed him to a narrow dirt driveway that looked long-ago abandoned. Overgrown bushes scraped the sides of the golf cart as they slowly made their way.

"Look at that," Katie said when they reached the end of the drive. "It looks worse than the Culpeppers' house. It looks like Godzilla attacked it."

Mary Ellen's Daufuskie Island house had been destroyed by the hurricane. The roof was gone. Large sheets of blue metal roofing were scattered everywhere.

"That looks like the blue metal in the marsh when we found the chest," Abby said.

The front part of the house and one of the sides were still mostly standing. Blue shutters framed broken windows. The front door was in the yard a few feet from the house. It too was blue.

Most of the Gullah houses on the island had blue doors and shutters. Evan knew that Gullahs believed the color blue protected them from evil spirits. But apparently not from hurricanes.

"Not just the roof," Caris said to Abby.

"I'm sorry. What?" Evan asked.

"It wasn't only sections of the blue metal roof that we found in the marsh." Caris stepped off the golf cart and picked up one of the nearby pieces of blue shutter. "It's like the wood I used to pry open the chest this morning."

She tossed the wood aside and walked through the front yard looking at the damage. Evan went inside of what was left of the house.

"Be careful," Caris said. "It looks like the rest of it could fall at any time."

Evan came out moments later into the backyard and walked around to the front where Caris and the girls were waiting.

"He's not in there," Evan said.

He came closer to Caris.

"You said at Natalie's that your wish might be all that Will has."

"If the wishes have to remain secret," Caris said, "let's not talk about my wish."

He looked at her. She caught his eye and held his gaze.

"Okay," he finally said, "I trust you."

He turned his attention to the sections of blue metal roof and broken blue shutters. "You saw this same blue roofing and wood this morning when you found the chest?"

"Yeah," Caris answered.

"Yeah," Katie repeated. "It was all over the beach road and marsh."

"I wonder if the chest and key came from here too," Evan said.

"That's exactly what I've been thinking since we got here," Caris responded. "On the way to the ferry dock, let's swing by the house."

"Why?" Katie asked.

"I want to get the chest. I think we should bring it with us to Bluffton when we meet her."

Evan climbed onto the golf cart. "You think this Mary Ellen has known for at least two decades that the storm last night would wash the chest into the marsh from her house and that you and the kids would find it? That doesn't make sense."

Caris looked at him. "Has anything made sense this morning?"

"I see your point," Evan agreed.

CHAPTER 8

AFTER PASSING THE ST. JOHNS ON THEIR WAY TO SEE NA-
talie, Kenny Shivers went directly to their beach house. He
had just enough time before he needed to meet Dan Rose
at the ferry dock, and he planned to use that time well.

Kenny had worked some of the last two summers on
the *Black Dagger*. The wooden chest Caris had been holding
in the field looked to Kenny like the treasure chests on that
pirate ship. He'd wanted a chest like it, but they were over
a hundred dollars. Nobody would spend that kind of
money on a treasure chest.

He imagined the St. John woman stealing it. Her husband
was an attorney in Charleston, or Charlotte, or Atlanta.
Wherever. It didn't matter. She could afford to buy one if
she wanted, but Kenny had a feeling she had somehow
managed to steal it from the *Black Dagger*. She probably
walked right off the pirate ship with it. She was a thief like
him. He was certain of it.

He went to the front door and knocked. Nobody answered.

He knocked again. Still no answer. He tried the handle.
It was unlocked. He opened the door a few inches.

"Hello, anyone here?"

No answer. He opened it a bit more.

Kenny was sure he'd seen the entire St. John family on their black golf cart when he passed them. Their jerk dad had even waved at him.

"Hello, it's Kenny Shivers. Y'all here?"

Still no answer. He opened the door the rest of the way and went inside. He walked through the hallway at the bottom of the stairs and stepped over the sleeping bags and towels on the floor.

Kenny's head had been itching throughout the morning. He hoped he didn't have lice again. He was prone to catching lice each summer.

He took off his baseball cap and fiercely scratched his head before going into the living room with the wall of windows at the back of the house. Not seeing what he was looking for in there, he continued into the kitchen. And there it was. The treasure chest. Right there on the kitchen table.

He came closer and admired it. This one was better than the one he'd wanted from the *Black Dagger*. And this one would not cost him a hundred bucks.

He thought again of Caris St. John walking off the *Black Dagger* with it. She must have stolen it to give to her kids. There were souvenirs the tourists were supposed to buy, not take with them. The nerve of these people.

He stood in front of the chest and set down his cap in order to use both hands to open the rounded top. He looked at the broken glass jar and the red cloth inside at the bottom.

And what was this?

A silver key.

Kenny took the key from the chest. He hadn't seen it on the *Black Dagger*. He looked closely at it. The numbers 1529 were engraved along one side. Maybe the key was worth some money.

This was turning out to be a pretty good day. The storm last night wasn't bad. Not bad at all. Kenny actually kind of enjoyed it. And now this morning, he finally had a treasure chest. The key was the frosting on the cake.

He put the key back into the chest, closed the rounded top, and left through the garage. Outside, he put the wooden chest onto the floor of his golf cart and covered it with a grimy beach towel. Yes indeed, he thought, this was turning out to be quite a nice day for Kenny Shivers.

CHAPTER 9

"DID WE LEAVE THE FRONT DOOR OPEN?" EVAN ASKED when they returned to the beach house for the chest. He pulled the golf cart into the driveway. "I'm certain I closed it before we left."

"Maybe one of the kids left it open," Caris said.

"Hey, don't blame us for everything," Katie shot back from the rear seat. "I didn't leave it open."

"Me neither," Abby said. "You blame us for everything."

"The door didn't open by itself," Evan replied. "Guys, come on. You have to close the door when you go outside. We'll get bugs in the house, or worse, a snake."

He parked the golf cart in the garage, and they headed up the steps into the kitchen.

Evan was the first to see it. Kenny Shiver's blue baseball cap with the red crab on the front. Right there on the kitchen table next to where the wooden chest had been before they left.

Evan picked up the cap for Caris to see. "Kenny Shivers."

"You don't think he broke into our house and stole it?" she asked with disbelief. "Why would he do that?"

"I don't know, honey. Why would that kid do any of the dumb things he does? Look around and see if he left the key."

"Evan, we need that key."

"Maybe Kenny's still at the dock meeting Dan." Evan checked the time. "The ferry from Hilton Head should be arriving about now."

"What if he makes a wish?" Katie asked. "He has the key."

Evan reached into his shorts pocket and took out the note Caris had found in the chest. "Without the note, I don't think he'd know to make a wish. Hopefully, he doesn't get lucky and turn out to have the best day of his life by making some boneheaded wish by accident that comes true."

The four of them went back into the garage and onto the black golf cart. Evan brought the baseball cap with him and stuffed it into the golf cart's storage compartment.

They were soon at the cart barn and onto the ferry dock. The ferry was there, but the passengers had already disembarked.

"It must have arrived early," Evan said.

They went into the welcome center. Natalie was getting herself situated at the large desk in the corner.

"I just got here," Natalie said. "I rode my bicycle."

"Was Kenny here?" Evan asked. "Kenny Shivers."

"Yeah, he was here with Dan Rose a couple of minutes ago."

"You know the key we were talking about?" Evan said. "The key from the chest. Kenny broke in while we were at your house and stole it. He took the chest too."

"No, he couldn't have done that. How do you know it was him?"

"He left his baseball cap on our kitchen table," Evan said. "The same one he was wearing this morning. Do you know where he went?"

"No, but you might try Mr. Rose's place. If he's not there, then maybe he went to his parents' house. Do you know where they live?"

"Yeah," Evan said.

Evan knew Kenny's parents, Randy and Crystal Shivers. They seemed like good people. Evan felt bad for them for having a son who had turned out like Kenny. He could not imagine the heartache that such a kid would cause his parents.

"I'll find Kenny and get the key," Evan said to Caris.

"The next ferry's not for another two hours," Caris said. "I'll take this one and head to Bluffton to speak with Mary Ellen. I wanted to go together, but you need to get that key, and I need to talk to her."

"You're okay going to meet her without me?"

"What other choice do we have?" Caris turned to Natalie. "Can I impose on you?" she asked.

"Of course," Natalie answered.

"Can you watch the girls until Evan gets the key from Kenny? Can they watch movies in the loft upstairs until then? I don't know that woman. I don't know what we're going to find out. I'm okay going by myself to meet her while Evan gets the key, but I'd feel a lot more comfortable if the girls stay here. Once Evan gets the key back, he can bring them over in the boat and meet me in Bluffton."

"Oh, Caris," Natalie said, "you don't have anything to be worried about with Mary Ellen. She's the sweetest woman you'll ever meet."

"That might be," Caris said, "but that's one less thing to worry about if the girls stay here until Evan brings them over."

"I'll watch them," Natalie said. "It's no problem. No problem at all."

"But we want to go with you," Katie interrupted. "We want to see if she's a witch and find out what she knows about Will."

"I need for you and Abby to stay here with Natalie," Caris said. "If anything else happens to any of you, I don't know what I'd do. You can come over on the boat with Daddy once he gets the key."

"If for some reason I can't find him," Evan said, "then go ahead and speak with her. We'll catch up. We might have cell phone service by then too."

Evan and Caris headed together down the dock to the waiting ferry.

"I wonder what I'm going to say when I meet her. Hi, I'm Caris St. John. We found the wooden chest you told Natalie about twenty years ago, and by the way, our son disappeared. Do you know where he is?"

"She obviously knew about the chest and the magic," Evan said. "If I can find that idiot and get the key, I'll be with you when you meet her."

"I'd like you to be there. You need to get that key."

"That's the idea," Evan said.

Caris stepped aboard the ferry. "I'll see you over in Bluffton."

Evan returned to Katie and Abby at the welcome center. "I want you to be good and listen to Natalie," he said. "She's in charge."

He gave them each a hug and kiss before heading back outside and onto the big black golf cart in the cart barn. He'd drive to Dan Rose's house first. He was friends with Dan. With any luck, Kenny Shivers and the key would be there too.

Dan Rose was a widower in his late sixties and lived alone on the island. He'd been a high school history teacher in Pittsburgh when his wife, Tammy, had been killed in a car accident. Tammy had been the love of his life, and following her death, Dan had given up living. Two summers later, at the suggestion and coaxing from a coworker that Dan needed to get away for a bit, he spent two weeks on Hilton Head.

One sunny afternoon on that trip, Dan had decided to check out Daufuskie. The island was well off the beaten path and had a certain allure. From the moment he arrived, the mystique and splendor of the island caught him. He found a place he wanted to call home.

Dan and Tammy never had kids, and with no ties left in Pittsburgh, his decision to stay had been an easy one. He soon found a job on Hilton Head as a history teacher and started the second chapter of his life. That had been fifteen years ago.

For the past few years, Dan had been retired from teaching and kept himself busy as a part-time contractor and handyman. Evan met him after the St. Johns' beach house was built, and the two had become fast friends.

Evan knew that Dan had a soft spot for troubled teens, and Dan had tried, without much success, to make a positive impact in the life of Kenny Shivers. Having Kenny help him on his latest project was a way for Dan to remain part of Kenny's life in the hope that Kenny would turn himself around and avoid prison, where Evan was fairly certain Kenny would otherwise end up one day.

Evan pulled his golf cart into Dan's driveway. The garage door was open, but Dan's golf cart was gone. He must have already been there and left. Evan wondered where Dan might have gone, but more importantly, he wanted to know where Kenny Shivers might be.

The island was a disaster from the hurricane. Dan and Kenny could have gone to a construction project, but Evan had no idea where it was. His only option was to head to Kenny's parents' house. Maybe Kenny would be there. If he wasn't, then maybe Kenny's parents might know where Evan could find their delinquent son.

As he approached the Shivers' house a few minutes later, Evan could see Kenny in the driveway. He was on his own golf cart, about to pull onto the sandy lane in front. Evan stopped at the end of the driveway and blocked him.

"I've been looking for you." The agitation in Evan's voice was more than noticeable.

"I wasn't lost."

"Let me have it," Evan said, as he stepped off his golf cart and moved toward Kenny.

"Have what?"

"The key."

"What key?"

"The one you stole from my house. The silver one. You know what I'm talking about. Hand it over."

"I didn't steal anything from your house. I can't believe you'd accuse me of that. I've never even been inside your house before."

"Is that right?" Evan said, returning to his golf cart. He took the baseball cap from inside the storage compartment. "Then what was this doing on my kitchen table?"

"I don't know. I've been looking for it. One of your kids probably stole it from me. You should be getting mad at them. Maybe your wife stole it." Kenny was still sitting on his golf cart. A smirk came across his face. "You're lucky I don't call the cops on them. Let me have my ball cap back."

Evan walked toward Kenny, who had his hand out to take the baseball cap. Kenny had a look of shock when Evan instead threw the cap at Kenny's chest and grabbed his extended wrist and shirt to pull him from the golf cart. Evan was six feet tall and a hundred and eighty-five pounds. Kenny was a few inches shorter and about thirty pounds lighter.

"Give me the key," Evan demanded.

In addition to his size advantage, Evan was furious. His adrenaline was racing. He grabbed Kenny more tightly by the shirt.

"I didn't take it!"

"We both know you did. Where is it?"

Evan hadn't been in a fight since elementary school. The last time he punched someone was Dean Holliday in the fifth grade. But he wanted to punch Kenny now. He could feel it. He needed the key, and this slug had taken it. Evan was going to get the key back even if it meant he needed to hit Kenny. Kenny must have realized it too.

"Okay, okay," Kenny blurted, "I took it. But you stole it first!"

"What are you talking about? I stole it first? Where's the key?" Evan tightened his grip on Kenny's shirt.

"You stole the treasure chest with the key in it from the *Black Dagger*. Or your wife did. I used to work on that boat, you know, and I've seen you and your family on it. You took that treasure chest from the *Black Dagger*."

"You're an idiot," Evan said. "My wife and kids found it this morning in the marsh. It didn't come from the *Black Dagger*."

As soon as he said it, Evan was sorry he mentioned it. No matter how Caris and the kids came to have the chest was none of Kenny's business. Kenny had broken into their house.

"If they found the treasure chest in the marsh," Kenny said, "then it's not yours anyway. Whether you stole it from the pirate ship or found it in the marsh, either way it's not yours."

"I'm not going to argue with you. It doesn't matter where the chest came from. It was in my house. You broke in and took it. You took the key too. Where is it?"

"I didn't break into your house. The front door was unlocked."

"Give me the key, and we'll forget the whole thing. For whatever reason Dan Rose has a soft spot for you."

"Keep Mr. Rose out of this."

"I won't call the police and have them come over here. We'll forget all of this. Just give me the key and the chest."

He let go of Kenny's shirt.

"Fine," Kenny said. "The chest is on my golf cart under the towel, but I don't have the key."

"What do you mean you don't have the key? Where is it?"

Evan grabbed him by the shirt again.

"I sold it to Mr. Rose," Kenny said.

"You sold it to Dan?"

"Yeah, I sold it to him before I dropped him off at his house."

"You better not be lying."

Evan released his grip.

"I'm not lying. I showed it to him when I was giving him a ride home from the ferry. He asked me where I got it."

"And what'd you tell him?"

"I said I found it. I could have found it. He was interested in it, so I told him I'd sell it to him if he wanted to buy it."

"You're a real piece of work. How much did you sell it to him for?"

"Twenty bucks."

"Give me the twenty dollars."

"What?

"You heard me. Give me the twenty dollars."

"You're stealing my money. Man, that's not right."

"Kenny, you're not keeping that money. You got it from selling the key that you stole from my house. I'm giving it back to Dan when I get the key from him."

Kenny reached into his front pocket and pulled out a crumpled twenty-dollar bill. He reluctantly handed it to Evan.

"If you're lying to me, I'm coming back here and breaking your nose. I mean it."

"I'm not lying," Kenny said pathetically.

"I went by Dan's house before I came here to find you. He wasn't there. Do you know where he went?"

Kenny didn't answer.

"Where is he?"

"I'll tell you for twenty dollars," Kenny said.

"You'll tell me now." Evan was losing his patience with Kenny. "I've about had it with you. Tell me where Dan is. This is your one and only chance."

"Okay, okay. When I dropped him off at his house, he got onto his golf cart."

"Did he say where he was going?"

"Yeah, I asked him. He said he was going to the light-house."

Evan thought of the silver door upstairs in the lighthouse with the cross etched into it. The numbers on the door could be 1529. The same as the key. The more he thought about it, the more he was certain those were the numbers. Maybe Dan knew of the key and the wooden chest. He'd been living on the island for years. He surely knew Mary Ellen Hadley.

"Kenny, did he say why he wanted the key?"

"Maybe he likes shiny things. I don't know."

Evan took the chest from Kenny's golf cart and put it onto the floor of his own golf cart. "You better not be lying."

"I'm not lying. Mr. Rose has the key."

"He better have it."

With the wooden chest on his golf cart, Evan left Kenny and headed to the lighthouse to find Dan Rose. On the entire drive there, he wondered why Dan had wanted the key.

CHAPTER 10

DAN ROSE'S GOLF CART WAS PARKED IN THE FIELD BEHIND the lighthouse. Evan knew it was Dan's from the bumper sticker of a red rose on the back. Although his golf cart was there, Dan was nowhere in sight.

Evan went around to the front porch and checked the door.

Unlocked.

"Dan," he called out, as he opened the front door, "it's Evan. Evan St. John. You in here?"

No answer.

"Dan, are you here?" Evan called a little louder.

He walked through the rooms of the first floor and to the bottom of the staircase to call upstairs for Dan. No response. The bedroom door upstairs with the numbers etched in silver filled Evan's thoughts as he ascended the steps.

There were two bedrooms on the second floor, as well as a narrower staircase on the second floor that wound its way up the lighthouse tower to the light. The door to the first bedroom was open. Evan entered and could see that Dan wasn't there.

The second bedroom was at the end of a short hallway around a corner. As Evan rounded the corner, he could see the door to the second bedroom was closed. It was the door with the rectangular area of silver.

The door was made of dark wood, maybe walnut. The area of silver within the door was much larger than Evan had remembered. In fact, the silver covered most of the wooden door and must have been at least five feet high and a little over two feet wide. There were only a few inches of the door's dark wood showing on either side of the silver.

The door reminded Evan of the back of Caris's and his bedroom closet door at home in Atlanta, which had an oversized mirror on the back that covered most of it. But instead of there being a large mirror on the door in front of him now, there was a large area of silver about the same size as the mirror at home.

Evan could see the cross etched into the silver. And directly above the cross were the numbers: 1529. Each number was about four inches tall.

Looking closer, Evan could see that the large section of silver had its own set of recessed hinges and a small silver doorknob with a keyhole under it. He realized the area of silver was itself a second door within the wood door.

He knelt down and examined the keyhole under the silver doorknob. The silver key from the chest might fit, and if so, Dan might have used the key to open the silver door.

He called again to Dan, and again, no response.

If Dan was in the bedroom, he would have surely heard Evan outside in the hallway calling for him. Maybe Dan had instead gone up the narrow, winding staircase in the tower and was outside on the observation platform below the lighthouse's light.

A thought popped into his head of young Maggie who had fallen to her death from the observation platform. Evan would check the tower next after making sure Dan wasn't in the bedroom.

He looked again at the door in front of him and its two doorknobs—one opened the wooden door, while the silver doorknob appeared to open the silver door. Thinking of the key and the strange events of the day, a feeling came over Evan that he should try the silver door first. He put his hand onto the silver doorknob and turned. It was unlocked. Maybe Dan had come this way. He pushed the silver door open, looking for Dan on the other side, and stepped through into the bedroom.

The bedroom was not as Evan remembered. The more he looked, Evan realized the room was not a bedroom at all.

There was a fire burning in a fireplace on the opposite wall, and two dark wooden chairs were in front of the fireplace. Bookcases were built into the wall on each side of the fireplace. A few books were on the shelves, and a wooden clock sat on the mantel. The word that came to mind as Evan looked about was "parlor."

The floor was made of dark wooden planks that sharply contrasted the white walls. There were two paintings of ships at sea on one of the walls, and on another wall were brass sconces. This was not the upstairs bedroom at the lighthouse. Evan had never been in this room before.

Along the wall that had the two paintings of ships, there was an arched opening to another room. Through the archway, Evan could see a large table in the adjacent room with chairs arranged around it. It looked like a kitchen.

On the same wall as the brass sconces, there was a door to the outside that was opened about a foot. There were windows on each side of the door, and Evan could see outside. This was not an upstairs room. He was instead in a first-floor room that he'd never been in before. Next to the door he had just come through was a staircase that went up to another floor.

The silver door he'd come through was still open, and he could see the upstairs hallway in the lighthouse on the other side of the doorway. But on this side of the door, he was not in the lighthouse.

"Unbelievable," he said softly.

He thought of returning through the doorway into the lighthouse. But he had a sinking feeling that Dan had come through the same door, and that Dan was somewhere on this side, wherever this place was.

Evan walked across the room to the exterior door and opened it the rest of the way to the outside. There was a small stoop and a brick walkway that led to a dirt road. Standing in the road at the end of the walkway was Dan Rose.

"Dan!" he cried out.

Dan turned and smiled broadly at seeing his friend.

"Look at this place," Dan called back to Evan. "Can you believe this? Where in the world are we?"

"I was going to ask you the same question," Evan said, as he walked toward Dan.

Across the road was a square field bordered by dirt roads on all four sides. The field was much smaller than the field near the Haig Point lighthouse. The first thing that caught Evan's eye was a large British flag in the middle of the field.

There were also several tents. He counted five rows of tents with five tents per row. They looked to Evan like oversized pup tents. They were dingy white and appeared to be made of canvas. Evan could also see three horses in the field that had their reins tied to an iron ring at the top of a short wooden post.

But he didn't see any people.

Several houses were located along the dirt roads on all four sides of the square field. Most of the houses were wood, but some were constructed of brick, similar to the house behind them with the silver door in the parlor. All of the houses had wood shingles, similar to the Haig Point lighthouse, which made them collectively resemble an old-time, pioneer village.

The largest house was on the opposite side of the field. Evan counted eight round, white columns in front of the house. There was a British flag on a tall flagpole near the front, and another Union Jack fluttered from a pole attached to one of the columns.

The leaves on some of the smaller trees were yellow, orange, and red. The colors of autumn. There was a slight chill in the air. It felt like morning on a crisp early fall day.

The air had a smoky smell from the chimneys of the houses, and there was an odor of horse manure from the large quantities of horse droppings in the dirt roads. The smell of the air reminded Evan of his uncle's farm in Massachusetts.

"Where do you think we are?" Dan repeated.

"I've been looking for you," Evan answered. He had no idea where they were, but all he wanted was the key and to get back through the silver door.

"You have?" Dan said. "Did you come through the lighthouse? Of course you did." Dan gave a small laugh. "Look at this place. How absolutely bizarre."

"I've seen my share of bizarre things today," Evan said.

"Look at those houses," Dan said, pointing to a handful of houses that appeared to have been exploded. Splintered wood and bricks were scattered near them. "They look like they were blown apart. I wonder if the hurricane hit them."

Dan began walking toward the closest destroyed house.

"Dan, stop for a second. Please. I need to talk to you. I've been looking for you. Kenny Shivers said you'd be at the lighthouse."

Dan stopped walking and turned to Evan.

"Kenny broke into my house earlier this morning. He stole something. Something important. He stole a key from my house. It's silver and looks kind of like a skeleton key. He said he sold it to you for twenty dollars. Do you have it?"

Evan reached into his shorts pocket and removed the twenty-dollar bill he had taken from Kenny. He held it out to Dan.

"Yeah, Evan, I have it. If it's your key, then it's your key, no problem."

"I need it back."

"I didn't know it was stolen," Dan said.

"I know."

Dan took the twenty dollars from Evan, put the bill into his pocket, and took out the key. There it was. Right there in Dan Rose's hand.

"I really had no idea it was stolen when I bought it from Kenny. I never would have bought something I knew was stolen. I've been trying to get him to turn his life around, and then he goes and does something stupid like this."

"Don't worry about it," Evan said. He took the key from Dan. "You have no idea how much trouble this thing has caused."

Evan put the key into one of the pockets of his shorts and thought of the words on the note about the holder of the key making one wish. He hoped that having the key in his pocket was not the same as actually holding it. He definitely didn't want to be the holder of the key. Not yet, at least. Not until Caris and he had spoken with Mary Ellen Hadley.

Evan had what he came for. "I think we should head back," he said to Dan.

"Head back from where? Where do you think we are?"

"I don't know," Evan answered. "This certainly isn't Kansas."

"You know," Dan said, appearing lost in thought, "if the key opens the door in the lighthouse, are you sure it's yours?"

In the distance, they heard a clap of thunder. They both looked up at the cloudless, blue sky. Two seconds later, there were four more thunderclaps in quick succession. The booming sound was like nothing Evan had heard before.

They both turned at the same time to see the front of a nearby house explode inward, shattering wood in all directions.

"Get down!" Dan yelled.

Dan dropped to the dirt road. Evan looked down at him dumbfounded.

"Evan, get down!"

"Huh?"

"It's not thunder. Those are cannons!"

Another house was hit.

Evan went to the ground next to Dan, trying to avoid a pile of horse manure. His mind was whirling, taking in what he was seeing.

Four men scrambled out of the canvas-looking tents in the field across from them and ran toward the large house on the other side of the field. Evan could not believe his eyes. They were wearing long bright red coats, black boots, white trousers, and black hats. Most schoolchildren would be able to immediately recognize what the four men were wearing—the uniform of British soldiers during the American Revolution.

Evan was on the ground beside Dan watching in disbelief. The four men reached the large house and raced up the wide steps, past the British flag attached to one of the columns.

"I think I know where we are," Dan said. "Look at the magnolia trees behind those houses and the live oaks draped with Spanish moss. It's familiar, isn't it? I taught American history in high school for over forty years with about ten of those on Hilton Head. I'm certain that's the royal governor's mansion. The royal governor of Georgia."

Evan had no idea what Dan was saying.

"Those four went into the royal governor's mansion." Dan pointed to the large house on the other side of the field in front of them. "Evan, I know this is impossible, but I'm pretty certain this is Savannah during the American Revolution. What we're seeing hasn't existed in centuries."

CHAPTER 11

KATIE AND ABBY WERE IN THE LOFT AT THE WELCOME CENter watching television. "I think I should go to Mary Ellen's house in Bluffton," Katie said.

"What?" Abby replied, as if her sister had just told her the most outlandish thing ever.

"I need to go. What if Will's at her house? What if she has him? I think I should go check."

"Are you nuts? Mom's on her way there now, and Daddy's bringing us in his boat when he gets back. Didn't you hear them? They told us to stay here. If Will's there, Mom will find him. We'll all find him when we get there with Daddy."

"But what if it's too late by then? I need to go now. Will might be there needing our help, my help."

"No," Abby protested. "We're supposed to stay here. And besides, we don't even have a way to get there."

"You don't, but I do." Katie held out her arms and flapped them like the wings of a bird.

Abby did not like where this conversation was going. She knew that once Katie got an idea in her head, she usually would not give it up.

"I'll probably be back before Mom even gets there. I tell you what, if Daddy gets here and I'm not back yet, you can tell him where I went. I should be on my way back by then anyway if I don't find Will."

"And if you find him there?"

"I don't know. I'll figure it out then."

"That's a dumb plan. I don't like this. We're supposed to stay here," Abby insisted.

"It's your fault he's gone," Katie said.

"I know." Abby began to cry again. "I didn't mean it. I don't want anything else to happen to him. I don't want anything bad to happen to you either. Please don't go. Stay here like Mom and Daddy told us."

Katie gave her younger sister a hug. "I'm sorry I said that. I know you didn't mean for Will to go away. Nothing will happen to me. Mary Ellen might not even be there. I'll go and be right back."

"You don't even know where you're going," Abby said.

"Sure I do. Bluffton. We've been fishing with Daddy a ton of times by the Bluffton Oyster Company. It's up the May River. You can see the river on the other side of Bull Island. You can see it from here." Katie pointed to a window in the loft in the direction of the Calibogue Sound to make her point.

"But you don't know where she lives."

"That's the easy part. Weren't you listening to Natalie? It has a blue roof. Remember Natalie said it's on Sycamore Street. I'll find it flying. It'll be easy."

"Please don't go," Abby tried again. "I don't want you to go."

"I'll be back in no time. Don't you dare say anything to Natalie."

Katie went down the stairs from the loft. Abby followed close behind.

"Miss Natalie," Katie said, "we're bored. Can we go out and play?"

"That'll be fine. But stay close where I can see you."

"Don't go," Abby pleaded one last time when they were both outside.

"I'll be back before you know it," Katie said and was in the air before Abby could object again.

CHAPTER 12

THE CANNON BOMBARDMENT ENDED, WHILE EVAN AND DAN remained motionless on the ground. Two more houses had been hit.

"This doesn't make any sense," Dan said. "I mean, I'm certain this is Savannah, but it can't be Savannah. This isn't possible."

"Maybe it's a reenactment," Evan suggested.

"If so, this is one heck of a reenactment." Dan pointed to the trees with their autumn foliage. "It's the first week of June. This isn't possible," he repeated.

Evan thought of Katie flying and what had happened to Will. Things that weren't possible had nonetheless happened. Maybe they really were in Savannah after coming through the silver door.

"Did you see the British soldiers?" Dan asked. "We're in Savannah. I was actually thinking of Savannah and the American Revolution earlier. Back at the lighthouse, I thought the numbers on the silver door could be a date. My mind was wandering through historical events. One of the traits of being a history teacher, I guess. The 1529 on the door made me think of 1492, you know, when Columbus sailed the ocean blue. That got me thinking of the British colonies that eventually followed, which made me think of the American Revolution and how Savannah must have looked at that time. We're in Savannah now. I'm certain of it."

"Then let's get back to Daufuskie."

They both stood up from where they'd been lying in the dirt road.

"Aren't you the least bit curious where we are and how we got here?" Dan asked.

"To be honest, I just want to get out of here. I'll explain later."

"Listen," Dan said, sounding like a history teacher, "of the thirteen colonies, Georgia had the smallest population. After the Declaration of Independence, Georgia threw out its royal governor who had been appointed by the English king. When the Revolutionary War started, the British easily retook Savannah and reinstated the royal governor."

Dan pointed to the large house on the other side of the field. "I think this is Telfair Square," he said.

"It doesn't look like Telfair Square," Evan replied.

"It used to be called St. James Square. There are twenty-four squares in downtown Savannah now, but there were originally only four. The royal governor's mansion was on St. James Square. The royal governor moved back into *that* house in June 1779.

"Later that same year," Dan continued, "the Americans developed a plan to retake the city in a joint operation with the French. It was called the Siege of Savannah. That happened in September and October of 1779. Judging from the fall leaves and the shelling, my guess is we're there now. October 1779. We're standing in Savannah in October 1779. Although it's impossible, that is the royal governor's mansion."

"Wait a minute," Evan said. "Maybe we're not actually in Savannah in 1779. Maybe that silver door acted like some kind of a window into what happened in the past. Maybe we're just seeing it."

"But we're here," Dan insisted. "I don't know how. But we're physically here. We're not just watching this. I can smell the air, the smoke."

Dan pointed to their right.

"The Savannah River is that way. Just before the riverbank, there's a forty-foot bluff almost straight down. I'm sure you've seen it when you've been to River Street. Most of Savannah's population hid along the bluff during the siege for protection. I'm guessing that if we walked over there now, we'd see the townspeople huddled there."

"Dan, I don't want to walk over there. I want to get out of here."

Dan looked to be in deep thought.

"I have to ask you something before we go," Evan said. "What do you know about the key?"

"The key?"

"Yeah," Evan said. "How'd you know it was the key for the door upstairs in the lighthouse?"

"Kind of a hunch," Dan answered. "Kenny had it this morning when he picked me up at the ferry. I saw the numbers engraved on the side and was pretty certain they were the same as the numbers etched into that door. They'd looked like a date to me, and I kind of have a knack for remembering dates. Anyway, I had asked Haig Point's general manager about the door a few years ago. He didn't know anything about it, and to the best of his knowledge, nobody had the key. When Kenny showed me the key this morning, my first thought was he'd found the missing key."

"Do you know anything about making wishes?" Evan asked.

"Wishes?"

"Yeah, wishes. Like a genie in a bottle. I know that sounds crazy."

"Kenny asked me if I wanted to buy the key, so I offered him twenty bucks. He probably would have taken five, but I knew he could use the money, so I made it twenty. Kenny and I were supposed to start a sun-room for Mrs. Lundh this week, and I wanted to make sure her house was okay after the hurricane. Since her place is over by the lighthouse, I told Kenny I was going to the lighthouse first to check out the key. Evan, I had no idea he stole it from you. How'd you get it?"

"It's a long story. I'll tell you when we're back, but I don't think you're going to believe all of it." Evan looked around again at the scene in front of them. "But then again, after seeing this, you might believe it. It's pretty incredible."

"I think that's not a bad idea to head back," Dan agreed. "And you're right. Judging from what I'm seeing, I think I'll believe about anything you say."

The two of them were about to return to the brick house with the silver door when they heard someone behind them with a heavy accent.

"You two," the man said, "what are you doing there?"

They turned to see a man about ten feet away coming in their direction. He looked to be a little younger than fifty and almost bald, except for short red hair above his ears and wide red sideburns. He was wearing a British uniform with a gold collar on the long red coat. Evan could see that the man's right arm was missing. A scabbard and sword hung from his waist.

"What are you doing there?" the man repeated.

Evan and Dan stood silent.

"I asked you a question," the man sternly said.

Evan and Dan could see six or seven more British soldiers coming onto the dirt road about a hundred feet away. The man turned around and walked toward them.

"I think we need to get out of here," Evan said.

"That's a good idea," Dan replied.

The man's back was to them as he approached the group of soldiers. Evan turned and saw another group of soldiers coming onto the road about two hundred feet in the opposite direction.

Evan thought of the key in his pocket and that he wasn't going to allow it to be taken. He was almost certain they'd be able to get into the house and through the silver door before either group could reach them. But if they couldn't, then Evan's only option was to make a wish with the key. He knew what he'd do. He'd wish for Will, Dan, and himself to be returned to the beach house. He suddenly liked the idea. It was a secret wish. Caris and the girls didn't know that his wish would include Dan. He reached into his pocket. Although he wanted to hear what Mary Ellen had to say, he would nevertheless make his wish if they wouldn't be able to get back through the door.

"Don't run," Evan said. "We don't want him to turn around. Walk quickly. We'll make it."

They were ten feet from the walkway.

The man's back was still to them. He was talking to the first group of soldiers. One of the soldiers pointed at them. The bald man turned and ordered them to stop.

"Keep going," Evan said. "We're almost there."

The soldiers in both groups began to run toward them. The front door of the brick house was still open from when Evan had come out looking for Dan.

"Lieutenant Mendenhall," the bald man shouted to one of the soldiers approaching from the other direction, "seize them!"

"Yes sir, Colonel Maitland!" the man yelled back.

Dan stopped. He looked at the bald man running toward them.

Evan reached the front door. He turned back and saw Dan had stopped a few feet away. "Dan! What are you doing? Get in here!"

Dan began running again and took his last few steps into the house, as Evan slammed the front door shut behind them. Evan put his hand on Dan's back and pushed him toward the silver door on the other side of the room.

As they crossed the parlor, Dan stumbled and bumped into the silver door. It swung shut. He grabbed the silver doorknob and yanked the door open.

"Go through!" Evan shouted. "They're almost here."

Dan went through with Evan following right behind.

CHAPTER 13

"WHOA!" EVAN GASPED.

Coming through the doorway behind Dan, Evan expected to be in the hallway of the lighthouse.

But they weren't in the lighthouse.

Instead, they had gone through the doorway but somehow ended up in the same room they'd just left. The silver door had acted like a magical revolving door bringing them back to the same room. But the room was different now.

The first thing that Evan noticed had changed was the furniture. Rather than the two dark wood chairs in front of the fireplace, there was a fabric-covered sofa. And the fire that had been burning in the fireplace moments earlier was out.

The paintings were different too. The ships had been replaced with flowers of pink, yellow, and blue.

The walls themselves were no longer white. They were covered with a pale blue fabric.

"We should be in the lighthouse," Dan said.

"Yeah, but we're not," Evan replied. "This room isn't right either."

Dan went to one of the windows and looked out. "You're not going to believe this."

"What is it?"

"It's definitely Telfair Square across the street. You have to see this."

"I think we should try the door again. The lighthouse has to be on the other side."

"But what if it's not? Do you know who that was who told us to stay there? That was John Maitland. He could be on the other side of the door right now."

"Who?"

"The bald guy in the British uniform who told us not to move."

"Huh? Wait. How do you know his name?"

"I heard one of the soldiers call him Colonel Maitland. Remember, Evan, I was a history teacher. Maitland commanded the British regiment where most of the fighting took place during the Siege of Savannah. It was one of the bloodiest battles of the American Revolution."

"The Siege of Savannah? Where we just were with the cannons?"

"Yeah. As I was saying earlier, the American and French undertook a joint operation to retake Savannah from the British. Remember what I said? Georgia threw out its royal governor once the Declaration of Independence was signed, but after the war started, the British retook Savannah and reinstated the governor. The American and French joined forces the next year to try to retake Savannah from the British. It was a total disaster. Not many Americans remember the defeats. It was one of the bloodiest American losses of the Revolution. The British ended up holding onto Savannah for the rest of the war. You didn't do very well in history, did you?"

"It was actually one of my favorite subjects," Evan said. "But, come on, it's been a few years since I took a history class."

"Fair enough," Dan said.

"So this Colonel Maitland, he commanded the British who won the battle? Are you sure that was him?"

"It was him," Dan said. "Did you notice that he only had one arm? He lost the other one in the French and Indian War."

"He lost his arm in battle?"

"Yeah. And he loses his life too."

"Excuse me?" Evan said.

"Yeah, about two weeks after the American and French gave up and withdrew from Savannah, Colonel Maitland died of malaria. You can look that up. It's true."

"I'm sure it is," Evan said. "It's amazing what people died of back then. I know you're a wealth of knowledge about Savannah history, but right now, I really need to get back to my family. How about we head through the door and go home?"

"But what if Maitland is on the other side when we go through? We kind of stick out like a sore thumb for that time period." Dan pointed to Evan's olive-colored shorts and faded orange T-shirt with Duxbury, Massachusetts, in large white letters across the front. "What we're wearing probably caught his attention in the first place. There were at least ten or more British soldiers coming after us, including Maitland. They could be on the other side of that door right now. I think we should wait here a bit. Let's give them some time to leave if they're still there."

"But, Dan, we're in the same room. This is the same room we just left. Wouldn't they be in here with us?"

"It might be the same room," Dan said, "but Maitland's not on this side of the door. This isn't his time."

"This isn't his time?"

Dan returned to the window and looked out.

"Maitland's time is during the American Revolution. That's not the time we're in now. Take a look outside."

CHAPTER 14

COLONEL JOHN MAITLAND AND THE BRITISH SOLDIERS FILED in through the front door of the brick house. The two strangely dressed men they'd been chasing weren't in the front parlor.

"Search the house," Colonel Maitland ordered.

Several of his men stormed through the archway into the adjacent kitchen and rooms beyond, while the rest of the soldiers searched upstairs. Maitland remained in the parlor by himself.

He saw a door near the stairway. A closet, Maitland thought. The door was made of dark wood with a large section of silver that covered most of the surface. There was a silver cross etched into the door with the numbers above it.

The two men could be inside the closet hiding. He put his one hand onto the hilt of his sword and demanded them to come out.

The men didn't respond. Maybe they weren't inside after all, but Maitland needed to make sure. He approached the door cautiously. As he neared, Maitland realized that the silver area within the dark wooden door was also a door. There was a silver doorknob.

He thought about the two men he'd encountered outside. They had such odd clothing. He was curious where they'd come from. Maitland was thinking that exact thought as he turned the doorknob and opened the door.

Instead of the closet that he expected, Colonel Maitland found himself looking at a hallway. Maybe it was a secret passage the two men had used to escape. He opened the silver door the rest of the way and stepped through.

He took a few steps down the hallway and rounded a corner. At the other end of the hall, he could see two staircases. One went up, and the other down.

Maitland had been suffering from a headache the last few days. His headache had grown worse from the sprint into the house following the two men.

He felt his neck and forehead. Both were warm, hot actually. He thought he might have a fever. His muscles ached. He needed a few moments to catch his breath. He was certain he'd feel better soon.

The horrible heat, humidity, and mosquitos of the South had plagued him since he'd been ordered to Charleston months earlier. His forced march to Georgia to bolster the defense of Savannah was no picnic either.

He needed a few moments to compose himself and leaned his back against a wall in the hallway. He could feel his legs giving way. Before he knew it, his back slid down the wall, and he was sitting on the floor.

A chill came over him. He was sweating now. Maitland closed his eyes and sat still. He was an officer in King George's army. Sitting here, regardless of his personal health, was not acceptable. What if his men saw him?

He gathered his strength and managed to stand. He pulled his sword from the scabbard, and using it like a cane, he staggered to the two staircases at the end of the hallway.

He was having a difficult time thinking of a reason why the staircases were there. Nonetheless, solely because going down would be much easier than climbing a flight of stairs, he decided to take the downward staircase. He stumbled down the last few steps, and at the bottom of the stairs, he could see a door open to the outside. He needed fresh air and went out.

Although he had no way of knowing, he was standing on the front porch of the Haig Point lighthouse over two hundred and thirty years from when and where he had opened the silver door in the brick house in Savannah.

The fresh, salty breeze from the Calibogue Sound was pleasant and made him feel a bit better. He pulled down on the front of his long red coat and tried to compose himself. He hesitantly returned his sword to its scabbard, thinking the men he was following would be here somewhere.

But they weren't.

To his right, he could see where the Calibogue Sound met the Atlantic. Maitland thought the ocean was too far from Savannah for him to be able to see it. Yet he could plainly see the ocean now.

Turning and looking up, he saw something even more unexpected—an American flag swaying on a tall pole about ten feet from the porch. The flag looked different, but there was no mistaking the red and white stripes of the American flag with white stars on a field of blue in the upper corner. Although the white stars were not in a circle that was familiar to him, he was certain the flag was American. He tried to get a better look, but the sun caused him to squint, compounding his headache.

If the Americans occupied this area, wherever this place was, he needed to keep his wits about him. He was the enemy.

He descended the few steps of the front porch and went around to the back. He looked upward and saw the observation platform. He saw the large lens above the platform too. He realized he had come out of a lighthouse. But how'd he get inside of it?

He wanted to think, but his head was aching like it had never ached before. He staggered a few more steps into the adjacent field, bent over, and vomited.

When he lifted his head, he caught sight of the Culpeppers' destroyed house. Having no idea where he was, he didn't know whether American, French, or British cannons had caused the damage. Illness or not, he needed to remain vigilant. Better yet, he'd go back the way he came and return with his men. He just needed a moment to catch his breath.

As he turned to head back inside, he noticed the most unusual carriages. One was black with three rows of seats.

The other was white and had some sort of small painting of a red rose on the back. He had never before seen carriages like these.

His head was hurting even more now, although Maitland didn't think that was possible. He broke into cold chills. He was going to collapse again. He could feel it. He took out his sword again and leaned against it to steady himself.

Kenny Shivers had thought quite a bit about what Evan St. John had said. *My wife and kids found that chest in the marsh this morning.*

That jerk didn't even own the chest. His wife and kids found it. And he had taken Kenny's twenty dollars. Who did that guy think he was?

Kenny was raised on Daufuskie Island. That guy and his stupid family weren't even from the island. If they found the chest in the marsh, then Kenny had more of a right to it than anyone. That included the silver key too.

That Evan St. John with his dumb Massachusetts T-shirt had gone to the lighthouse to find Mr. Rose. Mr. Rose had always been good to Kenny. That St. John had no right to the key. Kenny had sold it to Mr. Rose fair and square, and he was going to put a stop to any refund.

He drove his golf cart toward the lighthouse. He would talk sense to Mr. Rose.

Kenny drove across the field.

Who was that?

Oh great. What was that guy wearing? A British uniform from the American Revolution? Halloween was still months away.

Colonel Maitland thought he must be delirious. What was coming toward him? There was no horse pulling it. He managed to stand straight and wiped saliva from his mouth with the back of his hand.

Kenny stopped his golf cart a few feet in front of Maitland and climbed off.

"Hey, did you see two guys around here? Dan Rose and Evan St. John. Do you know them? Their golf carts are parked right there. Are they in the lighthouse? Did you see them go in?"

Maitland's head was pounding harder now. He clutched his stomach and leaned forward. He fell to both knees and vomited again.

"Oh, man, are you okay?"

That was the last Colonel John Maitland heard as he lost consciousness and fell to the ground.

Natalie had been right. Although Kenny Shivers made a lot of bad decisions, he had a good heart. At least sometimes on rare occasions. Cell service had been restored, and he called 911. Kenny waited with the unconscious man until paramedics from the Daufuskie Island fire station arrived minutes later.

The paramedics went to work attempting to assess the nature of the unconscious man's condition. It was more difficult in situations like this where the patient was nonresponsive.

When paramedics need to transport a patient off Daufuskie Island, there are generally two options. The first is a ferry ride to Hilton Head Island and an ambulance to Hilton Head Regional Hospital. That option is usually for non-life-threatening emergencies. The second option is LifeStar, which is a seven-minute helicopter flight to the Level 1 trauma center at Savannah Memorial Hospital. Assessing the unconscious man, the paramedics promptly decided upon the second option.

Minutes later, for the second time that day, a helicopter landed in the field near the lighthouse. Unlike the orange Coast Guard helicopter that had taken the Culpeppers to Hilton Head, this one was royal blue and was soon racing toward Savannah with a very sick man aboard. A man who was suffering from malaria contracted in the swamps near Charleston in the late summer of 1779.

Kenny Shivers watched the helicopter take off. He didn't know why Dan Rose and Evan St. John hadn't come out of the lighthouse when the helicopter was there. It was certainly loud enough. They must have heard it.

After the helicopter and paramedics left, Kenny checked inside. He couldn't find them and didn't know why they'd left their golf carts. But he was glad Evan St. John had left his. The treasure chest was still on the floor of the big black golf cart. And as an added bonus, the man wearing the crazy British uniform had dropped his sword. Kenny took them both.

The day was turning out well for Kenny Shivers after all. He had the treasure chest again, which he intended to keep. The sword was the cherry on top.

CHAPTER 15

"EVAN, YOU REALLY NEED TO SEE THIS," DAN SAID, AS HE opened the front door of the brick house. He went out and was standing on the walkway. It was the same brick walkway as before. Evan went to the open doorway and looked out.

The roads were dirt. The same as they'd been when Evan and Dan had stood in the road in front of the same house moments earlier. But the tents were gone from the field across the street. The British flag was gone.

Evan walked out to join Dan.

"Geez, it's cold out here. Come on, Dan, let's get back inside."

"Look across the square," Dan said.

The large house on the other side of the square, which Dan had called the royal governor's mansion, was no longer there. In its place stood a different, larger house.

Evan recognized the house immediately. He had been inside of it with his family.

"It's going to be the Telfair Museum of Art," Dan said.

"Going to be?" Evan asked.

"Yeah, and look over there," Dan said, pointing to a building about a hundred feet to the left of the house. The building where Dan pointed was light grey with two massive round columns in front. "It's Trinity Church."

Evan stared in disbelief at the church and house. There were flags draped from each of the two upper windows of the house. Confederate flags.

"That's the Telfair Mansion, and that's Trinity Church," Dan said. "There's no question about it. We're standing in front of Telfair Square."

Evan agreed. "I've been to the Telfair Museum with Caris and the kids. This is Telfair Square. But when? And why's it so cold? It feels like winter."

"It is winter," Dan said. "Look at that." He motioned toward a stand of trees that had lost their foliage. "And look over there. Those are Confederate battle flags."

"You're saying this is the Civil War?"

"Yeah. I don't understand how this is possible," Dan said.

"I'll try to explain as much as I can when we get back."

Dan walked a few steps ahead. "The Telfair Mansion doesn't become an art museum until the 1880s," he said. "It's a private home right now." Dan was smiling. He'd been a history teacher and was now living *in* history. "The Telfair family had deep roots in early Savannah. The patriarch, Edward Telfair, was a member of the Continental Congress during the American Revolution. He served as governor of Georgia twice after the United States gained its independence from England."

"Dan, how do you remember all of that? Why do you remember all of that?"

"I have history teacher blood in my veins."

"You're like a kid in a candy story," Evan said. "I guess this is every history teacher's dream."

"Yeah, I guess so," Dan agreed.

"What about this house?" Evan turned to the brick house behind them that had the silver door in the parlor. "I don't remember this house being on Telfair Square."

"This house doesn't have any historical significance that I know of," Dan responded. "In fact, in our time, this house isn't even here. Do you know what's here in our time?"

"I couldn't venture to guess," Evan replied.

"The Savannah field office of the IRS. I had some tax issues I needed to take care of a few weeks ago. I stood right here looking at Telfair Square. The same as we're doing now."

"You're kidding me," Evan said.

"No, I'm serious. I was in this exact spot."

"This really is amazing." Evan looked in all directions. "But we need to get back. At least I do. If you want to stay, you can, but I have to get back."

Dan looked around again too.

"Okay, I'm coming with you. I'm freezing. You promise to tell me how we got here?"

"I'll tell you everything I know."

"I'd like to get a picture of this place before we go. Nobody is going to believe me. I'm still not sure if this is a dream."

"More like a nightmare," Evan said. He reached into his shorts pocket, the pocket without the silver key, and took out his iPhone. "I'll get a few pictures of you, but please, let's hurry and get out of here." He pressed the camera app on his phone.

"Thanks," Dan said and walked to the closest building, about twenty feet away. It was three stories and made of a rust-colored brick.

As Evan was snapping a picture of Dan in front of a Confederate battle flag fluttering on a pole attached to the building, a man walked out behind Dan. He was wearing a grey Confederate uniform.

"You two," he said, "what are you doing there?"

He had a robust Southern accent.

Evan was certain he'd heard those same words spoken earlier by the British officer. But this situation was quickly turning out differently.

Three, four, five more uniformed men came out of the building and were now on both sides of Dan. The brick house with the silver door was too far. There was no way Evan and Dan would be able to make a break for the house and get to the silver door inside.

Evan thought of the key in his pocket. He had the same thought as earlier. He'd grab the key and make his secret wish for Will, Dan, and himself to be together safe in the beach house. Regardless of what Caris would learn from Mary Ellen Hadley, Evan had no choice. He had to make his wish now.

"Get your hands up," snapped the first man who had come out of the building.

Evan started to move his hand toward his pocket.

"I said get your hands up," the Confederate ordered again.

Two of the men who were standing with Dan had revolvers that were now pointed at Evan. One of the men cocked his gun's hammer.

Evan's iPhone that he had used to take the picture of Dan was in his right hand. The silver key was in the left-side pocket of his shorts. He was sure he wouldn't be able to move his hand quickly. He nevertheless considered dropping his phone and plunging his hand into his pocket for the key. He had to. It was now or never.

"If I have to tell you a third time to get your hands up, that's the last thing you're going to hear."

The man didn't sound like he was bluffing. There was no way Evan could reach the key before the man with the pistol could pull the trigger.

Evan raised his hands. The Confederate came closer and took Evan's iPhone.

"Keep your hands up until I determine this situation," he said. "There's something certainly amiss with the two of you."

The camera app was still open on the iPhone from when Evan took the picture of Dan. The man lifted the phone toward his face and was startled when he looked at the screen and could see Evan on the other side of it.

The man didn't say a word.

He stared at Evan intently for several seconds.

"Duxbury, Massachusetts," he finally said.

"What's that?" Evan responded.

He pointed at Evan's shirt and turned to his men. "I've never seen a contraption such as this. But looks to me like we have us a couple of Yankee spies."

About a hundred and fifty years into the future and quite a few miles away from where Evan and Dan now stood as captives of the Confederacy, the ferry that Caris had boarded on Daufuskie Island arrived at Hilton Head. She would be in Bluffton within twenty minutes and hoped that Evan, Katie, and Abby would be at the dock at the Bluffton Oyster Company waiting for her before going on to meet Mary Ellen Hadley.

Katie, however, was already there. She had flown up the May River and had easily found the oyster company. She had landed on the dock, paused for a few moments, and was in the air again looking for Sycamore Street and Mary Ellen's house with its blue roof.

At the same moment, a LifeStar helicopter landed at Savannah Memorial Hospital. The hospital's emergency medical services coordinator, whose job included assessing patients as soon as they arrived at the hospital by ambulance or helicopter, did a double take when she saw that the unconscious patient onboard appeared to be wearing a British soldier's uniform from the American Revolution.

And in a completely different time and place in the world, a seven-year-old boy named Will St. John was being comforted by an unfamiliar woman. The boy had no idea where he was or where his parents were. He had been crying, and the woman, who was a mother of her own three children, felt a motherly need to care for him. Although his appearance out of thin air had scared most everyone in the woman's village, the woman was not afraid. Whether the boy who had supernaturally appeared was a god or not, she didn't know. That was something to be determined by others. For now, she stroked his light blond hair and told him in broken English that everything would be fine.

CHAPTER 16

"WE'RE NOT SPIES," EVAN SAID.

"We'll find out soon enough," the Confederate officer replied. "Sergeant Higgins, please do me the courtesy of searching them."

"Yes sir, Major," a large man said. He put a beefy hand into Evan's pockets and took out the silver key. Evan's wallet was also soon in the man's massive hand. He searched Dan and easily found Dan's cell phone and wallet.

"Thank you, Sergeant," the Confederate officer said when he took all of the items.

He examined Dan's cell phone carefully for a few moments and put both phones into a pocket of his grey uniform. He placed the silver key into the pocket too.

He then opened the wallets and inspected the contents, removing Evan's Georgia driver's license and Dan's South Carolina driver's license.

"Georgia and South Carolina," he said, exaggerating his already strong Southern accent. "I don't recognize either of these papers. Are these some sort of identification? I would expect that if a couple of Yankees were going to have forged papers, they would at least look real."

133

He examined the licenses more closely.

"Odd," he finally said. "This material. It isn't paper."

"It's plastic," Dan said.

The man looked at Evan, as if to say something, and then stopped himself.

"Yeah," Evan said, "plastic. Actually, I think it's a plastic laminate. I'm not really sure."

The Confederate officer glanced again at the words Georgia and South Carolina written largely at the top of each driver's license.

"I'm from Charleston," he finally said, looking at Dan's South Carolina driver's license. "I haven't been home in over a year. My name's Nathan Childs. Major Nathan Childs of the Fifth South Carolina Infantry Regiment."

"South Carolina," Dan said. "I've lived there for the last twenty years. Evan here has had a house in South Carolina the last five years or so."

"You don't sound like you're from South Carolina," the major said, almost sarcastically.

"So you can tell," Dan said with his own hint of sarcasm. "I'm not originally from there. I was actually born in Pittsburg. I grew up in Pennsylvania and taught school before settling in South Carolina."

"Then where, sir, are your loyalties?" the major asked. "I love South Carolina and would give my life for her and the cause. Where do your loyalties lie?"

It took Dan a moment to realize that Major Childs was asking him if he supported the North or the South. Dan had almost an encyclopedic knowledge of American history from his forty years of teaching. He had, in particular, focused on Southern history and the Civil War following his move to Hilton Head after his wife's death. He tried to recall the name Nathan Childs from his vast memory. The name rang no bells, nor held any historical significance. Major Nathan Childs was instead one of thousands of officers in the Confederate army lost to history. Dan had no idea whether the man would survive the war.

And yet, here the Confederate officer was, standing with Evan and Dan on a dirt road across from Telfair Square in long-ago Savannah.

Dan took in the sights, smells, and sounds of the Old South. He had made South Carolina his home and loved living there, but the South Carolina Dan loved wouldn't exist for nearly another century and a half. The South Carolina that Major Nathan Childs called home was a land that included plantations and slavery.

Major Childs looked at Dan for several more seconds waiting for an answer. "That's what I figured," he finally said. "Your loyalty is not to the South."

"You know, Major, I've thought about your South Carolina over the years and your cause. You don't know this yet, and maybe you'll never realize it, but you're on the wrong side of history. The South Carolina that's your home is not mine."

"Whether it's your home or not," Major Childs said, "that's where you're going. I'm taking you both to Charleston to General Beauregard. I honestly don't care where you call home. But I do care about these devices you have.

I've never seen anything remotely like them. The general needs to see these for himself. After that, he'll make the decision on what to do with you."

"General Beauregard?" Dan said. "He's in Charleston?"

Now it was Major Childs's turn to not answer.

"Major," Dan said, "we've been traveling, and I'm embarrassed to say that I've become a bit confused on what day it is. If you don't mind me asking, what's the date today?"

"As this might be the day you're going to hang, you should at least know the date. Today's Sunday. It's December eleventh."

Major Childs did not say the year. He didn't need to. Dan realized the year. It was 1864. Confederate General P. G. T. Beauregard had been in charge of the defense of Savannah, and if he'd already left for Charleston, there was only one reason why. Union General William Tecumseh Sherman was about to complete his historic march to the sea across Georgia, and General Beauregard was in Charleston finalizing his plans to evacuate his ten-thousand-men Confederate garrison from Savannah before Sherman took the city.

CHAPTER 17

KATIE FOUND SYCAMORE STREET AND WAS CERTAIN SHE was at the right house. The blue roof from the air looked similar to the blue roof of Mary Ellen Hadley's destroyed house on Daufuskie Island.

She landed near the driveway and saw the number 320 on the mailbox. There was no question that this was the right place.

A bit of nervousness swept over Katie as she walked up the drive, looking at the house's blue shutters and front door. She stepped onto a small front stoop and knocked. The sound of movement came from somewhere inside.

Katie took a step back as the door opened, revealing an old woman with dark brown skin, black hair, and a face wrinkled from age.

"Are you Ms. Hadley?" Katie tentatively asked. "I'm looking for Mary Ellen Hadley."

"Well, you found her," the woman answered, moving from the house onto the front stoop.

The aged woman appeared to study Katie, taking her fully into view. Her intent gaze made Katie nervous and uncomfortable. Katie's nervousness soon gave way to a wave of fright. Coming by herself might not have been such a good idea after all.

But then a smile appeared on the woman's ancient face. A warm and inviting smile. She beamed at Katie radiantly.

"Oh, Katie, it's so good to see you again."

Katie hadn't expected that. She was certain she'd never met the old woman before.

Mary Ellen moved forward and wrapped her arms around Katie. "Oh, child, I've been so looking forward to seeing you again."

"How do you know my name?" Katie stepped away from Mary Ellen's embrace. "We've never met, have we?"

"Oh, we've definitely met. How else would I know who you are? You're Katie St. John, and you're eleven years old. I've been expecting you." The woman smiled again. "I've been waiting a long time for you. A very long time."

Katie suddenly felt like a child in a fairy tale. A fairy tale where a witch, acting sweet and happy, lures a child into the witch's house and cooks her. Katie had a cold feeling again that she shouldn't have come alone. She should have waited for her dad at the welcome center with Abby and Natalie. She should have listened to her parents and her sister.

"You look frightened," Mary Ellen said. "Oh, don't be frightened, my sweet child."

My sweet child. Wasn't that something a witch would say before springing a devilish trap on an unsuspecting youth?

Katie wondered if the woman had known she'd come alone. But even so, Katie had wanted to come by herself.

She wanted to meet this woman. She needed to know if Will was here. She needed to be brave. She thought of the hurricane that had battered the beach house and how brave her mother had been. Will was missing, and this strange woman might know where he was.

"I'm looking for my brother," Katie forced herself to say.

"I know you are. But Will isn't here."

"You know I'm here looking for Will? How do you know that?"

Yet the woman had said Will's name.

"Do you know where he is?" Katie asked. "Have you seen him?"

"Will's okay, child," Mary Ellen answered. "But he's not the one you need to be worried about right now."

Katie wondered what the woman was saying. Was she saying that Katie herself needed to be worried? Was that something a witch would say before nabbing a child and eating her? *You need to be worried about yourself, you little morsel of flesh and bones, because I'm about to put you in a pot of boiling water.*

"Who do I need to be worried about?" Katie asked. She hoped her voice would not reveal how frightened she was.

"Your father. He needs your help. You need to save him."

"Daddy," Katie said, surprised.

She was no longer scared. Whether Mary Ellen was a witch or not, the mention that her father needed her help caused Katie to put aside any fear.

"Is Kenny Shivers going to hurt Daddy?"

"Kenny Shivers? No, not that boy." Mary Ellen looked intently at Katie. "Your father is about to meet Mr. Rawlins."

"Who?" Katie asked.

"Mr. Gregory Rawlins. He may be the cruelest man who ever lived."

"Mr. Rawlins? I don't know who that is."

"You will, Katie, you will. You need to go. I want you to get into the air and fly to the lighthouse."

Katie stood silently.

"Oh, I know you can fly. I know a lot of things. And right now I know you need to get back over to Daufuskie Island and get into that lighthouse. You go upstairs. There's a door up there to one of the bedrooms. It's silver. It's a silver door framed within a wooden door. You'll see it. There's a silver doorknob. This is important, girl, so you listen well. You listen to what I'm telling you."

She held Katie's hand and squeezed it gently.

"I want you to take this hand and put it on that silver doorknob and turn it. It'll be unlocked. That's already been taken care of. When you open that door, you think of finding your father. Remember that. Think of going to where your father is. Don't think of anything else. When the silver door opens, you go through it. You hear what I'm saying? You go through that door to find him."

Katie nodded, having no idea why she was nodding or what the woman was telling her to do. She nodded nonetheless.

"Now when you get through the doorway, things won't appear right. You're going to be in a different place than where you thought you'd be. You'll see things that don't seem right. But, Katie, listen to me. You're a strong and brave girl. When you go through that silver door, you won't be in the lighthouse anymore. You'll be in Savannah."

"What?" Katie replied. "I'll be in Savannah?"

"Yes. It won't make sense to you, but you'll be in Savannah. For now, just listen to me. When you go through that door, I want you to find your way outside and get into the air. Don't you stop and talk to anyone. Don't let anybody talk to you. You step outside, and you start flying. I know this is a lot to take in, and you probably think I'm a crazy old woman rambling on about some nonsense, but Katie, I'm telling you what you need to do."

She put her hands on both of Katie's shoulders and looked steadily into Katie's eyes.

"I know that you, along with Will, Abby, and your mama, found that chest and made wishes on the key inside. I know you can fly."

Katie's full attention was now focused on Mary Ellen.

"I know that Will went missing. You'll see him again soon. I promise you. But right now, your biggest concern is finding your father. So when you get into the air, you need to fly right back to Daufuskie Island. That's where you're going to fly to."

"I don't understand," Katie said. "If I go into the lighthouse and come out of the lighthouse, won't I already be on Daufuskie Island?"

"You're not listening to me. You're going to be in Savannah. That silver door is going to put you into Savannah. I know this is difficult to take in, but that's the magic. Does it make sense you can fly? No, of course not. Yet you can. When you go through that door in the lighthouse, you're going to end up in Savannah. I know it sounds crazy, but that's where you'll be. And then you need to fly back to Daufuskie Island. I know this is asking a lot, but you can do it. You don't know this, but you've already done it."

"I've never done that."

"This is difficult to explain, so I'm not going to try. It will only confuse you more. It's almost time for you to be on your way. I have something for you first. Wait here."

Mary Ellen retreated into her house and emerged a moment later holding a black jacket.

"It's wool. I made it for you myself. You'll need it. It'll be cold where you're going."

"I'm still not sure I understand."

"It'll make sense when you're there. But now Katie, there's a little more to it. When you fly back to Daufuskie Island from Savannah, the lighthouse isn't going to be there."

"Now I'm totally confused. The lighthouse isn't going to be there? You just told me to fly back to Daufuskie Island to the lighthouse."

"The lighthouse won't be there when you fly back to Daufuskie Island because the silver door will not only take you to Savannah when you go through it, it'll take you to a different time. You'll be in the days of horses and buggies. Before the lighthouse was even built."

"The silver door is a time machine?"

"No, not a time machine. It's a passageway from one place in time to another."

The things the old woman was saying sounded ridiculous. Pure fantasy. Yet, at the same time, Katie knew the woman was speaking the truth.

"So when I go through the silver door, it will not only take me to Savannah, but it will take me back in time?"

"That's right. I knew you were a smart girl, Katie. When you fly back to Daufuskie Island, the lighthouse won't be there because at that time, the lighthouse hasn't been built yet. Standing in its exact spot will instead be a large house."

"A large house? You're talking about the Haig Point mansion. The lighthouse was built on the foundation of the Haig Point mansion. There's a sign next to the lighthouse that says it. That's where you want me to go? To the Haig Point mansion?"

"Oh my, you're full of surprises. Yes, indeed, you're a smart one. That's exactly where I want you to go. To the Haig Point mansion. But when you get there, Katie, do not go into that house. You know the tabby ruins of the slave quarters near the field where the lighthouse is now?"

"Yes," Katie answered.

"When you get to Daufuskie Island in that time, those ruins won't be ruins. They'll be fully intact slave quarters. I don't dare call them houses. There'll be a row of them, like the tabby ruins there now. I want you to go to the last one and sit right there, outside by the door. It won't be long before someone will come. That'll be someone you can trust. She'll ask you what you're doing there. You tell her your name and that you're there to help your daddy. She'll know what to do. She'll bring you to your father. And that's all you need to know."

"That's all I need to know? I don't know anything. What am I supposed to do when I find Daddy?"

"Oh, child," Mary Ellen said and hugged her again. "Trust me, you'll know what to do when you're there."

"How do you know all of this?"

Mary Ellen looked at her and smiled again. Another big, broad smile.

"People say you're a witch," Katie said, not really sure that was something she should have said.

"A witch? Do I look like a witch?"

"Well, kind of. Do you know all these things because you're a witch?"

"No, I'm not a witch."

"Then how do you know all this?"

"I'm—what's the word? Unique. I'm unique. I know a lot of things, Katie. And right now I know that you need to go back to that island and into the lighthouse."

"I don't understand why you want me to do this."

"There's a lot you're not going to understand right now. But you will. Your daddy is about to be in a whole pickle of a bad situation and needs your help. You need to get going. Just you. Just you, Katie. You need to do this on your own."

Mary Ellen walked Katie off the stoop and into her front yard. "Now quickly, tell me what you're going to do, so I know you got it."

Katie didn't want to do anything that Mary Ellen had said. But she knew she would. She would do everything she was told to do. It didn't make sense, but none of the magic had made sense.

"I'm going to the lighthouse and upstairs where I'll find a room with a silver door. You want me to open the door and go through in order to find Daddy. You say that it's going to take me to Savannah in the days of horses and buggies. I don't know why that'll happen, but I believe you. When I get there, you want me to fly back to Daufuskie Island. I've made that trip with Daddy a lot of times in his boat. I'll find my way. When I get there, I'll fly to the Haig Point mansion and the row of slave houses. I'll find them. I'll go to the last one like you said and sit by the door until someone comes and gets me."

"Perfect," Mary Ellen said. "That's exactly what you need to do."

"Who'll come and get me?"

"You'll see when you're there."

"And Daddy will be there?"

"Oh yes, he'll be there."

Mary Ellen helped Katie put on the wool jacket and kissed her forehead. "Now off you go."

Katie looked at Mary Ellen one last time before ascending into the air on her way to the lighthouse. She had more questions than answers. She was still scared, but not as much as she had been before. If her father needed her, she wouldn't let him down.

About fifteen minutes after Katie left, a white Suburban pulled into the driveway at 320 Sycamore Street. Caris turned off the engine and exited her vehicle.

Mary Ellen was on a rocking chair on the stoop waiting for her. "Hello, Caris," she called out.

The morning had been full of surprises. Yet the old black woman on the front stoop knowing Caris's name didn't come as a surprise. Caris thought about it and realized it would have been a surprise had the woman *not* known Caris's name.

She approached the stoop. "So you're Mary Ellen Hadley."

"I am."

"I'd ask if you know why I'm here, but I have a feeling you already know."

"You're looking for Will. I know that, Caris. You'll be with him soon. He's okay. I know your heart's been breaking."

"You know where he is?"

"No, I don't, but I know you'll be together again soon."

"What's that supposed to mean?"

"The two of you will be together soon. You're going to go where he is."

"And where's that? Is he inside? Do you have him?"

"Oh, no. I wouldn't be cruel like that. He's not here."

Caris was becoming annoyed. "You don't know where my son is, but you know he's okay and that I'll be with him soon?"

"That's right. I told Katie that too."

"Katie? Was my husband here with the girls?"

"No, Evan and Abby weren't here. Just Katie. She came to see me alone. She's already gone."

"Katie was here by herself? How? Why?"

"She flew here on her own. I know of her wish that she could fly. I know this doesn't make sense, Caris. It didn't make sense to Katie either. But you need to trust me. We're connected more than you know."

The woman had known that Caris would find the key. There was definitely more to Mary Ellen Hadley.

"Tell me then, how are we connected? And if you know where my son is, tell me."

"I'd tell you if I knew. I would. I know the pain you're going through. I only know that he's okay and that you'll be with him."

"If you won't tell me where he is, then tell me where Katie went. You said she's gone."

"I sent her to the lighthouse."

Mary Ellen didn't say which lighthouse. Caris already knew.

"You told her to go to the Haig Point lighthouse, didn't you?" Caris asked.

"I did."

"Why?"

"Because that's where she needs to be."

"You're speaking in riddles."

"I know it sounds that way. Stay with me for a few moments. We have so much to talk about. There is so much to tell you."

Caris thought of her earlier conversation with Evan about the lighthouse and whether the silver key from the chest was for the silver door. And now this woman had sent her daughter there.

"Tell me why you sent Katie to the lighthouse, and don't tell me that it's because she needs to be there. *Why* does she need to be there?"

"You're not going to believe me, but I'll tell you. Katie is going to go into the lighthouse, and when she comes out, she'll be in Savannah in December 1864. Evan is there now. He needs her help."

"What?" Caris asked in disbelief.

"That's what's going to happen. That's why I sent Katie. She's on her way to save your husband. She's on her way to save Evan."

Caris turned away from Mary Ellen and headed toward her Suburban.

"Caris, where are you going?"

"Where am I going? I'm headed back to Daufuskie Island and the lighthouse. Where do you think I'm going? I'm going to get Katie."

"You're not supposed to be there. Stay with me a bit longer. I have more that I need to tell you. You came here to hear what I have to say, and I'm telling you that you're not supposed to be where Katie's going, where Evan is now. This is something that Katie needs to do alone. She has a destiny that she needs to fulfill, and it does not include you being there."

"I know I've seen things today that I can't explain. And, yes, I came to see you for answers. So, please tell me, how do you know any of what you're telling me?"

"Because I was there. What is about to happen has already happened. Katie saves your husband. I was there.

You weren't. That's how I know you're not supposed to be where Katie is going. I lived it. You have your own path. It's a path that'll take you to your son. I don't know where he is, but I know your path will take you to him. This is Katie's path."

Mary Ellen rocked back in her chair. "Now come back and sit with me while we talk. You made me promise when we met before that I'd tell you everything you needed to hear in order for you to trust that what I'm saying is true and that Will is safe."

"But we've never met before."

"Oh, we haven't? I wouldn't be so sure about that," Mary Ellen said with a smile. "We've met. It was nearly a hundred and fifty years ago. I've been waiting since then for this day to speak with you again."

CHAPTER 18

COLONEL JOHN MAITLAND HAD DRIFTED IN AND OUT OF consciousness aboard the LifeStar helicopter. As he was wheeled into the emergency room at Savannah Memorial Hospital, he was unconscious again and entirely unaware of the triage nurse's attempts to assess his condition. His fever was 104 degrees, moving in the direction of fatal. His heart rate and blood pressure were poor. His breathing was shallow and labored.

"Let's get him into treatment room five," the nurse said.

"Interesting choice of clothes," Dr. Dwight Stephens commented, as he entered the treatment room to examine his latest patient. Dr. Stephens had finished his residency two years earlier and was the youngest emergency room physician at the hospital. "What do we know about him?"

"Not much," the nurse said. "LifeStar flew him over from one of the islands. Daufuskie, I think."

Colonel Maitland's coat had been taken off, and an emergency room aide removed his shirt, exposing where his right arm had been amputated. Dr. Stephens began a physical exam.

151

"His spleen's swollen," Doctor Stephens said, slightly pressing his patient's abdomen. "Liver too. We need to start ruling out causes. I want a full blood work-up. Let's get an RDT going."

An RDT, or Rapid Diagnostic Test, is used to quickly detect various bacteria, viruses, and parasites. Since an unconscious patient being admitted into the emergency room can turn into a life-threatening situation if a diagnosis is not timely made, an RDT may mean the difference between life and death.

A technician found a vein in Colonel Maitland's arm and inserted a needle. A small amount of blood was drawn for the RDT. Two full vials were also filled for additional testing.

"Well look at that," the technician said a few minute later when the RDT results came back.

"Let's get Dr. Hunter in here," Dr. Stephens replied. "He had a patient last summer with the same thing. I want to make sure he sees this."

Dr. Julius Hunter was sixty-two and the emergency room's chief physician. "What do we have?" he asked when he entered the treatment room.

"We just got the RDT results back," Dr. Stephens said. "It's malaria. I know you had that patient last summer from one of the cargo ships. From Malaysia if I remember correctly."

"Yeah, he contracted it abroad and was pretty sick when the ship arrived. How about this man, do we know where he contracted it?"

"No. He was unconscious on arrival."

"Go ahead and start a broad spectrum treatment until we know what species of parasite we're looking at here. When are the lab results going to be in?" Dr. Hunter asked the technician.

"Should be another few hours," the tech answered. "I wasn't working here last summer. I've never seen a malaria patient before."

"Well, as long as we start treatment early enough, there's a very strong survival rate. When a mosquito that carries the malaria parasite bites a person, the parasites are introduced. They then travel in the bloodstream to the liver where they reproduce. Headaches and fevers can progress to coma and death if not treated."

"I have a backup of patients injured last night in the hurricane," Dr. Stephens interrupted. "Any chance you interested in taking this one?"

"Yeah, I'll take him," Dr. Hunter answered. "We'll get intravenous quinine started. By the way, Dwight, what's the scoop with this guy's clothes?"

"Maybe he does reenactments."

"Yeah, maybe. But I'm more concerned where he contracted it." Dr. Hunter turned to the technician. "There's mandatory reporting of confirmed malaria cases. We're going to have to get his name and information when he regains consciousness. Where do think he's been to have picked up this bug?"

Chapter 19

EVAN AND DAN WERE TAKEN FROM TELFAIR SQUARE BY Major Nathan Childs and a detachment of eight men. Their hands were tied together in front of them for a half-mile march until they reached a wooden wharf along the Savannah River.

"Sergeant Higgins," Major Childs said to the big Confederate soldier who had searched Evan and Dan. "Keep them here. I need to confer with General Hardee."

"Yes sir," the sergeant replied.

Dan waited a few minutes after the major left. He spoke to Evan in a soft voice so the nearby soldiers couldn't hear.

"See those?" he said.

Near the riverbank, several pontoons and barges bobbed in the current of the Savannah River. Teams of soldiers were hammering planks across their tops.

"They're going to attach them together end to end," Dan whispered. "They're constructing a floating bridge over to Hutchinson Island." He motioned slightly toward an island in the river. "And from there to the South Carolina side. It's going to be the Confederate garrison's evacuation route before Sherman cuts them off and takes Savannah."

"Sherman?" Evan said in a low voice. "What Sherman? General Sherman?"

"Yeah, General Sherman." Dan looked to make sure their conversation could not be overheard. "We need to get back through that doorway. I figure we're in Savannah in December 1864. The city's going to fall to Sherman's army soon, and I don't think we should be around when that happens."

Major Childs soon returned with a few more soldiers, who climbed into two sailboats tied to the wharf. "Gentlemen," he said, "you two are in this one with me."

Evan and Dan were forced onto a wooden bench seat in the front of the smaller of the two boats, and both of the sloops were soon underway.

The December air was cold, especially in the middle of the river. Their shorts and T-shirts had been comfortable on Daufuskie Island on a warm June day, but now, Evan and Dan were cold and miserable. The wind picked up, and every few minutes, frigid spray from the river landed on their bare arms and legs.

Major Childs came to the front of the boat holding a wool blanket that he offered them. With their hands still tied, Evan and Dan accepted the blanket and tucked it in around them, which took away some of the chill.

"Major, where exactly are you taking us?" Dan asked. "Earlier you said Charleston to see General Beauregard. Surely we're not sailing to Charleston."

Major Childs, who had returned to the rear of the boat, looked away without responding.

"Evan," Dan said grimly, "the mouth of the Savannah River is controlled by the Union where it hits the Atlantic. We're in a Confederate boat."

"I'm assuming that's not good," Evan said.

"No, it's not."

"Well, who's this general we're going to see in Charleston?" Evan asked.

"His name is Beauregard. You've heard of Fort Sumter in Charleston Harbor, haven't you?"

"Yeah," Evan answered, "the first shots of the Civil War happened there."

"That's right," Dan said. "Beauregard ordered the attack on Fort Sumter."

"Is that right?" Evan asked.

"It is," Dan answered. "Let me give you a two-minute history lesson to get you up to speed on General Beauregard. I'll try not to sound like a history teacher."

"Teach away, my friend," Evan said. "I think we might have some time." He looked at the cold, grey sky.

"Okay, back in November 1860, Abraham Lincoln was elected president."

"Now him I've heard of," Evan said.

"As I'm sure you probably know, Lincoln opposed slavery."

"Yep, I knew that one also. I'm shooting two for two."

"South Carolina feared that Lincoln would outlaw slavery after taking office," Dan said, "so the state legislature called a convention to decide whether or not to stay in the Union. There was a unanimous vote to secede. You see,

157

their state had voluntarily joined the United States when our country was created, so they figured they had the right to leave if they wanted. Lincoln disagreed.

"Six more Southern states seceded right after that and created the Confederate States of America. The Confederacy then sent representatives to meet with Lincoln in order to negotiate a peace treaty and purchase Union properties in the South. But Lincoln thought that any negotiations would be viewed as recognizing the Confederacy and refused to meet. In response, the Confederacy forcibly took Union property.

"General Beauregard, who we're on our way to see, was in charge of South Carolina's military forces in Charleston. Fort Sumter in Charleston Harbor was one of the properties owned by the Union that the Confederacy wanted. When Beauregard demanded the surrender of the fort, and the fort's commanding Union officer refused, Beauregard responded by opening fire. That was April 12, 1861, the start of the Civil War."

"So Beauregard stayed in Charleston throughout the war?" Evan asked.

"Actually, no. He was appointed to various commands and ultimately ended up in Savannah to defend the city from General Sherman."

"You mentioned Sherman earlier and that he's on his way to Savannah."

"Yeah, I'm assuming you know about Sherman's march to the sea. After he burned Atlanta, he proposed a plan to strike out across Georgia with sixty thousand of his men and cause utter destruction of everything in his path from Atlanta to Savannah. He wanted to shorten the war by destroying the Confederate will to fight. He wanted to show the citizens of the Confederacy that he was free to march his army wherever he wanted and that the Confederate government was incapable of stopping him. In his own words, he wanted to make Georgia howl."

"And he's almost here now?"

"Yeah, remember earlier when Major Childs said the date today is December 11? Well, two days earlier, on December 9, 1864, Sherman reached and overtook the outer defenses of Savannah. On that same day, the Confederate general in charge of defending Savannah skedaddled."

"That's General Beauregard," Evan said. "The one we're on our way to see in Charleston?"

"That's right. Beauregard already regards Savannah as lost. He knows that his ten-thousand-man garrison won't hold out long against Sherman's battle-hardened army of sixty thousand. That's why he's having the pontoon bridge built. He's already left for Charleston and put one of his subordinate generals in charge. Did you hear Major Childs say he needed to speak with General Hardee? Hardee is under orders from Beauregard to defend Savannah as long as he can and to get the floating bridge completed."

"Sherman doesn't know about the bridge?"

"Nope," Dan said. "Sherman has no idea. And before his army is able to get their heavy guns into position, General Hardee finishes the bridge and gets his men across into South Carolina under cover of night. It's pretty amazing they were able to pull it off. The bridge's planks will be covered with straw to muffle the sounds of feet, hooves, and wheels, and ten thousand Confederates will secretly cross from Savannah into South Carolina. When the last man has crossed, the pontoons will be set on fire, and the cables connecting them will be cut."

"You're enjoying this, aren't you?"

Dan gave a smile.

"Is it that obvious?" he said. "This is history, and we're living it. I'm not too thrilled with being a captive, but yeah, I am enjoying this. It's amazing, and I have no idea how we got here."

"I'll tell you later," Evan said. "I don't want to risk any of them overhearing what I'll tell you."

The weather turned colder.

"What about Savannah's citizens?" Evan asked. "Did they cross the bridge too?"

"Actually, no," Dan answered. "The next morning, the citizens of Savannah will wake up, learn of the Confederate garrison's evacuation, and will feel completely betrayed. The city's aldermen end up riding out to meet Sherman to surrender. They'll plead with him to not burn Savannah, and unlike Atlanta's fate, Sherman agrees."

"If I remember my history," Evan said, "I think Sherman presents Savannah to Abraham Lincoln as a Christmas present."

"That's right," Dan responded. "I don't know about you, but for me, I think this is downright pretty cool to talk about history without it being past tense. I mean, these events that we've been talking about, they happened about a hundred and fifty years ago in our time. But for these people here, these are things that are *going* to happen."

"I know what you mean," Evan said. "And thanks for the history lesson."

"No problem."

Evan sat for a few minutes thinking.

"Listen, Dan, I really need to get that key back and for us to get out of here. Let's just say, for sake of argument, that we were able to give Major Childs some important information about what is going to happen in exchange for him taking us back to Savannah and giving us the key."

Dan looked at Evan skeptically. "You want to trade information? Maybe give Major Childs the Union's plans for a major battle that hasn't been fought yet? What you're suggesting could change the outcome of the Civil War. That would have significant repercussions. Haven't you seen *Back to The Future*? If Marty McFly's parents hadn't kissed at the Enchantment Under the Sea Dance, then Marty would never have been born. He'd be erased from existence. That was only a movie. This is real. You're talking about potentially changing the outcome of the entire Civil War. Don't you think that a different ending to the Civil War might affect something in our time?"

"Well?" Evan murmured.

"Well what?" Dan responded. "That's a bad idea. We can't get involved in history. What has happened once has happened."

"Okay, Dan, bad idea. You're right."

"You know what could actually change the outcome of the Civil War? A good set of walkie-talkies," Dan said. "If the Confederates had better communications, like at Gettysburg, they would've won those battles."

"Do you think he knows we're from the future?" Evan asked.

"He, who?"

"He, Major Childs," Evan said. "Our driver's licenses have our birthdates on them and the dates they were issued."

"I don't know. He's definitely not too talkative."

"Yeah, I guess it doesn't matter," Evan said.

Evan thought about the key and hoped Major Childs would not show as much curiosity in the key as he had shown with their cell phones. Evan padded the outer fabric of his shorts pocket. He could feel the note still inside that Caris had given him. The big sergeant had missed it when he had searched Evan and Dan. At least Major Childs would not know about making a wish from the note, and Evan hoped the Confederate officer would not start fumbling around with the key and inadvertently make a wish that could change the outcome of the Civil War.

Neither spoke again for several more minutes as they floated past random trees varying in size, draped with Spanish moss along the banks of the river. The miles of dormant winter marsh grass had a brown hue.

"We're passing Elba Island," Evan said. "That's Bird Island up ahead of us on the right and Jones Island on the left."

The two boats sailed silently toward the left side of the Savannah River to where the water forked around a low island. The river narrowed as the two boats took the left fork.

"You don't need to worry about us running into the Union navy," Evan said. "We're not heading to the Atlantic. We've just left the Savannah River. This fork is actually the Harbor River. It'll narrow more ahead and then widen out as it merges with the Cooper River on the other side of Turtle Island. The water gets pretty wide after that on its way to the Calibogue Sound. I came through here this morning in my boat. In our time, this is part of the Intracoastal Waterway. We're going to pass right by Daufuskie Island."

"Back to where we began. I'm just hoping the day is going to get a bit better soon," Dan said.

"I'm with you on that," Evan agreed. He turned and looked at Major Childs sitting at the back of the small sailboat. "Let's hope it gets better soon."

CHAPTER 20

EVAN COULD SEE DAUFUSKIE ISLAND AHEAD ON THE RIGHT and watched as they passed a few docks with various boats tied to them along the backside of the island. Minutes later, he could see the Calibogue Sound. Another dock came into view, and Evan realized it was in the same location where the Haig Point ferry dock would be built. The two boats came closer to land.

Three scruffy men wearing civilian clothing and thick wool coats stood on the dock. "I wasn't expecting to see you again so soon, Major," one of the men said.

Evan could hardly understand his Southern drawl.

"Any news from Savannah?" another man asked. "Have you come to tell us you've pushed back the Yankee invaders? Is it safe for us to return to our homes?"

"No such news," Major Childs answered, as they tied the two sailboats to the dock.

Two other men and a woman were now walking onto the dock.

"Your homes are safe, at least for now. Sherman is advancing. I wish I were here to tell you that his army has been defeated, but I'm afraid that's not why I'm here."

"Who are these two with you?" the woman asked.

Evan and Dan climbed out of the smaller boat and stood on the dock next to Major Childs. Their hands remained tied, and the wool blanket was left behind in the boat.

"They'll catch their death of cold," the woman said, examining their T-shirts and shorts.

"These two are the reason I'm here. I'm looking for William Graffin."

Evan was certain he'd just heard the name of the man who had signed the note that Caris had found with the key. The note now in his shorts pocket.

"Do you know where I might find him?" Major Childs asked the small group that had gathered. "I've been informed he was among you when you fled Savannah."

"The manor house," one of the scruffy men answered. "He's there. And Major, with all due respect, I have every confidence in your ability to defend our homes, but if Savannah falls and has the same fate as Atlanta—"

"Where may I find it?" Major Childs asked, cutting off the man.

"I'll take you," another man answered. "What business do you have with Mr. Graffin?"

"That's something I'll take up with Mr. Graffin."

The man led the way from the dock onto a dirt lane, narrower than the island roads that Evan and Dan had traveled so many times. The Confederate soldiers from the two boats accompanied them, except for a couple who stayed behind at the dock.

The narrow lane opened to several clearings. White pods of cotton sporadically dotted the landscape. It took

Evan a few moments to realize that he was looking at the dried bolls of Sea Island cotton. He knew that Sea Island cotton had been the backbone of Daufuskie Island's economy, and that the cotton industry in the Lowcountry had been decimated by the Civil War, never to return.

They continued through the abandoned cotton fields until reaching another field that had not been planted. Through a small stand of trees on the other side, Evan could see a large tabby house where the lighthouse should have been. Evan and Dan stopped walking and looked ahead at the Haig Point mansion.

They were standing in a field Evan knew well—the same field where his wife had set down the wooden chest. He looked far to his right. Sea Island cotton that would never again be harvested swayed in the winter breeze where his family's beach house would one day be built. He thought of Caris and his children. He desperately wanted to know if Caris had met Mary Ellen Hadley and whether she'd found Will.

"Keep moving," Major Childs ordered.

Evan and Dan were visibly trembling from the cold. Their summer clothing offered little warmth.

The Haig Point mansion was now in front of them with the expanse of the Calibogue Sound directly behind it. A cold December wind from the water stung their arms and legs.

As they approached the mansion, Evan could see two men standing nearby. The two men watched them approach.

"Are you William Graffin?" the major asked one of them.

"I am," the man answered.

He had a kind face. He was short, a little under five and a half feet tall. He appeared to be around sixty, although his age was difficult to determine. He had a head of white hair similar in color to the white bolls of the Sea Island cotton. His thick beard was the same white color, and he reminded Evan of a shorter, thinner version of Santa Claus.

"I'm Major Nathan Childs."

"A pleasure to meet you, Major," William Graffin said and extended his open hand.

The two shook hands.

"We have a situation," Childs said. "May I have a word with you?"

Major Childs glanced at the second man standing next to William Graffin. He was a big man, almost as big as Sergeant Higgins. Childs then turned to thank the man who had shown them the way to the mansion. He nodded and left.

"A situation?" William Graffin asked. He examined Evan and Dan, their hands tied in front of them. "You came from Savannah to have a word with me?"

"Indeed," Major Childs replied. "I wouldn't have come if it wasn't important. General Hardee agrees that it's important enough to have sent me."

"We can speak inside," William Graffin said. "That is, as long as Mr. Rawlins here doesn't mind. Gregory Rawlins is the overseer of the plantation. I'm sure these two want to go inside out of the weather."

"You may speak wherever you prefer," Gregory Rawlins said.

His voice sounded almost like a growl. An angry growl, Evan thought.

"We can speak out here," Major Childs said. "Mr. Graffin, do you know these men?"

"No, I've never seen them before."

"They were in your house in Savannah."

"In my house? Are you certain?"

"I saw them myself come out your front door," Major Childs responded. "One of my men knew the house was yours."

"Well now," William Graffin said. "Why would these men be in my home, and more importantly, why would a pair of burglars cause General Hardee to send you all the way out here from Savannah?"

"Do you deny knowing them?"

"Deny knowing them? Major, I said I've never seen them before. I'm sorry I cannot help you. I don't know them."

"I watched them from a building across the way after they left your house." Major Childs pointed his thumb toward Evan and Dan's clothing. "I think you'd admit they are more than slightly peculiar."

"I'm assuming there must be something you haven't told me," William Graffin said.

"They had devices with them. Also peculiar."

"So, these peculiar men had peculiar devices. And you think they took them from my home?"

"The thought did cross my mind. It crossed General Hardee's mind too. You have a reputation yourself for being a bit peculiar. He ordered that I bring you to Charleston. A messenger has been dispatched ahead of us, and General Beauregard will be expecting us."

"You're here to pluck me from Daufuskie Island and bring me to Charleston?" Graffin looked incredulously at Major Childs.

"Those are my orders."

"And if I don't wish to accompany you to Charleston?"

"You have no choice in the matter. You'll accompany me to Charleston, preferably as my guest."

"Major Childs, I must protest. I don't know what you believe these men took from my home, but I can assure you I don't know them, and there's nothing within my residence that would warrant a trip to Charleston to see General Beauregard or anyone else."

"You can explain that to the general."

William Graffin examined the ropes binding the hands of Evan and Dan. "Tell me, sir," he said to Evan, "what is it that the major believes you took from my home?"

Evan remained silent, thinking the best strategy for now would be to say nothing.

Gregory Rawlins glared at Evan.

"Major," Mr. Graffin said, turning toward the Confederate officer. "What did they have? What were the peculiar devices?"

Major Childs didn't respond. Evan didn't know whether the major was stoic or simply accustomed to giving orders without his orders being questioned.

"Major, I have no involvement in this matter. As long as you are nevertheless intending to bring me to Charleston, you can at least do me the courtesy of letting me know what this is about."

"That is a fair point," Major Childs said.

He took the two cell phones from a pocket of his uniform and held Evan's iPhone so that William Graffin could fully view it.

"And you believe I had this device in my home?"

"That is precisely the discussion we're going to have with General Beauregard."

"You're making a regrettable mistake. I haven't seen any such contraption before, nor these men."

"You can convince the general."

"I intend to do exactly that." William Graffin looked closer at Evan's phone. "I'll grant you that it is a peculiar object. Tell me, Major, did they have anything else with them when they were captured?"

"They had forged identification papers. One of them also had this." Major Childs removed the silver key from his pocket and held it for William Graffin to see. The numbers 1529 were clearly visible.

"That's the key the slave girl stole," Gregory Rawlins interrupted.

"You're mistaken," William Graffin said to Rawlins. He reached into his own coat pocket and lifted out an exact duplicate of the silver key. It even had the numbers 1529 along one side.

Evan stared at it. It was the same as the key that Caris and the kids had found.

"That's a key to my home," William Graffin said. "I don't know how these men came to have it in their possession, and I'm more than willing to take that up with the civilian authorities in Savannah. But in the meantime, if you don't mind, I'd like it returned. I don't see any reason why the Confederacy needs a key to my house."

Major Childs handed the silver key to William Graffin.

Evan considered snatching it from the man's hand and making a wish for Evan, Dan, and Will to be transported to the beach house. But this man, William Graffin, was the person who had signed the note in Evan's pocket. Surely he would have as much information as, if not more than, Mary Ellen Hadley. Evan needed to find a way to speak with him. And then Evan noticed that William Graffin was staring directly at him. Evan was certain the man likewise wanted to talk.

"Sergeant Higgins," Major Childs said, "I'd like you to secure our prisoners for a few hours."

He turned his attention to William Graffin. "The Yankees have control of Port Royal, so sailing to Charleston is not an option. Instead, after sundown, we'll sail up the May River. General Hardee will have horses waiting for us north of Bluffton, and we'll ride from there tonight to Charleston. You'll accompany us when we leave. In the meantime, I must insist that you not leave this property for the next few hours."

"And Mr. Rawlins," the major said to the large man standing next to Graffin, "if I may impose on your hospitality, can you show Sergeant Higgins a place to keep these two out of the weather until we're ready to depart?"

"I know a place," Gregory Rawlins said.

He moved in front of Evan and Dan.

"So you entered this man's house and helped yourselves to his property?" Gregory Rawlins said to Evan. "Do you know what we do with thieves?"

"That'll be all," Major Childs said with authority to Gregory Rawlins.

Ignoring him, Rawlins leaned in between Evan and Dan. "We whip them."

Rawlins put his finger onto Evan's Duxbury T-shirt.

"And if the thief is a Yankee, that'd be grounds for a hanging."

He took a step back and punched Evan square in the stomach. The blow was unexpected and hard. Evan coughed but managed to keep from falling.

"That's enough!" Major Childs shouted to Rawlins.

The big Confederate sergeant pulled Rawlins back, and Major Childs grabbed Rawlins by the arm.

Rawlins pulled away and laughed.

"Did I hurt you?" he taunted Evan.

"That's enough," Major Childs repeated.

"Follow me," Gregory Rawlins grunted, as he turned to Sergeant Higgins. "I know where you can keep them until you leave. But if it was my decision, I'd hang them both."

CHAPTER 21

THE LAB RESULTS FOR COLONEL JOHN MAITLAND'S BLOOD-work had returned and showed he'd been suffering from a deadly strain of malaria that would have killed him. Fortunately, his body was responding well to the intravenous quinine.

He'd been unconscious since being admitted to the hospital the day before, and early this morning, he awoke disoriented and confused. Dr. Hunter was making his morning rounds when he saw his patient's eyes open.

"We weren't sure you were going to make it," Dr. Hunter said. "You were unconscious when you arrived. You're at Savannah Memorial Hospital."

His patient looked at him blankly, trying to focus.

Dr. Hunter took a penlight from his breast pocket. Turning on the light, he placed it a few inches to the side of Colonel Maitland's right eye. He held up the index finger of his other hand.

"Look at my finger and follow it with your eye. Can you do that?" Dr. Hunter moved his finger from side to side.

Colonel Maitland closed his eyes without looking.

"Recovery is going to be gradual. You're going to be pretty groggy for the next day or two. That's normal. If you want to go back to sleep, that's normal too."

"Where am I?" Colonel Maitland asked, opening his eyes. He spoke slowly with a dry mouth and a thick accent.

The accent sounded Irish, maybe Scottish, Dr. Hunter thought. Dr. Hunter was well aware that there are many places in the world where someone can be exposed to malaria. He also knew that the disease had been almost eradicated from the United States in the 1950s, but in the last decade, malaria was making a weak, but steady, comeback. Identifying the place of infection was thus crucial to prevent the malaria parasite from being reestablished. Dr. Hunter needed to know where his patient had contracted the disease.

But that conversation would need to wait for now. His patient was again asleep.

As Dr. Hunter left the room, he passed a small closet. The door was open, and a bright red coat caught his eye.

Savannah is sometimes referred to as Hollywood of the South since several movies have been filmed in and around the city over the years. Maybe his patient was an actor in a movie about the American Revolution. That would certainly explain the uniform hanging in the closet.

Dr. Hunter regarded his patient. With his missing right arm and accent, the man certainly looked and sounded authentic enough to play a British soldier.

Colonel Maitland opened his eyes several hours later. He had no idea where he was. He ached everywhere.

He had a disconnected memory of following two men into a house and emerging out on a hot summer day. It was more like a dream than a memory, or more like fragments of a dream.

He recalled that a machine had come out of the sky and that people had put him aboard the machine. The machine had flown. He was almost certain of it.

He realized he was in a bed. He pushed back the blankets to reveal his hospital gown. Nothing was familiar.

Dr. Hunter entered the room. Colonel Maitland eyed him cautiously.

"I see you're awake again."

"Am I a prisoner?"

"A prisoner? No, not at all. You're a patient. You're at Savannah Memorial Hospital. My name's Doctor Hunter, Doctor Julius Hunter. Do you remember I spoke with you earlier today when you first woke? What's your name? You didn't have any identification when you arrived."

The colonel did not respond.

"Someone from administration will be up to get some information from you. You were unconscious when you arrived, and from what I understand, nobody has come to check on you. I'm not sure if anyone knows you're here. If there's someone you'd like the hospital to notify, let administration know. In the meantime, if you don't mind, I'd like to get your name and where you've been."

"My name is Maitland. Colonel John Maitland of the First Battalion of the Seventy-First Foot. Fraser's Highlanders. And if I'm not a prisoner, then I'd like to be allowed to leave."

"You're recovering from malaria. It's a little too soon for you to be discharged."

"Then I am a prisoner?"

"No, you're not. Legally, you can discharge yourself from the hospital at any time, but your recovery is far from over, and it would be against my medical advice."

Colonel Maitland attempted to sit from his inclined position in the bed and found he had no strength.

"Don't overexert yourself. Your strength and alertness will return. Give it some time. If you're intent on leaving, administration can contact someone to come for you. But again, I strongly recommend against that. Malaria is serious business. We weren't sure at first whether you were going to make it. How about you stay put and work on your recovery?"

Colonel Maitland didn't sense he was in danger, but at the same time, he didn't want to be here.

"I'd like to talk about where you might have contracted malaria. I'm required to ask you some questions. Have you traveled abroad lately?"

"Traveled abroad?"

Colonel Maitland was beginning to feel slightly better, although his entire body was sore. He wanted to know where he was. He wanted to hear something that made sense.

"Where is this place?"

"Where are you from?" Dr. Hunter continued. "Your accent sounds Scottish, maybe Irish. You said you're a colonel. Are you active-duty military?"

"Scottish," Colonel Maitland said. "I'm from Scotland, not Ireland. Now I've answered your question. Please answer mine. Where is this place? Where am I?"

"You're in a hospital in Savannah. You've been treated for malaria. You're lucky to be alive."

"This isn't Savannah."

"Are you supposed to be somewhere other than Savannah? What countries have you visited within the past six months?"

Colonel Maitland had no interest in revealing where he'd been. Giving his name and rank was all that was required.

"Look, I'm not trying to pry. You either contracted malaria abroad or, although unlikely, here in the United States."

"The United States?"

"Right, I need to know whether you contracted malaria here or abroad."

"If I'm not a prisoner, then I'd like to be returned to my battalion."

The energy needed for the conversation was exhausting him.

"Like I said, you'll need to speak with administration about that. You shouldn't be discharged until you've recovered, but if you're going to leave anyway, I'll need to note that you self-discharged against medical advice. Before then, I really need to know where you contracted the infection."

Dr. Hunter saw that his patient had fallen asleep. "We'll talk later," he said to the sleeping man. As he was leaving the room, he again saw the bright red coat in the open closet. He turned and looked back at his sleeping patient.

CHAPTER 22

GREGORY RAWLINS LED THE WAY FROM THE MANSION. A small unit of Confederate soldiers followed behind escorting Evan and Dan until they came to a tabby outbuilding a few hundred yards from the Calibogue Sound. It looked like a large shed.

"This is as good a place as any," Rawlins said.

"Inside," Sergeant Higgins ordered.

The door had been removed, revealing various tools and farm implements housed inside. Sergeant Higgins tied Evan and Dan to a support post in the center of the shed and left without a word.

They sat back to back on the cold dirt floor with their hands bound behind them to the post. Frigid wind blew into the shed bringing a few dried leaves whirling about.

"This is a fine mess," Dan sighed and shivered. "It's going to be a while before we leave for Charleston."

"I'm freezing," Evan said. "I thought the Union occupied Daufuskie during the Civil War. That Major Childs sure didn't seem concerned about running into any Union troops."

"The Union did occupy the island," Dan replied. "There were about sixteen hundred Union soldiers on Daufuskie, but that was early in the war. They're not here anymore. I wasn't aware that civilians from Savannah hid on Daufuskie to avoid Sherman's army. I guess that makes sense."

"One of them was William Graffin," Evan said. "He's the man Major Childs is taking with us to Charleston. Is there anything that stands out in history about him?"

"I've never heard of him before today," Dan said. "It sounds like he owns the house in Savannah with the silver door we came through. I'm sure he has some answers. I'd like a few minutes with him."

"Yeah, me too."

"I can't believe that was the Haig Point mansion," Dan said. "There's not a lot of known history about it."

"I know the lighthouse was built on its foundation," Evan said.

"Yeah, it was one of the biggest tabby houses ever built, and no one really knows whether it was destroyed during the Civil War or afterward. Most of the houses and the eleven plantations that were on the island during the war were dismantled for their lumber by the Union army."

"What'd they want the lumber for?"

"In order for the Union to take control of the mouth of the Savannah River, they needed to take Fort Pulaski near Tybee Island. To take that fort, the Union's heavy guns needed to be brought into range. Daufuskie was a bit too far, but Jones Island that we passed earlier was close enough.

The problem was that Jones Island was too boggy. The heavy cannons kept sinking in the mud, so the Union troops cut trees on Daufuskie to make a timber road. The soldiers soon realized it was a lot easier to take wood from the houses than to cut trees. Most of the plantations on the island were stripped of their timber for the road on Jones Island. By the time the Union forces withdrew after Fort Pulaski's surrender in the spring of 1862, there weren't too many houses left standing on Daufuskie."

"Well, the Haig Point mansion is definitely still here," Evan said.

"Yeah it is," Dan agreed.

About twenty minutes later, Evan heard someone approaching from outside. He turned to see William Graffin enter the shed.

"There's no one standing guard," he said. "Major Childs and his men went back to the dock. There was no one guarding me either."

He had two heavy coats. He pulled a short knife from the inside of his own coat and cut the ropes that tied Evan and Dan.

He offered one of the coats to Evan. "You had the key. You came through the Schottenklein door?"

"The what door?" Dan asked, as he accepted the other coat.

"The Schottenklein door," William repeated. "The silver door in my home. You must have come through it."

Evan reached into his shorts and took out the note. "You wrote this." Evan handed him the paper.

William read aloud:

The holder of the key of Schottenklein Abbey, created in the Year of Our Lord 1529 by Abbott Friedrich Kragh and blessed by God for the defense of the City of Vienna against the onslaught of the Ottoman Empire, may be granted one wish made in private known only to God. Beware to enter with care and vigilance through the Schottenklein door.

William Graffin
March 25, 1875
Daufuskie Island, SC

"This is my handwriting and signature," William said, "but I didn't write it. It's signed more than ten years from now. How curious. I assume I'll write this in the future."

"Wait a minute," Dan interrupted. "The key mentioned in the note. Is that the key I bought from Kenny?"

"Yeah," Evan said. He turned to William. "We came through the door about a century and a half from now. But I don't know how much care and vigilance we used."

"Then we need to get you back through to where you belong," William replied. "It's not safe for you here."

"You're telling me," Evan said, as he rubbed his still-aching stomach where Rawlins had punched him.

William moved the few feet to the door opening. He looked out and motioned them forward. "We need to leave."

"Hold on," Evan said. "My wife and children found that key in a wooden chest on the island, this island, Daufuskie. The key and this note were in a glass jar inside the chest. They read the note and made wishes. They each made a wish, a secret wish. Just like you wrote in the note. They were playing, but as I'm sure you know, wishes come true when you hold the key."

William stepped back toward them from the door opening. "Do you know their wishes?"

"Our son is missing. He disappeared. My nine-year-old daughter wished that he'd go away. Will, my son, is only seven. They'd been arguing, and my daughter wished that he'd go away. She didn't think the wish would come true, of course, but now he's gone. We don't know where he is. I was planning to use the key to wish him back to us."

"You can't do that," William said.

"Why not?"

"Because you cannot change another person's wish. The key doesn't work that way. If your daughter wished for your son to be gone, then you cannot use the key to wish him back. You need to find where he is and bring him back."

"That's not what I wanted to hear," Evan said.

"I'm sorry, but you cannot interfere or change another person's wish," William replied.

"What's this all about?" Dan asked. "Are you seriously saying that key is able to grant wishes?"

"Dan, hold on a minute. Back in our time," Evan said to William, "my wife is going to see a woman who knows about the key. Her name is Mary Ellen Hadley. She knew that our son would disappear. We were hoping she'd be able to help. Do you know her?"

"I don't," William said. "I've never heard that name."

"She knew that my wife and kids would find the key. She knew Will would go missing."

"Then we need to get you to her. I learned a long, long time ago of the interactions people have with each other through the key. That woman is connected to you, maybe in a way you don't yet know."

"I know Mary Ellen," Dan said. "She used to live on Daufuskie. She lives over in Bluffton now."

"That's right, she does," Evan said. "Caris was on her way to Bluffton to see her. I was going to get the key from Kenny and take Katie and Abby over in the boat to meet up with her. Then it turned out that Kenny sold you the key and that you went to the lighthouse. I've been a bit detoured since then."

"Will disappeared?" Dan asked. "Mary Ellen knew that?"

"Yeah, she told Natalie Larkin over twenty years ago that a woman would find a wooden chest with the key in it and for Natalie to tell the woman not to worry because her son was okay. Natalie told us that this morning. The woman who found the key was Caris."

"That's creepy," Dan said.

Evan moved toward William. "Can you get us back to our time?"

"You need to pass through the Schottenklein door. It's a portal from one time and place to another. The door has been moved throughout the years. It's in my house in this current time. Where's the door in your time?"

"The Haig Point lighthouse," Evan said.

"It'll be built on the foundation of the Haig Point mansion in about ten years from now," Dan added.

"I see," William said. "When you opened the Schottenklein door in your time, you came through to this time. I must say that it's fortunate you didn't come through to the other side of the door in its original location."

"Where was that?" Dan asked.

"As the note states, the door originated in Vienna. You could have easily opened the door in your time and come out on the other side in Austria during the Siege of Vienna in 1529."

"We actually went through the door more than once," Evan said.

"Yeah, we were also in your house in 1779," Dan added. "We came through the door while Savannah was under British occupation during the American Revolution. We might have missed the Siege of Vienna, but we had a firsthand view of the Siege of Savannah."

"And you locked the door behind you?" William asked.

"No," Dan answered.

"No," Evan repeated, looking at Dan as if everyone knows that you need to lock a magic door once you've gone through it. "I didn't know we were supposed to."

"That could be unfortunate," William said. "The door should never be left unlocked. But let's not worry about that now. You need to be on your way to where you belong and to meet that woman. She might very well know where your son went."

William went back to the opening of the shed and out into the cold December air. Evan followed.

They heard a scream in the distance. A woman's scream.

William hurried ahead down a path toward the sound. He moved quickly for his age. Evan followed closely behind.

The path led to an opening that had another, smaller shed. Next to it, a young black woman was tied to a wooden structure that reminded Evan of a stockade from colonial New England. She was wearing a long grey skirt and a white blouse that was pulled up in back, revealing a deep, bloody cut across her lower back.

Gregory Rawlins, the man who'd punched Evan, stood several feet behind her. A whip hung from his right hand.

"You'll get ten more if it kills you," he screamed at her. Spit flew from his mouth as he yelled. "You didn't think I'd catch you stealing. But I did. I did, and now it's time to pay the price."

He pulled his arm back to deliver another lash from the whip.

In an instant, Evan sprinted forward past William.

Gregory Rawlins heard the footsteps and turned in surprise as Evan barreled into him, knocking the bigger man to the ground. The whip flew from his hand.

William grabbed a small log from a nearby woodpile. Evan turned to look at William, giving Rawlins the break he needed. He started to get up.

He was nearly standing when William swung the chunk of wood at Rawlins. It smacked against the back of the big man's head. He went limp and collapsed.

Dan arrived in time to see Rawlins fall. He felt for a pulse and found one.

Evan went to where the woman was tied. "Hand me your knife," he said to William.

Tears ran down her cheeks.

"I'm going to cut you loose," Evan said, taking the knife.

He cut her free and took off the coat William had given him, putting it around her.

There was rope near the small shed that William used to tie Rawlins's legs and arms tightly behind him so he wouldn't be able to stand. He then used an extra length of rope and tied it around Rawlins's head and open mouth, fashioning a gag to keep him quiet when he regained consciousness.

"I think we need to bring her with us," William said to Evan and Dan. "He might kill her when he eventually gets loose. We'll get her back to my house, and I'll arrange travel for her to the North once the two of you are safely back where you belong."

"Do you want to come with us?" Evan asked her.

She nodded.

"I'm Evan St. John," he said.

"I'm Mary Ellen. Mary Ellen Hadley."

CHAPTER 23

"COME SIT WITH ME," MARY ELLEN SAID TO CARIS. SHE patted the chair next to her on the small front porch of her house in Bluffton.

Caris was still a few feet from the stoop, where she had been when Mary Ellen informed her that Katie had gone to the lighthouse and that she and Caris had met before. Not sure what to believe, Caris hesitantly took the seat next to Mary Ellen.

"I'm so glad to see you again," Mary Ellen said.

"Tell me what you know. You said we've met before and that you promised then to tell me what I need to know to believe you now. So, tell me. Tell me what I need to hear because I don't understand any of this."

"You and your children found the silver key in the chest in the marsh. The chest came from my house on Daufuskie Island. I know you found it because you told me that."

"Did Natalie tell you that this morning? Did she call you? I didn't think you had a phone."

"Caris, I'm over a hundred and seventy years old."

"You said you were going to tell me something that makes sense." Caris thought of getting up and leaving, but she needed to hear what Mary Ellen wanted to say, even if it was the ranting of an old, deranged woman.

"I was born into slavery on Daufuskie Island. I was born on the Haig Point plantation on New Year's Day, January 1, 1842. I've been alive since then."

Caris gave her an unbelieving frown. She had come to Bluffton to learn about Will, not to hear this.

"You don't believe me? I don't say that I blame you. It sounds like a concocted story. But it's true. I've got a lot to tell you. Whether or not you believe me is up to you, but every word I say is God's honest truth.

"That silver key that you found, I made a wish too. That was so long ago. I made my own secret wish during the Civil War. Back then, of course, folks on Daufuskie didn't call it the Civil War. It was the War of Northern Aggression. I was only nineteen.

"Not long after the war began, Union soldiers came to Daufuskie. They had splendid blue uniforms. The plantation owners and most of the white folks had fled the island by then. The Yankees came and said we slaves were free. I still remember that day."

She looked into the distance as if looking over the years of her life.

"The soldiers stayed on the island for months. And then they left. Some of the Southern white folks came back when they felt it was safe. One of them was Gregory Rawlins. He'd been the overseer of the Haig Point plantation. Oh,

Mr. Rawlins returned. He brought his hatred and his whip. He said the Yankees had left Daufuskie because they'd lost the war. He ordered all of us to return to the plantation and to life as it had been.

"But several of the slaves had already left. Some joined the Union army. Some simply left Daufuskie with their freedom. That didn't sit well with Mr. Rawlins. He saw red when he heard that. In his rage, he took his whip. He was like a man possessed with evil. When he'd finished, two men were dead. He whipped them to death, Caris. Those poor people. I remember their screams.

"Then one day Mr. Rawlins overheard a boy, maybe ten or eleven, just a boy, say that he kept seeing Yankee ships passing by the island, so maybe the Yankees hadn't lost the war after all. Mr. Rawlins had the boy point to the ocean where he said he'd seen the ships. When the boy did, Mr. Rawlins cut off the boy's finger so he could never point again.

"Those days with Mr. Rawlins were hard. Without anyone in charge at the plantation over him, he had free rein to be as cruel as he pleased. He called us his slaves, and he would beat his slaves whenever he wished.

"After a while, he didn't care about the upkeep of the plantation. Crops weren't planted. Cotton wasn't harvested. We lived mostly on what we caught from the sea.

"We continued that way during the war, and then we heard that the Yankees were coming back again. Word came that the Northern general, General William Sherman, the one who'd burned Atlanta, was on his way to Savannah.

"When General Sherman was only days away from Savannah, several families left the city to come to Daufuskie. They came to wait until General Sherman and his army left. He had put so much of Georgia to the torch. The people of Savannah feared for their children and their homes. They feared General Sherman would burn their city too.

"A man I'd never seen before arrived at the plantation. His name was William Graffin. He was with the group of folks who came from Savannah."

"What was his name?" Caris interrupted.

"You heard right. It's William Graffin. I know you know his name. He's the one who wrote that note you found with the key."

Caris thought of Evan. The last she had seen the note was at Natalie's house when Evan was writing Mary Ellen's address on the back of it.

"Go on," Caris said.

"Mr. Graffin had been friends with Herman Blodgett. Do you know that name, Herman Blodgett? He'd been the owner of all of Haig Point in the years before the war. Any friend of Mr. Blodgett was always welcome at the plantation.

"By the time Mr. Graffin had come to the island in December 1864, much of the mansion had already been rebuilt. You see, the Yankees needed the wood and had destroyed most of it before they left years earlier. After Mr. Rawlins returned to the island, he constantly demanded boards be milled and that the plantation house be rebuilt to new again. I believe to this day that Mr. Rawlins intended to live in that house as if it was his own.

"Mr. Rawlins at first wouldn't allow Mr. Graffin to stay, but then he thought better of it and decided it would be in his best interest to display hospitality to Mr. Blodgett's friend. A few days after Mr. Graffin arrived at Haig Point, I overheard him speaking with Mr. Rawlins and another man. They didn't know I was in the next room.

"That other man was an alderman on the Savannah city council and had come to Daufuskie with the others. His name was David Boyd. He said he was worried that Savannah would be burned by General Sherman. Mr. Graffin told him that he thought he'd be able to help and asked if he believed in magic. Mr. Rawlins laughed at that and said they were carrying on like schoolchildren. He didn't want to hear anymore nonsense and left. I was so thankful that he didn't come through the next room where I was standing because I'm sure he would've punished me severely for listening to them.

"Mr. Graffin and Mr. Boyd continued to talk. I heard Mr. Graffin say that all Mr. Boyd had to do was make a wish while holding a key—a secret wish that included Savannah being saved. He just needed to keep the wish secret. I poked my head around the corner so they couldn't see me, and I saw Mr. Graffin give him a silver key. Mr. Boyd was quiet for a moment with his eyes closed and then gave the key back.

"The next morning, I heard that Mr. Boyd had left early to go back to Savannah. I don't know whether he believed his wish would come true, but General Sherman never did burn the city.

"As for me, I believed what I overheard Mr. Graffin say about making a secret wish. I believed it. Later that morning, I was cleaning Mr. Graffin's room. He wasn't there, but on the dresser was the silver key. The same key I saw them with. I made a wish that day, Caris. I made a secret wish. I wished for a long, free life. That's what I wished for. A long life, free from slavery."

Mary Ellen looked again into the distance and then at Caris.

"Mr. Rawlins walked past while I had my eyes closed making my wish. He saw me holding the key and thought I'd snuck in to steal it. He hit me. He hit me and knocked me down. He took me out of the house and tied me to a wooden beam. I was tied there for hours. He came back later for me with his whip and told me I needed to be punished for what I'd done. He said stealing would not be tolerated on his plantation and that he was going to whip me until he was done, whether it killed me or not.

"And that's when your husband appeared and stopped him. Evan cut the ropes that bound my hands to the post. Your husband saved my life. He freed me, and I've been free ever since."

"Evan? That can't be right."

"Every word I've told you is true. He was there. He set me free. This is the first time I've told anyone my wish. It's been a secret since the day I made it. If telling you my wish will end it, then I'm ready for that. I'm ready for my time to come to an end. I've seen so much."

Caris could tell that the woman believed what she was saying. Caris thought of the impossible things that had already happened today with Katie flying and Will vanishing. All because of the magic.

"You told Katie to go to the lighthouse," she said. "Why?"

"She needs to go through that silver door. You know the one I'm talking about. That's how Evan was able to come to my time. Evan wasn't alone. Dan Rose was with him. The two of them came together, Evan and Dan. I sent Katie back because she needs to save them. It will happen. It's already happened. It happened in December 1864. Katie was there. She needs to be there again."

"You sent my eleven-year-old daughter?"

Caris stood from the rocking chair and started down the steps of the stoop.

"Caris, wait. You have a different path. Katie has her path. You have your path. A path that will lead you to Will."

Caris stopped and turned around.

"Tell me about my path."

"I don't know much. I can tell you that you're going to go through the silver door, and when you do, you'll find Will. When you come through again to where we meet, he'll be with you. Will was with you when we met. So was Abby. And another."

"Another? Another who?"

"That's really all I can say," Mary Ellen answered. "That's everything you made me promise to tell you."

"I don't believe any of what you told me."

"You and I both know that's not true. I know you believe me. Do you know how I know that? Because when you get back to Daufuskie Island, you're going to go to the lighthouse and through the silver door. And the reason you're going to do that is because you trust what I'm saying is true."

"I don't think so," Caris replied.

"Oh, I know so," Mary Ellen said. "You'll go through the silver door like I said. That's how I met you a hundred and fifty years ago. You just don't know it yet."

CHAPTER 24

ODD DREAMS AND IMAGES FILLED COLONEL MAITLAND'S restless sleep. He awoke midafternoon.

A nurse entered his room. "Food service asked about you a few minutes ago. I'll let them know you're awake. I'm sure you're getting hungry."

He was hungry.

"Dr. Hunter left you something," the nurse said. "He asked me to make sure you get it."

The nurse handed him a bag. Inside was a book, along with a handwritten note taped to the cover.

Colonel Maitland accepted the book from the nurse and read the note to himself.

The more you exercise your mind, the quicker your recovery. Based upon what you were wearing when you were admitted, I thought you may enjoy reading this.

I would like to know where you contracted malaria. The information you provide may be helpful to prevent others from also being infected. If you'd like to talk about your recent travels before you leave, I would appreciate that.

Dr. Julius Hunter

Colonel Maitland set the note aside and focused on the title printed on the book's cover. *Independence: A History of the American Revolution.*

"Dr. Hunter bought it when he went to lunch," the nurse said. "He's gone home for the day and will be back tomorrow morning. I know he wants to speak with you when he makes his rounds tomorrow."

"Please convey my appreciation and gratitude," Colonel Maitland responded.

"You can tell him yourself when you see him tomorrow. Between us, I've never seen Dr. Hunter give anything to a patient before."

Colonel Maitland knew he was in an American hospital. He didn't know why or how, but this was an American hospital. Everything was so strange. So foreign.

He asked the nurse the date. When she said June 9, he asked her the year. The year she told him could not be true.

"I'll be back in a few minutes," the nurse said. "If you need anything before then, press the red button on the side of the bed. I'll make sure food service knows you're awake."

The nurse left his room.

Colonel Maitland set the note aside and opened the book. He flipped through the pages, not at all certain what to think.

He was either a prisoner in an elaborate hoax to trick him, or, he thought, he was really here. The latter made no sense, no sense at all. But here he was.

He opened the book and read the account of Bunker Hill and the opening days of the American Revolution. The information in the book was accurate.

Turning page after page, he skimmed random paragraphs. There were battles he knew, and battles that had yet to be fought in his time.

Toward the end of the book, he came across a chapter with the heading *Yorktown*. He read intently.

He learned that after British successes in South Carolina and North Carolina, Lord Charles Cornwallis was ordered to Virginia to wait for the Royal navy. Cornwallis selected the town of Yorktown on the Chesapeake Bay. Maitland read of how a combined force of the American Continental army led by George Washington and the French army had marched to Yorktown, and that the French navy had arrived in the Chesapeake Bay. The Americans and French had surrounded Cornwallis.

The stinking French, Maitland thought. They were helping the Americans in Savannah too.

Maitland continued reading about the three-week siege on Yorktown and of Cornwallis's surrender of his army of over seven thousand men on October 19, 1781. The colonists had done it. George Washington had done it. The British had been defeated. So it ends at Yorktown, he thought.

Maitland stopped reading and set aside the book. The Americans would win their independence.

Dr. Hunter had given him the book. The book was a road map of events that were to happen in his time. Maitland knew the mistakes the British would make—mistakes that would cost them the war. He also now knew the mistakes that the colonists would make. Mistakes that could be exploited.

He needed to return to Savannah with this book. He needed to share this information with the British generals.

He picked up the book again and flipped pages until the word *Savannah* caught his eye. He began reading.

After failed military campaigns in the northern colonies early in the American Revolutionary War, British military planners decided to embark on a southern strategy to conquer rebellious colonies with the support of loyalists in the South. Their objective was to take control of the southern ports in Savannah and Charleston. In December 1778, a British force under command of Lieutenant Colonel Archibald Campbell took Savannah with modest resistance.

Maitland had been part of the Southern campaign. He knew Colonel Campbell. He continued reading.

By the following summer, the Continental army began devising plans to take back Savannah. The endeavor would be a joint effort by the American and French.

There were the French again. Maitland wondered whether the outcome of the war would have been different without the French. Of course it would. The Americans owed their independence to the French. The Americans must love the French, he thought.

British troop strength consisted of twenty-five hundred regulars at Savannah and another nine hundred men forty miles away at Beaufort, South Carolina, under the command of Colonel John Maitland.

His own name. There it was on the pages in black and white. He was included within the book.

The French navy began landing troops on September 12, 1779. Four days later, the combined Franco-American assault force was within striking distance of Savannah. Rather than attacking the British when they had the advantage, however, the French admiral in command of the operation agreed to give the British a twenty-four-hour truce to

consider surrendering. This allowed Colonel Maitland to bring his forces undetected the forty miles from Beaufort to Savannah to bolster the British defenses. With the additional troop strength, the British refused to surrender.

Colonel Maitland thought about how he was able to make it to Savannah in time.

Irritated by the lost opportunity to attack when they had the advantage, the French bombarded Savannah from October 3 to 8, 1779, and caused significant damage. There was hardly a house that had not been shot through, wrote one British observer. When the Siege of Savannah did not result in a British surrender, the Franco-American force prepared for all-out direct attack. The assault began in the early morning of October 9, 1779.

What Maitland was reading had not yet happened, at least for him. In Maitland's time, the date had been October 7, 1779, when he had followed the two men into the brick house. The American and French attack would not occur for two more days from then.

He thought of the silver door. He remembered it clearly. He had followed the two men into the brick house. The silver door was in that house. He'd thought the men were hiding in a closet. He'd stepped through into this place. This time.

The memory came back to him of staggering outside and looking up at the observation platform. He'd come out of the house in Savannah into a lighthouse in this time. The same silver door was in the lighthouse.

He had no idea how it was possible. But it had happened. There was no denying it had happened.

He wanted to know the outcome of the battle that he was going to fight. Maitland continued reading.

> **A redoubt is an earthen fortification. The redoubt known as Spring Hill was located near the center of the British defenses less than a quarter mile from the center of Savannah. Incorrectly believing that the Spring Hill redoubt was minimally defended by local loyalist militia, the French and Americans concentrated their attack at that point. The Spring Hill redoubt was instead strongly defended by Scottish regulars under Maitland's command. Within fifty-five minutes of fighting, eight hundred French and Americans were dead, resulting in the bloodiest hour of the American Revolution. After the hour of carnage was over, the assault was ended. Savannah would remain in British hands for the remainder of the war. Had it not been for Maitland's timely arrival at Savannah and his defense of the Spring Hill redoubt, the Franco-American assault would have likely succeeded with the British losing the city.**

Maitland felt a sense of pride at the actions he had taken throughout his life and the actions that were to occur.

History, the history he read in the book, had regarded him well. His life had meaning, purpose, and honor.

He needed to return to his own time. He thought of the lighthouse and the silver door inside.

Before the nurse had left his room, she had said that someone was going to bring him food. That had been thirty minutes ago. His stomach rumbled. He felt as though he had not eaten in days, which, he thought, could be correct.

Maitland decided to read a bit more. Other than being hungry, he felt terrific. He focused again on the book.

Colonel John Maitland did not, however, live to celebrate the victory. He had suffered from malaria, contracted in the swamps near Charleston before the Siege of Savannah, and died on October 22, 1779, at the age of forty-seven.

He closed his book and set it down on the bed. His appetite was gone.

CHAPTER 25

"YOU'RE MARY ELLEN?" EVAN ASKED.

She nodded.

She was young and beautiful. She looked to be the same age as Kenny Shivers, no more than nineteen.

"I told you your lives would intersect," William said. "This is the time, and this is the place."

Gregory Rawlins moaned and moved slightly as he began to regain consciousness. With his feet and hands tied tightly behind him, there was no way he'd be able to stand.

"We need to go," William nonetheless said. "Follow me."

He led them to the nearby plantation stables. The wood of the barn looked new. A large, wood-framed door was closed, and three horses were saddled and tied to a long, horizontal rail outside. William went into the barn and came out with a thick cotton shirt that he offered Evan.

Evan put it on over his T-shirt. The heavy sleeves came almost to his fingers.

"I saddled the horses for the three of us. After what she's been through, I'm not sure if she'd be able to ride on her own anyway. Can she ride with you?" William asked Evan.

"I think so," Evan answered.

"We need to get to a boat and off the island," William said. "I saw a few earlier." He glanced back at where they'd left Rawlins. "With luck, by the time someone finds him, we'll be halfway to Savannah."

They followed William on horseback away from the stables, and Evan was struck by the vast areas of land that had been cleared for cotton. Haig Point had been a plantation after all, but in his time, these planted fields no longer existed. Sea Island cotton was gone, and the entire island had been largely reclaimed by nature.

Major Childs was a curious man. It didn't take him long to figure out that the one button below the screen on Evan's iPhone activated the contraption and illuminated little pictures with words under them. Although many of the words were not familiar, such as Pandora and Facebook, there were many that he knew, such as Calendar, Clock, and Notes.

He touched the picture above Calendar to see what would happen, having, of course, no idea that the picture was called an icon and no idea what would happen when he touched it. Evan's calendar appeared.

He saw the month and year in the upper left corner. That was odd.

He pressed the one button on the bottom of the screen again, bringing up the earlier menu of pictures. One of them had the word Photo under it. He pressed it. Evan's camera roll with more than fifteen hundred pictures was displayed. He touched random pictures, which enlarged to fill the screen. The photos were mostly of Evan and his family. Several included them in a Jeep Wrangler they'd rented over the kids' last spring break. Major Childs was amazed at the images.

He remembered the wallets and spent a few minutes examining the contents of each, including the dates of birth shown on each driver's license. The younger of the two men would supposedly not be born for more than a hundred years from now.

Not only was Major Childs a curious man, he was an intelligent man. But the thought that these men were from the future was too outlandish to consider. Was it? He had no doubt that General Beauregard would want to question them personally, but for now, he had custody of the men and would talk to them himself.

Sergeant Higgins gave him directions to the shed where the sergeant had tied Evan and Dan to the interior post, but when the major went inside, all he found was cut rope on the hard dirt floor. He went back out and saw Sergeant Higgins and two of his men approaching.

"They're gone!" Major Childs announced.

"What? When?" Sergeant Higgins answered.

"I don't know."

The four of them hurried down a pathway that led to another opening and shed. Gregory Rawlins was on the ground with his legs and feet tied together behind him.

Rawlins was fully conscious and fully furious. Higgins cut him loose.

"I'm going to kill them," Rawlins said when he managed to pull the gag from his mouth.

"You'll do no such thing," Childs responded. He noticed the whip not far from where Rawlins had been. "What happened here?" he demanded. "Were you going to whip my prisoners?"

"Graffin freed them. They attacked me. It must have been no more than ten or fifteen minutes ago."

"We'll find them," Childs said.

"I'll find them myself," Rawlins shot back.

"That's not going to happen," Childs replied. "You're staying here while we find them."

Rawlins glared at Major Childs. Then, without a word, Rawlins picked up his whip from a few feet away and headed back to the Haig Point mansion.

"We'll need to keep an eye on him," Childs said to Sergeant Higgins. "I don't want him anywhere near them."

"I agree," the sergeant said. "I've known men like him."

"I have also," Childs said. "As for our escapees, the way I figure, they must realize we're not leaving without them. That means they'll need to get off the island before we find them. They'll either leave now if they can secure a boat and take their chances with us seeing them on the water, or they'll wait until nightfall. Either way, we need to find them as quickly as possible."

He turned to one of the two Confederate soldiers who had come with Sergeant Higgins. "Go back and tell the men what happened. I want this island searched."

"Yes, sir," the man answered and departed.

They found the stables nearby and quickly saddled the three remaining horses. "If Rawlins is correct," Major Childs said, "they only have about a fifteen-minute lead on us. We'll find them."

William led the way from one trail to the next until they came to a clearing. A tree near the clearing had been struck by lightning years earlier, and the dead tree looked like the neck and head of a giraffe. There was a wide pathway next to it.

William dismounted. "I was riding by here a few days ago. There's a dock down that way and a few boats."

"This is Finley Hammer's property," Mary Ellen said. "He has boats."

"I want to make certain nobody's down there," William said and handed his reins to Evan. "Stay here with the horses."

He returned a few minutes later.

"I didn't see anyone," he said. "There are two boats tied to the dock. One of them has sails that'll get us nicely to Savannah. I'll make sure Mr. Hammer gets his boat back once we're done with it."

"What about the horses?" Evan asked.

"We'll leave them at the dock," William answered.

William took his horse by its reins and walked on the pathway toward the dock. The rest of them remained on the two other horses and followed behind him.

About fifty yards down the pathway, Evan thought he heard a cough coming from the water ahead of them. "Hold up," he said.

"What's wrong?" Dan asked from the horse behind him.

"I thought I heard someone."

William halted. "You certain?"

"I think so," Evan answered.

Near the side of the pathway was another clearing with a two-story tabby building. The roof was gone, but the tabby walls remained.

William motioned them to the structure.

"That was Mr. Hammer's storehouse where he'd collect cotton bales before shipping them to Savannah," Mary Ellen said quietly to Evan.

The rear door of the building was gone, and William led them to it. Evan and Dan slid down from their horses. Evan led his horse with Mary Ellen still on it into the storehouse, and William and Dan tied their horses to a railing outside, a few feet from the back doorway.

Once inside, they helped Mary Ellen from the horse.

The front of the structure faced the water more than a hundred yards away, and the door on that side of the building had also been removed, likely taken during the Yankee occupation of the island earlier in the war.

The three men walked softly to that open doorway.

"We can see the dock and boats from here," William said. "Let's wait to make sure Evan didn't hear anyone down there."

He looked at Evan, almost studying him. He then took both of the silver keys from his coat pocket. "The Schottenklein key," he said and offered one to Evan. "Take it with you back to your time."

"How do you know which one is the Schottenklein key?" Evan asked.

"It's the same key," William answered, pulling back the key he had offered to Evan and extending the other one. "It doesn't matter which one you take."

"But there are two of them," Dan remarked.

"It only appears to be two," William said. "I've had the key for quite some time. In about a hundred and fifty years from now, you said that your wife and children will find it. When you and Dan come through from your time, you'll bring it with you. While it may appear there are two keys now, they're the same key."

Evan accepted one of the keys from William and placed it into his shorts pocket. "I think I understand," he said. "You'll keep one here, and I'll bring the other back with us."

"Yes," William responded. "And remember, you can't make a wish for your son to return. You said earlier there's a woman in your time who knows that your son disappeared."

They all looked at Mary Ellen, who had gingerly walked over to join them at the open doorway.

"The overseer, Gregory Rawlins, was hurting you," William said to her. "Why was that?"

Mary Ellen looked away.

"Earlier today, he said that a slave girl had stolen my key. Is that why he was hurting you?"

"I didn't steal it," Mary Ellen replied. "I overheard you yesterday telling that man from Savannah about making a secret wish with the key to save his city. I saw it in your room this morning. Mr. Rawlins thought I was stealing it. But I wasn't. I promise."

William regarded her. "You made a wish, didn't you?"

She didn't answer.

"Whatever you wished for, keep it a secret," he said. "You don't know it yet, but your wish has come true."

A tear came to her eye.

"Evan and Dan aren't from here, as I'm sure you've figured out by now. They've come a long way. Do you know anything about Evan's son?"

"No, sir," she said. "I'd tell you if I knew."

"I don't think she knows anything," William said to Evan. "Whatever she learns about your son hasn't happened yet."

"Mary Ellen," Evan said. "Dan and I live in a place very different from here. I don't know your wish, but it enables you to be when and where we're from. When I return there, I'll find you. Promise me that when I do, you'll tell me whatever you learn."

"I promise," she said sincerely.

Evan knew that although Mary Ellen Hadley would someday have information that he needed to know, she didn't have that information now. He needed to get through the door and to Bluffton. He would meet Caris, and the two of them would speak with Mary Ellen. He couldn't imagine how she'd look in his own time. She'd be over a hundred and fifty years old.

"Back at the shed," Dan said to William, "you mentioned it would be unfortunate if Evan and I had left the door unlocked. I've been thinking about that. What'd you mean?"

William rubbed his white beard. "If the door is left unlocked, then anyone may enter through it."

"Like we did?" Dan said. "What an amazing experience. Just think about it. A person from the past showing up in modern days. It'd be incredible."

"And also potentially unfortunate," William said. "Potentially very unfortunate."

Dan looked at him for a moment. "What you're saying is that someone could learn how history unfolds and bring that knowledge back to his own time?"

"Precisely," William replied. "I've traveled to your time and to your future. I've been there as only an observer. The Schottenklein door should remain locked when not in use because another person could come through with different intentions than being a mere observer."

"You're saying a person could affect history?" Evan asked.

"Yes," William said.

Evan thought of the Schottenklein door that Dan and he had unwittingly left unlocked. A thought occurred of Kenny Shivers going through the door looking for Dan. Kenny was such a screw-up. He'd surely do something to mess up history if he went through the doorway.

Dan must have sensed what Evan was thinking. "We need to get back and lock the door," he said. "If Kenny comes looking for us at the lighthouse, he'll be in for the surprise of a lifetime if he checks the upstairs bedroom. Other than Kenny, I can't think of anyone who'd have any reason to be in the lighthouse."

"I think we've waited long enough," William said, changing the subject back to their immediate concern of escaping the island. "I haven't heard or seen anyone down by the dock. I don't think there's anyone there."

"Dan and I will go first to make sure," Evan said. "If there's someone there, I don't think Mary Ellen would be able to get away quickly enough." The back of her shirt was stained from the blood. "If there's nobody at the boats, we'll signal you to come down."

"There are not that many docks on the island," Major Childs said to Sergeant Higgins and the other Confederate with them.

The three had searched the first one closest to the Haig Point plantation without success, and Childs intended to continue down the backside of the island until they had searched them all. This part of the island had paths and trails that led to the water, and they stopped in a clearing near a dead tree that strongly resembled a giraffe.

There was a slave coming into the clearing from the opposite direction. He was as large as Sergeant Higgins. Major Childs guessed he was in his midtwenties. He looked up at the Confederates on their horses and coughed. He coughed again.

"Is there a dock down that way?" Sergeant Higgins demanded, pointing to the pathway that led from the clearing.

"Yes, sir. Belongs to Mr. Hammer. He told me to cut back the vines growing onto it. That's where I'm going now."

Sergeant Higgins kicked the side of his horse and steered the animal's head toward the path. Major Childs and the other soldier followed him down the wide pathway.

From inside the storehouse, William and Mary Ellen heard the unmistakable sound of horse hooves coming fast down the pathway. Evan and Dan were on the dock. There was no way they'd be able to get away.

William and Mary Ellen moved from the front doorway and went to the rear of the structure. The horse that Mary Ellen had been on was in the building with them, but the other two were still tied out back.

Through the back doorway, Mary Ellen glimpsed the three Confederates galloping past. William joined her. A few moments later another man came into view. Mary Ellen knew most of the other slaves on the island, including the man looking at William and her now. Bear Shires had been sweet on Mary Ellen the last few years since she'd turned sixteen. He stared at William and her.

Mary Ellen brought her index finger up to her closed lips and whispered, "Shhhhhh."

Major Childs saw two horses tied outside the tabby building as he passed. He wanted to get to the dock as quickly as possible.

As his horse carried him the last hundred yards, he saw his quarry. The two men he first encountered in Savannah were untying one of the boats. They saw him, and their eyes widened in surprise.

Major Childs and his two men halted their horses at the edge of the dock. "You can jump and swim, but I don't recommend it," he said. "Sergeant Higgins is the best shot I've known. I don't think I've ever seen him miss, even at targets in the water."

The big sergeant's revolver was pointed toward Evan and Dan.

"I know our initial introduction was less than cordial," Major Childs continued, "but I give you my word you'll be treated well."

"You're pointing a gun at us," Evan responded.

"Whether that's needed depends on you. Stop what you're doing and come off the dock."

The key was in Evan's pocket. He thought of the wish he wanted to make for Will to be returned. But he'd learned from William that such a wish wasn't possible.

"I examined your devices and looked through your identification," Major Childs said. "I saw the dates your identification states you were born. I'd like to speak with you."

Evan looked toward Dan, who shrugged his shoulders.

"I don't think we have much of a choice," Dan said quietly to Evan. "That water's pretty cold, and I really don't want to be shot at."

Evan dropped the line to the boat he'd been untying. "We're coming," he said to Major Childs.

"Where's William Graffin?" the major asked. "Rawlins said he freed you and that the three of you attacked him. I don't remember the last time I've seen anyone so angry."

"Rawlins said we attacked him?" Dan replied.

"It doesn't matter," Major Childs said. "Where's Graffin?"

The slave they'd seen earlier arrived at the dock.

"Where is he?" the major repeated to Evan.

"Are you looking for a man with white hair and a white beard?" Bear Shires asked Major Childs.

Childs nodded. "Have you seen him?"

"Yes, sir, I have. He was on a horse riding to Todd Salley's dock." Bear Shires pointed down the island's shoreline in the direction of the next dock. "I seen him myself about five minutes ago. He was riding hard that way."

"Go and find him," the major said to Sergeant Higgins and the other Confederate. The two of them spun their horses and headed back up the trail at full speed.

Bear Shires looked toward Evan and Dan and smiled slightly.

"I saw your horses up the trail," Childs said. He pulled out his own revolver and ordered Evan and Dan to walk that way.

Bear Shires went past them onto the dock to cut the vines he'd been instructed to clear. He didn't look back.

William and Mary Ellen were still in the storehouse and coaxed the horse with them into a recessed interior area of the building.

"I don't think they know you're with us," William said. "So stay out of sight with the horse. I'll try not to get caught, but if I do, I don't want them finding you too."

He moved toward another area of the structure where he was able to look through the rear doorway and see the two horses tied outside. A few moments later, he heard Major Childs and could see Evan and Dan untying the horses and getting onto the saddles. As they rode up the trail, William could see that Major Childs was several feet behind them on his own horse. His gun was unholstered. There was no way that Evan and Dan would be able to ride off without becoming perfect targets.

CHAPTER 26

KATIE EASILY FOUND HER WAY BACK TO DAUFUSKIE ISLAND after leaving Mary Ellen Hadley's house in Bluffton. The silver door was there on the second floor of the lighthouse just like Mary Ellen had said.

Katie placed her hand on the silver doorknob and turned the handle thinking of her father. She stepped through the doorway, closing the door behind her.

On the other side, everything was like the old woman had described. Katie walked out of the brick house into horse-and-buggy times. Although she'd been told ahead of time what to expect, it did little to lessen the amazement.

Pulling the wool jacket around her, she flew high above Savannah, studying the brick house from above to memorize how the area looked from the air. The Savannah River was easily in view, and she followed it toward the ocean. Daufuskie Island would be one of the larger islands to her left the closer she came to the Atlantic. She'd find it. She thought of her father needing her help and flew as fast as she could.

They came for Will in the late morning. The crowd was led by a powerful shaman. Will's miraculous appearance from nothingness, which occurred during the same hour as their king's death, convinced the shaman that Will had been sent to them by the gods.

Fifty years earlier, their religion had been outlawed — a decision made within six months of their then king's new rule. But illegal or not, the religion of their ancestors hadn't vanished. Traditions survive, and many villages had a shaman to communicate with the gods.

The shaman who led the crowd coming for Will was named Poipu, and the god with whom Poipu communicated most often was Ku, the god of war and prosperity. Even though many of the people's lesser gods had been abandoned over the past decades, the older villagers remembered Ku. Ku was a god that would not be forgotten.

Poipu and his followers brought Will to their capital city, a place where customs and rituals had survived the strongest and where the latest king had sought to preserve the traditional religions. The woman who had comforted Will earlier in the day had objected to them bringing Will there, but she'd known that her protests would be ignored. Will saw her crying when they took him away.

News of the fair-skinned boy with the light hair made its way from village to village, and by the time they arrived at the main temple in the capital, throngs of onlookers had lined the way.

A four-year-old girl had also been brought. Will's eyes met hers. They both looked terrified.

The girl was named Grace, but she was called Ono. The nickname came from the *ono*, a fish found in abundance in the local waters. Almost a year earlier, the girl had fallen overboard from an outrigger canoe and had swum to the surface like an ono.

Ono's father had been a Christian missionary from America and had married a woman from one of the villages. Poipu had objected to their wedding, of course, but his objections had been overruled. And now, both of her parents were dead. They'd drowned in the same hour as Will's appearance.

The shaman believed Ku had cursed Ono's parents and caused their boat to capsize. There was no other explanation as to why their boat would overturn when the seas were as calm as they'd been.

The girl, who was the only survivor, had cheated death. Twice now within a year, the gods had called her into the water to be drowned, and twice she had swum like the ono fish. The shaman would not permit her to escape death again. She would need to be sacrificed to Ku. The shaman was certain of it.

The arrival of the light-skinned boy earlier in the day was more confusing to the shaman. The boy hadn't been there, and in an instant, he was standing before more than twenty villagers. They were horrified. Ku must have sent the boy. Poipu could think of no other explanation. But why?

Poipu ordered that both the girl and boy be brought to the temple. The villagers complied. He knew they would.

He was convinced that the god of their forefathers required the sacrifice of the girl. There was no question about that. But as for the boy, the shaman was not yet certain. He would enter the temple with the boy and wait for enlightenment from Ku. Ku almost always revealed himself and his wishes if Poipu waited long enough. The shaman would know in due time whether the boy too was to be sacrificed.

CHAPTER 27

CARIS DROVE HER SUBURBAN TO HILTON HEAD FROM MARY Ellen Hadley's house in Bluffton. She had been so intent on meeting the woman on her drive to Bluffton that she hadn't fully taken in the destruction from the hurricane. Fallen trees and debris were everywhere.

Onboard the ferry going back to Daufuskie Island, Caris played the conversation with Mary Ellen over again in her head. So much of what she'd said seemed like gibberish.

None of it, of course, would have made sense yesterday. But today was not yesterday. Yesterday had brought a hurricane. At that time, Caris had experienced the greatest fear of her life, a fear that her children would be harmed. Today brought magic and the disappearance of her son. Her greatest fear was being realized. She hated today. She flat out hated it. She wanted her family together.

As the ferry approached the island, she could see Abby and Natalie waiting for her on the dock. Caris had hoped to see Katie and Evan waiting with them, but she knew they wouldn't be there. She didn't want to believe Mary Ellen, although part of her knew the woman was telling the truth. She didn't know why she knew it, and she wouldn't have been able to explain to anyone why such a thing could be possible, yet she knew that at least part of what the old woman had said was true.

The ferry docked. Abby ran ahead to her mother.

"I told her not to go." Abby was crying again. "I told her to stay and wait for Daddy."

"Sweetie, I know Katie went by herself to Bluffton. Has she come back? Have you seen her?"

"No," Abby sobbed.

Natalie caught up to them.

"I let the girls go outside to play. Miss Abby came back in, but Miss Katie was gone. I should have checked on them. Knowing what I know about Miss Katie being able to fly, I should have checked."

"It's not your fault," Caris said. "You wouldn't have been able to stop her. She went to Bluffton."

"To see Mary Ellen by herself?" Natalie asked. "Don't tell me that's what she did."

"That's exactly what she did. She got there and left before I arrived."

"So you met Mary Ellen?"

"I did. I don't know what to think. If Evan comes here, tell him we're at the lighthouse. Mary Ellen sent Katie there. She might be there now, but if she shows up here, tell her to stay put and wait for me."

"She sent Katie to the lighthouse? Why'd she do that? Did she tell you where Will is?" Natalie appeared to want answers almost as much as Caris wanted them.

"She said a lot of stuff. I'm not sure what to believe."

She took Abby by the hand. The walk to the lighthouse wouldn't take long.

Abby was only nine. She was too young to stay at the beach house alone, especially taking into account the strange events. And what if Mary Ellen was right? What if the silver door took Caris to another place, another time? How long would she be gone? How long would Abby be left alone?

Caris would bring Abby with her.

They arrived at the lighthouse a few minutes later.

On the second floor, Caris led the way down the hall and around the corner. The silver door was directly in front of them.

Caris thought of what she was doing. Why was she here? If the old woman was right, then going through the doorway with Abby didn't seem like a good idea. Caris should instead go back to the beach house and wait. But wait for what? For Evan and Katie to return? Return from where?

Caris moved the few feet toward the silver door. Her heart was beating faster. This is crazy, she told herself. It's just a room on the other side. A room in the lighthouse.

Mary Ellen had said that Caris had her own path to follow. A path that would lead her to Will. She thought of finding her son and turned the silver handle, pushing open the door.

Abby was behind Caris and could see the room on the other side of the open doorway. She came and stood next to her mother.

"What's that room?" Abby asked.

"I don't know."

For a moment Caris stood undecided. She was a deer in headlights, not knowing if she'd go through the doorway and into the strange room, or if she'd close the door and take Abby back to the beach house. But she knew the answer. She would go through and keep Abby with her. Wherever Will, Katie, and Evan had gone, she had no idea. But she needed to keep an eye on Abby. She needed to have her daughter with her and to keep her safe.

"Whatever that room is," Caris said, "I want you to stay next to me. You got it? You stay next to me."

Abby nodded.

Holding hands, the two of them stepped through the doorway into the room beyond.

The floor beneath them swayed.

"I think we're on a ship," Abby said.

It was impossible, but true. The only wooden ship that Caris had ever been on was the *Black Dagger*, and that was a modern boat only made to look like a wooden ship. This was the genuine article. Even the smell was how Caris imagined a wooden ship would smell. They were in a cabin of an old-time wooden ship.

The motion of the waves caused the silver door behind them to close. It didn't slam, but Caris saw it close. She considered opening it and returning to the hallway in the lighthouse. But she wanted to see where she was. Mary Ellen had been right. The door was a portal. But a portal to where? To the path that would lead her to Will?

There was a doorway open on the other end of the cabin. Through it, Caris could see the wooden deck, as well as ropes and sails tied back out of the way. They were definitely on a ship.

Caris and Abby walked through the open cabin door onto the deck. The ship was in a bay. They could see land a few hundred yards away. There were hills and mountains. The vegetation was tropical, green, and lush.

The blue water of the bay was a deeper blue than the Calibogue Sound. This wasn't Daufuskie Island. This wasn't South Carolina.

The breeze was warm and refreshing. Caris could see palm trees on the land, and even at the ship's distance, she could see that hanging from the palm trees were coconuts. Most of the palm trees had coconuts.

Beyond a row of coconut-laden palms was a town. There was a pier also, and at the far end of the pier, Caris could see a worn path under the palm trees. She thought of her own path, the path that would lead her to Will. She needed to get off the ship.

There must be a small boat, a rowboat of some sort, that she and Abby could use to get across the bay and onto the path. Caris was looking for it over the ship's railing when she sensed movement behind her. There was a man behind them.

"Caris St. John," the man said. "Hello to you too, Abby. I was wondering when the two of you would show up. Welcome to Hawaii."

CHAPTER 28

CARIS HAD READ *THE LION, THE WITCH AND THE WARDROBE* to the kids. She now felt like Abby and she had climbed through the wardrobe into Narnia. But there was no talking lion. No Aslan.

Instead, there was a man on an old-fashioned sailing ship standing before them. He was shorter than Caris. She estimated he was slightly under five and a half feet tall. He had a head of cottony white hair and a thick white beard.

"I can imagine this all comes as a surprise," he said. "Introductions are in order. My name is William Graffin, and although we've met before, of that I can assure you, that event has not yet occurred for you."

Here we go again, Caris thought. The man reminded her of her conversation with Mary Ellen Hadley. He spoke in riddles.

He held a large grey envelope. He reached in, retrieved a small slip of paper, and handed it to Caris.

The paper was aged. At first glance, it appeared to Caris to be the note she and the kids had found in the glass jar in the wooden chest. But that was impossible. Evan had the note.

"If you please," William Graffin said, "turn it over to the reverse side."

On the back of the note, the words 320 Sycamore were written in Evan's handwriting—the beginning of Mary Ellen's address in Bluffton.

"Evan gave me this. That was eight years ago."

"You must be mistaken," Caris said, although she knew the impossible could be true.

"Today is December 14, 1872. I met your husband and daughter, Katie, nearly a decade ago in December 1864."

Caris felt a lump in her throat. "There was a woman I met who told Katie to find Evan," she said. "That he was in trouble."

"Katie found him. And Dan Rose."

Caris realized she was still holding Abby's hand. She held tighter not wanting Abby out of her sight.

"Do you know where you are?" he asked.

"You said Hawaii. But how? Why?"

"You're in Honolulu Bay." He motioned toward the land. "That's Honolulu."

Caris looked at the land with the mountains and hills in the background and a town near the water. She noticed for the first time there weren't any cars. All of the streets were dirt. There were no traffic lights. No pavement. No signs. No telephone poles.

The thing she found most unusual was the number of horses. She had never seen so many horses in one place at one time. There were people in the town moving here and there, shuffling about doing whatever business they did. It looked like a town from the 1800s.

Caris turned the paper over and reread the note that she and the kids had found in the marsh.

"You're William Graffin?"

"I am."

"You said we're in 1872." She put her finger on the date written across the bottom of the note. "The note is dated 1875."

"Yes, peculiar, isn't it. Truth is, I won't write this note for a few more years."

"I'm really not following. If you haven't written it, then how's it here?"

"Because your husband gave me the note nearly a decade ago."

"He traveled back in time and gave you a note?" Abby asked.

"Honey, Daddy didn't travel back in time."

"I think we just traveled back in time too," Abby told her mom.

"You came through the Schottenklein door," William said. "You came through the door seeking Will."

"How'd you know that?" Caris asked.

"I'm here in this time and this place because this is where you told me in 1864 that you found Will. I'm here now because of you."

"We haven't been to 1864," Caris said.

"Not yet, but you will. I'm here to help you."

"Help me?"

"Yes, I'm here to help you. I promised you and Evan eight years ago that I would. I sailed to Hawaii to be here on this date."

Will could not have known that less than a half mile away, his mother and sister were on a ship in Honolulu Bay, and that they'd come through a magical silver door looking for him.

Will and Ono had been brought into the main temple and forced to sit near the altar. Poipu accompanied them. He was shirtless, barefoot, and wore only a dark red skirt. To Will, Poipu's face looked strikingly how he'd envisioned Dracula to look. The thought of the shaman Poipu as a vampire horrified him.

Poipu sat near the children and meditated with his eyes closed for nearly an hour. When he opened them, he declared that he'd had a vision from Ku that both of the children were to be sacrificed after sunset.

A handful of shamans from other villages openly disagreed with Poipu's vision of Ku's intention. The most outspoken was Keoni.

Keoni tried again and again to convince the growing crowd that the murders of the children would not appease the gods. That was not what Ku wanted. Killing the children would cause only wrath from their ancestral deities. Ku had, after all, delivered the boy to them. The boy had been a gift from the gods. He was not to be harmed. And Ku had saved the girl twice from drowning. She too was not to be harmed.

But Poipu would have none of it. He convincingly justified his revelation that Ku required the blood of the boy and girl. They would be sacrificed to Ku once the sun had set. Far too many years had passed without a human sacrifice. Poipu was going to change that in a few short hours. The death of the children would usher in a reawakening of the people to the gods of their past. A reawakening of their traditional religion. A reawakening of the power and authority of the shamans. And yes, Poipu thought, he would be the one to lead them.

CHAPTER 29

DR. JULIUS HUNTER ENTERED COLONEL MAITLAND'S ROOM at Savannah Memorial Hospital. He'd been looking forward to checking in on his patient this morning.

The bed was empty.

Dr. Hunter's name was printed neatly across an envelope resting on the pillow. He opened it and removed a hand-written note.

Sir, I am unable to adequately express my gratitude for all you have done. You saved my life when I am certain in every way possible that I would have died but for your intervention and care. I am truly thankful.

You have asked that I inform you of where I traveled in order to have contracted malaria. I

237

believe the answer to your inquiry is Charleston.

The note was not signed. Dr. Hunter left the room and went to the nurse's station down the hall.

"Vicki, have you seen my patient in room 308?"

"He came by earlier this morning and asked for an envelope," the nurse responded.

"He hasn't discharged himself, has he?"

"Not that I know of."

Dr. Hunter returned to his patient's room. The closet door was still open, but the red coat and uniform were gone.

Colonel Maitland exited the hospital at the same moment that Dr. Hunter entered his vacated room. His gift from the doctor, *Independence: A History of the American Revolution*, was with him in the bookstore bag.

The colonel's uniform caused more than one head to turn. Although the sight of a man wearing a colonial-era British uniform was certainly uncommon, the sights Colonel Maitland viewed were even more astonishing.

While in his room, he had marveled at the devices and technology, especially after the nurse had told him the date. Now, on the sidewalk outside the hospital, the cars drew his attention. He was fixated on them. What strange and wonderful machines.

There was a parking lot across from the hospital, and Colonel Maitland spent several minutes examining the cars. He wanted to know how the things worked.

A woman was parked three spaces from where he was standing and waved at him. These Americans were quite friendly.

The nurse had told him yesterday that he'd arrived by helicopter from Daufuskie Island. Colonel Maitland remembered being on the machine that lifted into the air. He thought it had been a dream.

He could also now clearly remember the silver door. The silver door was in a lighthouse. He had seen the observation platform when he was outside. The helicopter had taken him from Daufuskie Island where the malaria had been killing him. He needed to return to the island and find the lighthouse.

He was curious if traveling through time was as common for these Americans as traveling in one of their cars. He'd like to know that. There were so many things he wanted to know about this place and time.

He felt good, and the early June morning made him feel better. He was alive. He felt delighted.

That was the word that best described him. He had somehow managed to escape death. The malaria that would have killed him, according to the history book, was no more. He would not die of malaria within weeks. He was delighted he would live. He was delighted to be here. Delighted to see the things he was now seeing.

While still examining the cars in the parking lot, he spotted something on the ground. It was a tourist pamphlet of

Savannah. One side of the pamphlet included an enlarged map of the old city with its squares shown in green. The opposite side comprised a map of greater Savannah.

He was studying the enlarged map, half watching where he was walking, when he found himself on the sidewalk along Waters Avenue. He saw the name on a street sign. He looked for the street on the map, and there it was, not far from the historic city center.

He studied the map. The Colonial Park Cemetery was shown in green, and he wondered whether any of the hundreds of Americans and French who fought and died during his time would be buried there.

He also saw the Savannah History Museum and Visitor Information Center on the map. It did not look too far from where he now stood. He was a visitor to this place and in search of historical information. Surely that's where he needed to go.

Along the way, several drivers honked and waved at him. He became acutely aware that his uniform was far from ordinary in this place. When he finally reached the museum, more people were looking at him. A few children stared. He smiled disarmingly at all of them.

In the information center, he found a small bookstore with books primarily about Savannah, which, of course, made sense because he was at a Savannah history museum. There was also a section of books on American history.

A big leather chair was empty, and after considering that it'd be a splendid place for him to read, the colonel selected two books with the intention that he would not move from the chair until he'd absorbed both of them cover to cover. He set his own book in its shopping bag onto a side table.

The first book he selected was on American history from the Revolution through the 1970s. The book included page after page of amazing pictures. The Americans had traveled to the moon.

The subject of the second book was World War I and World War II. When he read the words World War in the title, he'd wrongly assumed the first world war must have been referring to the American Revolution. Men from so many nations were involved in that conflict. The British were against the Americans in the war for America's independence. The French were with the Americans. Hessians from Germany fought on the side of the British against the Americans.

World War I had not, however, been about the American Revolution. The Americans, British, and French were instead fighting the Germans. The three nations as allies. That was an unexpected surprise. World War II saw more of the same with the British and Americans as close allies. The Americans had come to the aid of Great Britain against the Germans.

That couldn't be right. But was it? There it was in black and white. He continued reading for another hour.

"Do you work here?" a man asked. He was with two children.

Colonel Maitland looked up at them and didn't respond.

"I thought because of your uniform that you might work here. I'm looking for the Spring Hill redoubt and know it's close by. I thought you might be able to show us where it is."

241

Colonel Maitland shook his head no, and the man and his children walked away. He thought of the battle that he'd fight at the Spring Hill redoubt. The battle described in his book. He decided he needed a break from reading.

Taking his own book in its shopping bag and leaving the two other history books behind, he went outside. He turned to his right and crossed the street to Tricentennial Park.

To his astonishment, there was a fully intact earthen fortification—a redoubt—in the park. An information marker next to the redoubt stated it had been constructed in 2006 as a replica and that the actual battlefield where so many had died was directly in front of the redoubt.

The information marker also included the British battle plans. There was a map showing each of the fourteen redoubts the British had constructed to defend Savannah against the American and French siege. The plans and map had been a military secret in his time, vital to the British defense of the city. Now, they were on display in a park for the entire world to see. There was, of course, no need for them to be kept secret anymore. The battle had happened over two hundred and thirty years ago.

Colonel Maitland looked across the battlefield, and about a hundred yards away, there was the remnant of an earthen work. He walked to it, and another marker showed that it was the remains of the actual Spring Hill redoubt. The exact place where he was to fight the Americans and French.

"The British are coming. The British are coming," came an accented voice from behind him. The voice sounded

Scottish. Colonel Maitland turned to see a man several years older than himself.

"Ah, you're in dress of one of Frasier's Highlanders," the older man said, examining Colonel Maitland. "Good choice. Good choice, indeed."

The colonel was not certain what to make of this. His first thought was that the man must have also come through the silver door in the lighthouse.

"My great-great-great-grandfather fought here," the man said. "He was on the British side, of course. His name was Thomas Egan."

Colonel Maitland knew Thomas Egan.

"He serves under my command," the colonel said. "You should be proud of his service to the king."

"So you're going to stay in character," the man replied with a smile. "That's good. Makes it authentic."

Colonel Maitland was a smart man and realized the older Scotsman believed the colonel to be some sort of an actor.

They spent the next half hour talking. They had both been raised in the same area of Scotland, although centuries apart, which was a fact that the colonel did not share.

The older man now lived on Hilton Head Island and had been to the museum a few times. When the colonel wanted to know more about the relationship between the British and the Americans, the man spoke in detail that the people of the two nations had so much in common. The Americans had come to the aid of the British in both world wars, and the two nations were the closest allies of any two countries in history.

Colonel Maitland immensely enjoyed speaking with the great-great-great-grandson of Thomas Egan. He marveled at the idea of what Thomas Egan would say if he could see them.

The topic eventually moved to Daufuskie Island, and Colonel Maitland asked whether he'd be able to attain passage on a helicopter. The man laughed a little at that.

When the colonel later mentioned that he did not have a car, Thomas Egan's descendant offered him a ride to the Haig Point embarkation center on Hilton Head Island. The man told Colonel Maitland that he'd probably be able to catch a ferry to Daufuskie Island from there.

This news was simply delightful to Colonel Maitland. He would soon be back on Daufuskie Island, and along the way to Hilton Head, he would have an opportunity to ride in a car.

CHAPTER 30

EVAN AND DAN RODE ABOUT TEN FEET IN FRONT OF MAJOR Childs until they arrived back at Haig Point. Sergeant Higgins was standing near the stables when they returned.

"You find Graffin?" the major asked his sergeant as he dismounted.

"No, sir," Higgins responded. "We rode back to see if you or anyone else had him. We must have missed you. I'll organize the men to search again."

Gregory Rawlins emerged from one of the paths and came toward them.

"What's that for?" Major Childs asked.

"Protection," Rawlins answered. He slapped the side of a holster on his belt with the palm of his hand. A large revolver was in the holster. "They attacked me once. I want to be ready if they make that mistake again." He looked up at Evan and Dan on their horses and sneered.

"I'll organize the men," Major Childs said to his sergeant. "You stay here. It'll be dark before long, and with any luck, we'll find him before then. If we don't find him, I'll be back in a couple of hours. In the meantime, tie these two in the barn. I'll speak with them once I'm back."

He gestured toward Rawlins.

"And whatever you do, don't let him into the barn."

William and Mary Ellen reached Haig Point without running into Major Childs or any other Confederate soldier. William found a place out of sight and helped Mary Ellen from the horse after tying its reins to a tree.

They decided to split up to search for Evan and Dan and to meet back at the horse. William would search the eastern side of the plantation, including the stables, outbuildings, and sheds. Mary Ellen would search the western side, including the plantation mansion, slave quarters, and dock.

In the growing dusk, William checked the shed where Evan and Dan had originally been tied. When he saw it was empty, he quietly followed the path to the shed where they'd earlier come upon Mary Ellen and Gregory Rawlins. There was nobody there either.

He made his way to the barn. From the bushes, William could see Gregory Rawlins and Sergeant Higgins and assumed Evan and Dan were inside. While circling around to a side door of the barn, William stepped squarely on a branch that snapped in two.

The sound caused Rawlins and Higgins to look in his direction. William froze in place, concealed in the bushes and shadows. He was only forty feet away.

William was certain he could remain as still as a statue for as long as it took to make sure the men didn't see him. He didn't have to wait long. They'd seen him and were now moving in his direction.

"Don't move," Sergeant Higgins commanded.

Rawlins was the first to reach William.

"You cracked that piece of firewood right across here," Rawlins said, moving his finger along his head. He made a fist. "Maybe it's time you knew how that felt."

Sergeant Higgins had his revolver out of his holster. He aimed it at Rawlins, making it clear that Rawlins was not to harm the man.

"I'll take him," Sergeant Higgins said. He ordered William into the barn and tied him to the railing of a horse stall across from Evan and Dan.

Rawlins remained outside, his temper boiling.

Mary Ellen searched the dock first. The two boats were there. The Confederate soldiers were not.

She then made her way to the mansion. In the days before the war, the great house was always alive with people. Now, it was as quiet as a graveyard.

She left the mansion and kept to the shadows on the edge of the field. In the growing darkness, she headed to the tabby slave quarters.

There were five of them in a row. When she reached the last one, she could see a girl sitting with her back to the wall near the door.

Mary Ellen had never seen the girl before.

Still in the shadows, Mary Ellen viewed the area and eventually decided to approach. She walked cautiously toward the girl. The girl was no more than ten or eleven.

The girl watched Mary Ellen approach.

"Are you the person I'm supposed to meet?" the girl asked.

"I don't think so," Mary Ellen replied.

"Oh, I thought you might be. A woman named Mary Ellen Hadley told me that I'm supposed to wait here until someone comes to get me."

"Mary Ellen Hadley told you that?"

"Yes."

"I don't think she did."

Katie looked closely at her. She looked familiar. Katie had met a much older version of the same woman. She was certain of it.

"Are you Ms. Hadley?" she asked.

"I am."

"Do you know who I am?"

"I've never seen you before, child."

The way she called Katie child. The voice was the same. There was no mistaking it.

"You sent me. You were the one who told me to wait here."

"You're mistaken," Mary Ellen responded.

"You sent me here," Katie insisted. "You were much older. You said Daddy was in trouble and needed me. You told me a bad man was going to hurt Daddy."

"A bad man is going to hurt your father?" There was a look of recognition on her face, as if she'd solved a difficult puzzle. "Follow me," Mary Ellen said, already heading toward the eastern side of the Haig Point plantation.

Sergeant Higgins came out of the barn after tying William near Evan and Dan. Gregory Rawlins was outside waiting for him.

"You heard the major say he'd be back when he found Graffin," Rawlins said, walking toward Sergeant Higgins. "He also said that if he couldn't find him, then he'd return in a couple of hours. Since we have Graffin, the way I see it, Childs won't be finding him on the island. That means he won't be returning for a while."

"Make your point," the big sergeant said impatiently.

"My point?" Rawlins snarled and quickly drew his revolver. He raised it and fired directly at Sergeant Higgins's chest.

Higgins stumbled back with a look of shock. He put his hand onto his bleeding chest and was able to stumble a couple of steps toward Rawlins before he hit the ground with a heavy thud.

Rawlins knelt beside the dying man.

"My point is that I'll need to inform Major Childs that the prisoners overpowered you and took your revolver. One of them, maybe Graffin, was able to get off a shot." Rawlins unholstered Higgins's gun and fired it into the air. He threw the gun a few feet away. "That shot fatally

249

wounded you. You'll be dead by the time Childs returns. But I was able to fight them off. Unfortunately for them, I had to meet their use of deadly force with deadly force of my own. When Childs returns, I'll need to report that all three of them, plus you, of course, were killed in their escape attempt. That's my point."

He stood and headed toward the barn door.

Mary Ellen and Katie had reached the back of the barn when they heard the first gunshot. The two of them entered the barn through the side door.

"Katie!" Evan's eyes lit up in disbelief when he saw his daughter. "How'd you get here? Is Mommy with you?"

"I'm here with her," Katie answered, motioning toward Mary Ellen. "She told me to come when I spoke with her in Bluffton."

"Bluffton? Mommy came back and took you with her to Bluffton?"

Katie didn't answer.

He looked at her. "Listen, I need to get out of these ropes. There's some tools over there. See if there's something over there you can use to cut them."

Katie came back a few seconds later holding an ax.

A second gunshot sounded from outside the barn.

Evan stretched the rope in front of the railing and pulled his hands behind the wood for protection. Katie whacked at the rope with three slight blows, making only small cuts each time.

The front door of the barn began to slide open.

"Cut the rope," Evan said. "Hit it harder!"

Katie swung the ax with all her might. The blade landed into the wood railing cutting through the rope.

Evan jumped over the railing, grabbed the ax, and sprinted to the barn door.

As the door slid open, Gregory Rawlins was on the other side. But before he could react at seeing Evan, Evan slammed the butt of the ax's wooden handle into Rawlins's jaw.

The jawbone in the human body is called the mandible. When it's struck hard enough, the impact can cause a person to become unconscious. The blow to Gregory Rawlins's jaw instantly knocked him out cold.

Evan came back into the barn to Katie and hugged her tightly. "What are you doing here?" he said.

"She told me to come," Katie answered, again pointing at Mary Ellen. "She said I needed to save you."

Mary Ellen looked at both of them and shrugged her shoulders in a look of confusion.

Evan had no doubt that Katie was telling the truth and that the older version of Mary Ellen in their time had sent his daughter through the Schottenklein door.

He used the ax to cut Dan and William from their ropes, and leading them out of the barn, he stepped over the unconscious Rawlins. Sergeant Higgins's body was in a pool of blood a few feet away. Evan turned Katie away to protect her from the gruesome sight. The mystery of the two gunshots moments earlier appeared to have been solved. Gregory Rawlins had shot the Confederate sergeant.

"There's nobody at the dock," Mary Ellen said. "I was just there a few minutes ago."

"The boats are still there?" William asked her.

"They are."

"Then I suggest we be on our way," he replied.

CHAPTER 31

THE TWO BOATS WERE TIED TO THE DOCK WITHOUT ANYONE in sight, exactly as Mary Ellen had said. Evan helped Katie get aboard the smaller boat. He grabbed the wool blanket Major Childs had given Dan and him on their trip to the island and tucked it around her.

"I've got an idea," he said to Dan and untied the second boat from the dock. "Help me push it into the current."

The two gave the empty boat a push, and then Dan climbed onto the smaller sloop.

With everyone else aboard, Evan untied the final line and joined them on the sailboat. He took a seat opposite Dan, and the two of them put oars into the oarlocks and began rowing.

William began working on the rigging to hoist the mainsail and soon had all the sails unfurled. They were fully underway toward Savannah, already a quarter mile from the Haig Point plantation.

Daufuskie Island paralleled them to their left about fifty yards away, while miles of dormant marsh grass stretched to their right.

Evan turned his attention to Katie, who was sitting across from him, and Katie relayed how she'd flown to Bluffton on her own to find Mary Ellen and hopefully Will. She made sure to emphasize that she only disobeyed because she was trying to find Will and that Abby was against the idea. There was no need for both of them to get in trouble.

Katie explained how Mary Ellen had told her to fly to the lighthouse and to go through the silver door. She explained how the door opened into an unfamiliar house and that she had to find Daufuskie Island and sit by the door of the last tabby slave house until someone came for her. She had no idea that the person who would come for her would be Mary Ellen herself.

Mary Ellen sat in the front of the boat and heard everything Katie said. She didn't say a word in response. She simply listened.

Darkness was approaching. Through the fading light, Evan thought he saw someone move on the shore to the left of the boat. He again looked closely. Someone was there.

It was one of the Confederate soldiers who'd accompanied them from Savannah with Major Childs.

Evan saw a flash followed by a boom.

"Get down everyone!" Evan yelled, realizing what he'd seen.

The flash had been the black powder igniting in the man's muzzle-loader rifle.

Evan lurched forward from his seat and pulled Katie to the deck of the boat, hoping the low hull would provide cover. He put his body over his daughter.

Dan turned toward the sound of the gunshot. A minié ball tore into his upper chest near his shoulder. He slammed back into the boat.

The soldier reloaded and fired again. The second shot hit the metal oarlock on the left side of the boat.

Although the boat was cutting swiftly through the water, it was not a speedboat. Evan figured they'd be within range of fire for several more minutes. Longer if the man ran along the shore keeping pace with them.

He fired again.

The third shot hit the upper left of the boat, splintering part of the wooden side.

William crawled over to Dan and pulled back the heavy coat he'd given him. He lifted Dan's shirt. Evan could see him well, and the wound was worse than Evan feared. A large chunk of tissue had been ripped from Dan's body. He was losing a lot of blood. Katie saw it too.

And then she was gone.

"Katie!" Evan yelled.

He looked up, and there she was.

She was two hundred feet, now five hundred feet straight up. She was so fast.

She flew toward the shore high overhead in a sweeping arc so she came at the man on the shore from behind. The bottoms of both her shoes struck him squarely in the back of the head. He went down, the gun falling from his hands.

Katie landed and grabbed the rifle by the wood stock and swung it into the water, where it landed with a splash about ten feet from shore. The threat from the man firing at them was over.

The man staggered to his feet and lunged himself onto her. He grabbed her from behind and tried to pick her up.

Katie's immediate reaction was to fly.

She soared several feet above the shore and over the water. The man held tighter.

He was not a big man, but he was a fully grown adult. The realization struck her that she was able to fly with him holding onto her. There was no way she would have been able to pick him up while she was standing, but her ability to fly enabled her to carry substantially more weight than her own body.

The man got his right arm around Katie's neck. He was trying to choke her.

Katie flew in fast body rolls toward the water like an alligator rolling with prey. She bit his arm and elbowed him in the ribcage. His grip loosened, and he fell about ten feet into the dark water.

Katie saw him come to the surface and swim toward the shore as she flew back to the boat.

"Don't you ever do that again," Evan scolded when she landed aboard.

"But, Daddy," she started.

Evan held out a hand to stop her.

"How were you able to fly with him?" William interjected.

"I don't know. I just was. He wasn't heavy at all."

"She could carry him," William said to Evan.

They both looked at Dan.

"No," Evan said.

"He may otherwise die," William replied. "She needs to bring him to a hospital. One of *your* hospitals."

"Dan, can you hear me?" Evan asked his friend.

Dan's eyes rolled back.

Evan had no medical training. William and Mary Ellen appeared to have even less.

"Is Mr. Rose going to die?" Katie asked.

She was still so young. But Evan couldn't watch Dan die. His daughter had found Daufuskie Island on her own, had rescued them from the barn, and had single-handedly disarmed the Confederate soldier on the shore who was shooting at them.

"You were able to fly with that man as if he didn't weigh anything," Evan said. "Do you think you'd be able to fly Mr. Rose? He needs to get to our time through that door and to a hospital. You're the only one who can get him there quickly enough."

"I think I can," Katie said. "Maybe."

"Listen, if you don't think you can, then I don't want you to go. But if you really think you can make it, you're Mr. Rose's only hope."

Katie nodded. "I need to try."

"I love you," he said.

Evan used William's knife to cut a few sections of rope from the boat's lines.

"William, help me get him up."

They carefully wrapped Dan in the wool blanket and used the sections of rope to tie Dan to Katie. When they were finished, Katie lifted with ease a few inches above the deck of the boat to make sure she could fly with Dan's weight.

"Daddy, he's not heavy. I can make it. I know I can."

"Stay above everyone," Evan said. "You don't need anyone in this time to help you. Get him to our time. Get him through the door."

"I know where it is," Katie said. "I didn't know if I'd be going back there, so I made sure to look at landmarks from the air just in case. I can find it."

"I love you," Evan said again.

"I love you too, Daddy. Don't worry."

Evan would, of course, worry. He did not want his daughter to leave, but he knew she must in order to save Dan.

Before Katie left, William put a hand on her arm.

"When you open the silver door in my house," he said, "it is of the utmost importance that you think of your own time. Do not let your mind drift to any other thought. You must focus on your own time."

"I will," she said.

"Make sure you do," William said before Katie lifted into the air and raced Dan toward Savannah above the dormant marsh grass. "Make sure you do."

Major Childs returned to the stables sooner than he'd planned. The rest of his men were still in their search parties scattered around the island.

Sergeant Higgins lay dead near the barn.

Gregory Rawlins was unconscious. Major Childs poured a bucket of water over Rawlins's face to wake him.

He came to and told his tale that Sergeant Higgins and he had caught William Graffin attempting to free the two prisoners and that the prisoners attacked them. He lied that Sergeant Higgins had been shot by Graffin.

The only part of the story different than Rawlins originally planned to tell was that he'd been hit in the face and knocked unconscious. He had the injuries to prove it.

"I'm sure they're trying to get back to Savannah. They won't stay there long after this," Major Childs said. "If I catch them on the water, there'll probably be a fight."

"Then I'm coming with you," Rawlins offered. "You have no one else but me."

"No," Childs answered.

"You've seen what Graffin did. The three of them should hang for that. Whether you hang them or I do, it doesn't matter much."

"My orders are still the same. I'm taking them to Charleston. Do you understand that?"

Rawlins nodded. "I understand."

"As long as you do," the major said. "This goes against my better judgment, but I'm trusting you."

Childs and Rawlins headed toward the dock.

The smaller of the Confederate boats was gone. The second one had been untied and allowed to drift in the current, but it had come to rest about twenty yards down shore in an oyster bed. The two men were soon in the boat.

"At least they left the faster of the two," Major Childs said.

Gregory Rawlins had no idea how to sail, and his head throbbed. He needed Childs to sail them to Savannah.

He wanted to kill the three men who'd escaped. And of the three, he mostly wanted to kill the one who had hit him in the face with the butt of the ax handle. He wanted to kill the man with the orange Duxbury, Massachusetts, shirt.

Rawlins had said what he needed to say to assure Major Childs that he could be trusted and to get aboard the major's boat.

When they arrived in Savannah later tonight, he would find all three of them and kill them. He would kill the slave girl too. He had been to Savannah several times and had friends there. He'd find out where William Graffin lived.

CHAPTER 32

"WILL IS HERE?" CARIS ASKED WILLIAM GRAFFIN. "HE'S HERE in Hawaii?"

"He's close," William confirmed, looking toward the town. "I need to lock the Schottenklein door before we leave the boat. It's unwise for it to remain unlocked for any length of time."

He held the grey envelope that had the note. He reached in and took out a silver key.

"The key!" Abby announced.

"You have the key," Caris said. "Back on Daufuskie Island, there was a teenage boy who stole it. Evan went to find it."

"He found it," William replied. "In fact, Evan still has it."

"If Daddy still has the key," Abby said, "then how do you have it too?"

"One of the complexities of moving through time and space. Your father has the key from your time period, while this, my dear Abby, is a key from my time period."

"You're going to lock the door?" Caris asked, changing the subject. There was a hint of worry in her voice. She didn't like the idea of the door being locked.

"Yes," William answered. "The door has been unlocked for most of today because I knew that today was the day Abby and you would come through. The door used to be in my home in Savannah. I moved it onto the ship and sailed to Hawaii in order to be here when you arrived."

"Why does it need to be locked?" Caris asked. As best she could tell, returning through the door was the only way for them to return to their own time.

"If the door remains unlocked, then anyone may pass through. I had a similar conversation eight years ago with Evan and Dan. Don't be concerned." He handed Caris the key, apparently understanding how uneasy she felt about the door being locked. "Keep the key with you as long as you're here. You may unlock the door and leave whenever you wish. Until then, I'd be more comfortable with the door locked."

Caris returned with Abby to the cabin and locked the door.

She suddenly felt vulnerable, like it was a risky move to lock their only way home. But at the same time, she felt she needed to trust William Graffin. He knew where Will was, or at least, he claimed to know where Will was. He had the note from Evan. And if he was being truthful, he had sailed all the way from Savannah to Hawaii to help Caris find her son.

After locking the door, they came back onto the deck from the cabin. William was at one of the railings looking over the side of the ship.

"I'll row us over to land," he said.

Caris and Abby joined William at the railing. Caris had looked for a rowboat earlier and had been in this exact spot. She was certain the rowboat now bobbing in the waves tied next to the ship wasn't here earlier.

Caris turned behind her to take in the full view of the ship. It was massive with three tall masts. She didn't sail. She knew nothing of boats, and nothing about wooden sailing ships. Yet something wasn't right. The crew, she thought. There was no crew. William Graffin was alone on the ship.

"Where's your crew?" she asked.

"I have no need for a crew."

"You don't need one? This is a pretty big ship. You sailed all the way to Hawaii by yourself?"

"I did."

William set a rope ladder over the edge of the ship's railing to the rowboat below.

"You found the Schottenklein key in the chest, and you've been through the door," he said. "You've seen wonders that could not be real or explained, yet they are real. Many years ago, I too had my first encounter with the Schottenklein key and door. As you know, the wish that one makes must remain secret, known only to God. Without revealing the details of my wish, let us say that I'm able to sail this ship without a crew."

Caris believed him. She had seen the magic herself.

William turned his attention to Abby.

"From what your father told me, and from what I've been able to deduce, you wished for your brother to go away. I know you didn't wish your brother ill intent. You unwittingly wished him here."

He turned to the land on the edge of the bay.

"You must've been thinking of Hawaii."

"Did he go through the door too?" Abby asked.

"No, he didn't," William replied. "You wished him here. Although you might not have intentionally meant it, that was your wish. He arrived here instantaneously when he disappeared from your time. Your brother didn't come through the door to get here, but he'll go through it with you when you go back.

"Now Katie's wish," William continued. "That was quite a wish. I've seen her fly myself. And Will—he had the innocent wish of a child. He wished for the return of his father. That's a wish I could have used myself many, many years ago. And as for you, Caris, that has never been discussed. I have to admit that over the years I've been curious of the wish you made."

"I did make a wish," Caris confirmed.

"Say no more. Whatever your wish, the curiosity of an old man doesn't warrant you revealing it, or me asking anything further about it."

William descended the rope ladder into the rowboat and held it tight for Caris and Abby to climb down.

They pushed off from the ship. The water was calm, and to the west, Caris could see the beginning of a beautiful sunset. The colors were glorious.

She thought of the wish she'd made on the beach road. At the time, it had been the first thing to pop into her head. She now realized she would not have made any other wish no matter how much time she'd been given to think about it. She had made a wish, and she knew it would come true.

She would find Will and bring him home.

CHAPTER 33

EVAN THOUGHT OF KATIE AND PRAYED SHE'D BE ALL RIGHT.

He was still wearing the thick cotton shirt from the stables over his T-shirt, which helped take away the chill.

His thoughts turned to the silver key in his pocket.

He could have used it to make a wish for Dan to be transported to the hospital. That would have eliminated the need for Katie to take him. Or, thinking it through more, he could have simply wished that Dan hadn't been shot.

Could that have been his wish?

He knew from William that using the key to undo another person's wish wasn't possible. But how about changing events that had already happened?

He thought of Katie and suddenly had an uneasy feeling.

William had given her instructions. He'd been very specific. *When you open the silver door in my house, it is of the utmost importance that you think of your own time. Do not let your mind drift to any other thought. You must focus on your own time.*

He moved toward the back of boat where William was navigating.

"How does the door work?" he asked. "You instructed Katie to think of our own time."

"That I did. When you make a wish with the key, only God must know your wish. Otherwise, the wish will not be granted. The same is true with the Schottenklein door."

"The door takes you to where you wish to go?" Evan asked.

"In a way, yes, and in a way, no. The door is fixed at one location at any given time. Someone entering the door at one location can only pass through to the other side at a location where the door has been in the past, or where it'll be in the future."

"I'm not sure I follow," Evan said.

"Right now, we're in December 1864, and the Schottenklein door is in my house in Savannah. Yes? In your time, the door is in the lighthouse. You were able to go through the door from your time into my parlor because the door is physically here. You couldn't go through the door in the lighthouse and come out in Canada, for instance, because to the best of my knowledge, the door has never been in Canada. You can only go to where the door is, was, or will be."

"But I didn't wish to be in your parlor in this time, or any other time. I've never been in your house until today and didn't even know it existed."

"Then where did you wish to go when you passed through the door? What exactly were you seeking when you opened the Schottenklein door in the lighthouse?"

"I wasn't seeking anything," Evan said. "I was looking for Dan. When I went into the lighthouse and through the door, I was trying to find Dan to get the key back."

"And the door brought you to where you'd find him, did it not?"

"I guess that's true. Dan had gone through the door before me and had come out in your house. He was standing in the road when I came through looking for him."

"There you go. You were seeking Dan, and the door opened to where you'd find him. But why was Dan there? What was *he* seeking when he stepped through before you?"

"I don't know," Evan said. "He could've been thinking of anything."

"Did he say anything when you met up with him?"

Evan thought a moment.

"Actually, he did. He thought the numbers 1529 above the door and on the key were a date. Dan said he'd been thinking of the American colonies and Savannah during the American Revolution. I remember that. The door brought him to your house where the door had been located during the American Revolution. That's what he was seeking, and he didn't even realize it. When I went through the door looking for Dan, I ended up where he already was."

"You told me earlier in the shed that you'd gone through the door twice," William said.

"Yeah," Evan responded. "After I met up with Dan outside your house, we ran into a British officer. Dan recognized his name. He was a British colonel. We were able to get back into your house and through the door. Dan went first.

He must have been thinking of Savannah again but during the Civil War when he opened the door the second time."

"That's entirely possible."

"So when Katie brings Dan through the door on the way to the hospital, you gave her instructions to think only of our own time."

"Correct. As long as she is thinking of your time when she opens the door, she will come out on the other side where she belongs. She'll come out in the lighthouse."

"You could have been a little more clear on that point," Evan retorted.

"I thought I had."

Katie flew with Dan Rose high into the air above Savannah. It was practically dark when she located the brick house on Telfair Square.

Dan was no longer conscious. The bleeding had eased a bit.

After giving a quick survey of the area from the sky to make sure there was not anyone around to cause her problems, Katie landed with Dan a few feet from the front door of William's house. As soon as she landed, all of Dan's weight pulled her to the ground. She lifted herself back into the air, and his weight lightened. If she stood on the ground, there was no way she'd be able to support him. But as long as she levitated a few inches above the ground, she was able to manage.

Even so, he was becoming heavier as the time passed.

Katie was able to get Dan into the house and close the front door behind them. It was dark inside.

She thought she heard a noise from upstairs and waited a moment, suspending both of them inches above the parlor floor to make sure they were alone in the house. She saw the silver door on the other side of the room.

Reaching the door, she started worrying that she wouldn't be able to fly him to the hospital. He was getting heavier.

She also realized for the first time that she wasn't sure where the hospital was, or whether she was supposed to take him to Hilton Head or Savannah. That was a detail that had been overlooked in the hurry to get Dan help.

She pushed the door open seeking help. She thought of her own time. She needed help to get Dan Rose to the hospital.

The sky was dark and eerily lit by a crescent moon. Due to the multiple times Evan had made the crossing between Daufuskie Island and Savannah over the years in his own time, he was fairly certain they were approaching the Savannah River.

"Where'd the door come from?" Evan asked William.

"Do you read the Bible?" William answered.

Evan hadn't expected that response. "Not as much as I'd like," he answered.

"In the Sermon on the Mount described in the Gospel of Matthew, Jesus said to his followers, 'Ask, and you will receive. Seek, and you will find. Knock, and the door will be opened to you.'"

"Are you saying the silver door is the door Jesus was talking about?"

"In a way, yes."

"In what way?"

"You asked where the door came from. In the late fourteen hundreds, around 1490, a young man took his vows to become a Benedictine monk at a monastery in Vienna. The man's name was Friedrich Kragh. The monastery was the Schottenklein Abbey. It was a repository of knowledge and books in a very dark time in world history."

Evan recognized the name of the abbey from the note Caris had found. He thought he recognized the name Friedrich Kragh too.

"Are you familiar with grace?" William asked.

Evan was familiar. The St. Johns regularly attended church.

"Grace is a gift from God," Evan said. "Forgiveness for our sins."

"That's right," William agreed. "The young monk focused on the door as a metaphor for grace. Christ was using the door as an example to show that He is there all along on the other side, and that in order to gain salvation into the Kingdom of Heaven and be forgiven of sin, all one needs to do is accept Christ. But the monk also began to take the words of Jesus to mean that a door could be created through which a person could literally ask for and receive anything from God that the person sought."

"That doesn't sound like very good theology," Evan said.

"Nonetheless, over the years, the monk gained influence at the Schottenklein Abbey and was eventually elected abbot. The abbot is the head of the monastery. The monk had become convinced that not only could such a door be created, but a key to unlock the door could also be created and could be blessed by God to possess certain powers."

Evan could feel the weight of the silver key in his shorts pocket.

"By the fifteen hundreds, when the monk had been the abbot for several years, the Ottoman Empire was expanding to the west. A great conflict between the faiths of the Christians and Muslims would occur in 1529 in Vienna. In the spring of that year, the sultan of the Ottoman Empire had amassed three hundred thousand men in Bulgaria with the intent of expanding Islam into central Europe. Vienna stood in the way.

"The abbot feared the monastery would be overrun and burned, so before the sultan could attack, the abbot set about to create the Schottenklein door and key. His plan was to enter through it with the collected storehouse of books. He would enter the door with the intention of seeking a safe location where the knowledge of the abbey could be kept safe."

"I take it he succeeded," Evan said.

"Yes, he succeeded in creating the door and key. The door was placed into the abbey, ready to be opened when needed. But as history revealed, the door wasn't necessary. The Ottomans were unable to take the city. The Siege of Vienna was not successful, and the sultan retreated."

Evan recalled Mary Ellen saying that she'd overhead William telling a man to make a wish for the safety of Savannah.

"Did the abbot make a wish with the key for the safety of Vienna?" he asked William.

"I don't know. It's possible."

"What happened to the abbot?"

"He was hanged."

"What?" Evan replied in startled surprise.

"Yes, hanged. In constructing the door and key, the abbot required a large quantity of pure silver. He was accused of stealing and hoarding silver for his personal wealth. He didn't defend himself from the accusations by showing his accusers the door and key. He feared how they could be misused. He instead hid the door behind a fake wall. After the abbot was executed, the door and key would have remained concealed for all time."

"But they weren't," Evan said.

"No, they were not."

William shifted the rudder and navigated into the Savannah River. A cold December breeze from the Atlantic caught the main sail. Regardless of the thick cotton shirt he was wearing, a chill ran through Evan.

"Would you like to know when I first learned to sail?" William asked.

"Okay."

"I was fourteen. The year was 1764."

"So if you were fourteen in 1764, that means you were born in what, 1750?"

"Yes, in Hamburg, Germany. I was Wilhelm Graffin then. My mother died during childbirth. My father was often at sea. He owned a shipping company. Having lost his wife, he was overly protective and almost never allowed me onto the ships. I was all he had left. But when I turned fourteen, my father decided the time had come for me to learn to sail. I studied well. In the winter of 1765, my father's ship was lost at sea. I never saw him again.

"My father's brother, my uncle, was a monk at Schottenklein. He was able to secure my placement into the abbey with the intention that I too would become a Benedictine monk. That was not what I wanted for myself. I wanted to run my father's shipping company. But I had no say in the matter.

"I spent considerable time exploring the grounds. One day, in my third or fourth month, I came upon the hidden writings of an abbot, an abbot who had been hanged nearly two hundred and fifty years earlier. His writings concerned the Gospel of Matthew and a silver door and key that had been constructed and blessed by God.

"The abbot had left a description of where the door was hidden. I searched for weeks until I found the false wall that concealed the door. The door was locked. But following the abbot's writings, I was able to eventually find the key. Do you know what I did with it?" William asked.

"You unlocked the door?"

"That is precisely what I did. I unlocked the door and stepped through into another time and place. There was someone on the other side of the door waiting for me."

273

"Who?"

"I met myself."

"Come again."

"I met myself. When I went through the doorway in 1765 at the age of fifteen, I came out into the parlor of my home in Savannah in 1775, ten years later. The same house in Savannah where we're heading now.

"The William Graffin who lived in Savannah in 1775, who was very much me, explained to the younger Wilhelm Graffin, who had come from Vienna in 1765, that I had been thinking of my own future when I stepped through the door. I thus arrived on the other side of the door seeking myself.

"I learned from speaking with my older self that I would leave the abbey against my uncle's wishes and go into the shipping business like my father before me. My father's estate had been quite extensive, and I would purchase a ship with my inheritance.

"Knowing this information about how my life would unfold from speaking with myself ten years older, I returned to the abbey by again stepping through the Schottenklein door. Once there, I left the abbey, purchased a ship, and sailed to Savannah, where I would build the exact house where I met myself on the other side of the silver door."

"But how'd the door get into your house in Savannah? You said earlier that the door must be in a different location in order for a person to open it on one side and come through in a different place on the other side. If the door was in the abbey when you unlocked it, how'd you end up on the other side in Savannah?"

"That's why I needed to put it there."

"*You* put it there?"

"That I did. Although the door was in the abbey in 1765 when I too was at the abbey, by the time 1775 arrived ten years later, the door was safely installed in my parlor in Savannah because I put it there."

"You stole the door from the abbey?"

"Of course not," William replied. "I didn't steal anything. The door has no owner."

"That's one way to look at it," Evan said. "But you did take it from the abbey and moved it to Savannah."

"I did," William answered. "The key too."

"Did you make a wish with it?" Evan asked.

"I certainly did. One known only to God. I thought about the wish for many days before making it. I'm still living my wish and very much intend to keep it known only to God."

"I'm still a bit confused," Evan said. "If you were living in Savannah in 1775, what are you doing here? It's December 1864."

"I didn't remain in 1775 for long. I was, at first, living comfortably in Savannah. I was there in 1776 when the Declaration of Independence was signed in Philadelphia. But then war came to Savannah. The Americans, the British, the French. I don't care for war.

"So I went through the Schottenklein door thinking again of my own future, looking for a peaceful time. I emerged on the other side of the door in my very own parlor about eighty years later in 1855. I didn't know, of course, that another war would come again to Savannah a few years later. I could not have known that Americans would be fighting themselves, North against South."

"You've lived an amazing life," Evan commented.

"I still am," William said. "I do wish I could help you find your son." He gestured toward Mary Ellen at the front of the boat. "Go back through the door. Find her in your own time. She may have the answers you need."

In another twenty minutes, Savannah appeared.

Ahead of them, they could see soldiers illuminated by lanterns hurriedly lashing barges together to construct the floating bridge for the evacuation of the city's Confederate defenders. Careful to avoid being spotted, William brought the boat to the side of the river, well away from the downtown wharfs.

They tied the boat to one of the small docks. Coming ashore, William led the way under cover of night toward his house on Telfair Square.

CHAPTER 34

PRIOR TO TODAY, THE FASTEST COLONEL JOHN MAITLAND had traveled was on horseback. That was before his first car ride, which he thoroughly enjoyed.

The older Scotsman had dropped him off at the Haig Point Embarkation Center on Hilton Head Island. Not knowing whether he would need fare for the ferry, Colonel Maitland managed to slip aboard while the ferry mate was helping another passenger. The mate saw him, of course, but mistakenly believed the man in the colonial-era British uniform had been hired for some entertainment purpose by the Haig Point Club.

Minutes later, as the ferry made its way across the Calibogue Sound, Colonel Maitland could see Daufuskie Island ahead in the distance. The Haig Point lighthouse with its observation tower soon came into view.

The colonel contemplated all he'd learned and seen since arriving. The Americans had done very well for themselves. He wanted to dislike them. But he didn't. They had colonized a new world far from home and thrived.

Colonel Maitland had long thought that the Declaration of Independence had a certain flair, although when he had first heard of it, he was horribly offended. British subjects airing their grievances to the king of England and telling—no, dictating—to the king that the colonies were to be free and independent states, that they were absolved from all allegiance to the British Crown, and that all political connections between themselves and the sovereign nation of Great Britain were dissolved.

What appalling gumption the colonists had to decide for themselves that they'd start their own country.

But they had.

And as the colonel now knew, they had been successful.

When they should have lost the Revolution, they prevailed. When the rebellion should have been quashed and its leaders hanged for treason, Providence had other plans.

He had no personal animosity toward the Americans. Their sheer resourcefulness would create a new nation. A great nation. A nation that would come to the aid of his own country in two world wars.

He set his bag onto one of the benches on the ferry and removed the book. Several of the pages of *Independence: A History of the American Revolution* caught in the wind and flipped open.

Colonel Maitland had enjoyed reading the gift from Dr. Hunter. The information in the book could be used to change the outcome of the war in his time. He knew it.

In his own time, there were nearly two years left of the Revolution before Cornwallis's surrender at Yorktown. History could be changed. The existence of the United

States could be torn from the pages of time, as easy as the wind was now blowing the pages of the history book.

But he knew he wouldn't use the information. He would fight the battle at the Spring Hill redoubt. He would do his duty. That battle had already been fought according to the book. Nothing would be changed.

Yet there would be one change. He would live. He would not die of malaria weeks after the Siege of Savannah. He would live solely because of the American doctor who had saved his life.

Colonel Maitland would take no action to change history. He would keep quiet about what he had learned and seen. And when it was time for the war in his time to end, he would return home to Scotland and live out the remainder of his days in peace. He stood at the railing of the ferry, looked again at the lighthouse ahead, and dropped the book into the Calibogue Sound.

CHAPTER 35

THE FERRY DOCKED, AND COLONEL MAITLAND DISEMBARKED. At the end of the dock, he looked through the window of the welcome center and saw something familiar. In fact, he had thought about this very item several times over the last few days. The nurse at the hospital hadn't known anything about it when he asked her, and there hadn't been any report of the thing coming with him when he arrived in the emergency room.

But there it was. Kenny Shivers was holding Colonel Maitland's sword. He was showing it to the dark woman sitting at the desk.

Colonel Maitland entered.

"I believe that belongs to me," he said.

"Kenny, where'd you get that?" Natalie asked.

Kenny insisted at first that he'd found it, but then argued that since he saved the man's life by calling 911, the man should at least let Kenny keep it.

Colonel Maitland explained that he was not quite finished with the sword, but if he had been, he would have allowed Kenny to have it in appreciation for the role that Kenny had played in getting him to the hospital.

"That's just wrong," Kenny said. "You owe me the sword."

"I am quite sorry," the colonel replied.

Kenny gave him the sword and sulked toward the door. "I'm going to the lighthouse to see if Mr. Rose's golf cart is still there. That's strange he hasn't come back for it yet."

"The lighthouse," Colonel Maitland said. "May I impose on your hospitality to show me the way?"

"I'll take you there if you give me your sword," Kenny said before walking out the door and letting it slam behind him.

"It's not a far walk," Natalie said. "Take that path out the door. You'll come to a big field. The lighthouse is right across it."

Katie opened the silver door in William Graffin's house in December 1864 thinking of her own time and seeking help to get Dan to the hospital. As she and Dan passed through the doorway, they came out on the second floor hallway of the lighthouse.

Although it had been night in Savannah, it was day here. Sunlight streamed through the lighthouse's windows.

In the hallway, Katie lifted Dan and flew him a few inches above the floor toward the stairway. She managed to get him down the stairs and out the front door.

The Calibogue Sound was directly in front of them. Katie could feel the familiar warmth of early June.

Dan's weight was becoming unbearable. She was now floating only about an inch above the ground and didn't know how much longer she could hold him.

Coming around to the rear of the lighthouse, she noticed her family's black golf cart parked near the edge of the field. The key would probably be in it. Her dad had shown her how to drive it, and she was certain she'd be able to get Mr. Rose to the welcome center on the cart. Hopefully Natalie would be working.

But Dan's weight was too much. She fell to the ground.

With her eyes closed, trying to summon the last amount of strength to get them both into the air, she heard a sound in the field. She looked up, and there was Kenny Shivers approaching. He was driving his golf cart directly toward them.

Kenny had a look of terror on his face when he came nearer. Dan appeared to be dead. The wool blanket was soaked in blood.

"What happened?" Kenny shouted.

"He's been shot."

"Your dad shot him?"

The pilot of the orange Coast Guard helicopter who had spotted Jerry and Emily Culpepper the morning after the hurricane was on duty again today. He was flying the same pattern along the northern end of Daufuskie Island when he saw a young girl and an older boy with long blond hair waving to him. There was a man on the ground wrapped in what appeared to be a blood-soaked blanket. He brought the helicopter closer.

The pilot was at the right place at the right time. Katie had no idea that days had passed in her own time since she had entered the lighthouse following Mary Ellen's instructions to find her father. But this is where she found herself when she came through the silver door seeking help. There was help here. The Coast Guard was the help she needed to get Dan to the hospital.

The first one from the helicopter to reach Dan was the team's rescue swimmer and EMT. He had helped the Culpeppers.

Pulling back the blanket, he saw the gunshot wound to Dan's upper chest. Katie's clothes were covered in Dan's blood, and the man made sure that she too was not injured. Other than answering that she was okay, Katie didn't want to answer any of his few other questions.

Kenny shouted that the injured man was Dan Rose and that Evan St. John had shot him. Katie shouted back that wasn't true and that she needed to get back to her father. The rescue swimmer told them that the police would sort it out and that his immediate priority was to get Dan to the hospital.

The flight mechanic joined them with the same collapsible stretcher they had used to move Jerry Culpepper. Telling a lie that he was Dan's nephew, Kenny was allowed to join them on the helicopter.

At Savannah Memorial Hospital's trauma center a few minutes later, Dr. Stephens, the young emergency room doctor, examined Dan. When an x-ray showed what looked to be a minié ball in his patient's chest, Dr. Stephens thought of the man who had been admitted earlier in the week wearing a colonial-era British uniform.

Dr. Stephens would spend the next few days trying to find out if a movie was being produced in the area that involved the Revolutionary War or Civil War. His search would come up empty.

Katie had watched the helicopter take off with Dan and Kenny onboard. She was exhausted and sat on the field with her head down and her arms pulled in around her knees.

A few minutes later, she stood and flew inches above the ground toward the lighthouse. Once inside, she headed upstairs to the Schottenklein door.

On the other side of the field, Colonel Maitland emerged from the bushes and trees after walking from the welcome center. He had heard the helicopter ahead of him and was able to get a glimpse of it as it flew away above the trees.

He saw a girl in the field sitting with her head down. She didn't see him.

When the thumping from the machine's rotary blades had faded into the distance, Colonel Maitland watched the girl head to the lighthouse and turn the corner to where the front faced the water. The girl had moved so effortlessly that she seemed to Colonel Maitland to be floating on air.

CHAPTER 36

KATIE OPENED THE SILVER DOOR SEEKING HER FATHER. SHE stepped through the opening into William Graffin's parlor. She looked around the dark room and heard the front door open.

Three people came in. Even in the dark, she recognized her father as one of them.

"Am I glad to see you," Evan said when he saw her. "Were you able to get him to the hospital without any problems?"

"Kenny Shivers was outside. He thought you shot Mr. Rose."

"That kid's an idiot."

"I know," Katie agreed. "But then a helicopter came. It was the same Coast Guard helicopter that helped Mr. and Mrs. Culpepper. They took Mr. Rose. Kenny went with them."

"You did great, Katie. I'm proud of you."

William led her into the adjoining kitchen. "Let's get you cleaned up a bit and something to eat before you go back."

Evan and Mary Ellen joined them.

At the same time Katie had come through the Schottenklein door into William's parlor, the boat with Gregory

Rawlins and Major Childs was nearing Savannah. The crescent moon was hidden by clouds.

"I want to be clear," Major Childs said, "those men are my prisoners. I know what they did, and I know how you feel. When we arrive in Savannah in a few minutes, you're welcome to accompany a patrol to find them. But you are not to harm them in any way. Do I have your agreement on that?"

Gregory Rawlins did not agree.

There was no way Rawlins was going to allow Major Childs to take the three men. Rawlins wanted them. He could taste the hate. The Confederate major had done his part by sailing Rawlins to Savannah. Major Childs now needed to be dealt with before they came closer to the city. Before they were spotted. Before the major's men could help him.

Rawlins had watched how Major Childs had raised the sails. He knew he'd be able to lower them on his own.

"Do I have your agreement?" Major Childs asked again, getting irritated.

Rawlins took one of the heavy oars, as if to place it into an oarlock.

"You don't need that," the major said. "I'll put us to the wharf."

Those were the last words Major Nathan Childs would speak.

Rawlins swung the oar striking him on the side of the head. Major Childs collapsed into the back of the boat.

Gregory Rawlins lowered the sails and found the boat's heavy anchor. He tied it around Major Childs's lifeless body, cut the other end, and pushed him over the side. The major sunk into the black water, taking the twenty-first-century cell phones and wallets in his coat pocket to the bottom of the Savannah River.

Rawlins set the oars into the two oarlocks. The moon had come out again from behind the clouds, providing just enough light for Rawlins to see the other sailboat a couple of hundred yards away from where the Confederate soldiers were working on the pontoon bridge. He rowed toward it.

After tying the larger sailboat next to the smaller one, he set out to find William Graffin. He was certain his friends in Savannah would be able to tell him where Graffin lived. He'd find Mary Ellen Hadley and the three men, in particular the one with the orange shirt. He smiled when he thought of what he was going to do to them.

CHAPTER 37

WILL AND ONO WERE NEAR THE ALTAR IN THE TEMPLE. SUP-
porters of Poipu stood near the children keeping guard.

The shaman Keoni could no longer tolerate what was
going to happen. Poipu was going to sacrifice the children
once the sun set. Poipu had headed to Honolulu Bay with
several followers to pray to Ku. They would return soon.
Keoni needed to act. He needed to act now.

He left the temple to confer with two of his closest allies
and devised a plan to save the children.

"Poipu requires them to be brought to see their last
sunset," Keoni lied to the men guarding Will and Ono.

"Where's Poipu?" one of them questioned.

"He wants them by the water," Keoni responded.

Keoni's plan was to take the children to the bay less than
a quarter mile away, and along the route, a faction of his
own supporters would ambush the guards. Keoni would
be able to get the children to safety.

Three of Poipu's men brought Will and Ono from the temple.

They began their route downhill toward the bay. Keoni
walked in front. The plan would work. Less than a hundred

yards in front of him, Keoni could see a handful of trusted men from his own village in the thin crowd. They would attack the three men who guarded Will and Ono.

And then a sickening feeling overtook Keoni as his gaze went beyond the men from his village toward the water. Poipu, in his dark red skirt, was leading over thirty men up the hill from the bay.

Coming from opposite directions, Keoni and Poipu were the same distance from the place where the ambush was to occur. Keoni did not have enough men. Poipu and his followers would easily overpower them.

William fastened the rowboat to one of the Honolulu docks. Caris could see a large crowd up the hill from the water. The men were shirtless and wore colorful skirts. The women wore brightly colored dresses. It made Caris think of a luau.

"Do you know where Will is?" she asked William.

"I know he's in Honolulu. You told me when we met before that there was some sort of ceremony when you arrived."

For Caris, that conversation had not yet occurred.

"I didn't tell you where we actually find Will?"

"No, I didn't want to know too many details. You were referring to an event that had not yet happened for me. I've traveled through the Schottenklein door over a lifetime. I don't believe it's wise to know too many details of what you'll do in the future."

"Where exactly we find Will is kind of an important detail," Caris said.

"It will work out. Have faith."

William noticed a large group on the hill ahead of them. A man with a red skirt was in front.

"Maybe we should follow them," Caris said.

Keoni, the children, and the guards continued down the hill toward the bay. They were within ten yards of the planned ambush. The men from Keoni's village were on both sides of the road mingling with the sporadic crowd.

Poipu and his followers were the same distance from the ambush spot coming up the hill. Poipu saw Keoni. He saw the two children.

"Keoni!" Poipu shouted.

But before Poipu could do anything further, the men from Keoni's village pounced upon Poipu's three men who were guarding Will and Ono.

Keoni turned to Will and Ono.

"Run!"

Poipu's forces bolted up the hill to aid their three friends who were being attacked. In the commotion, Poipu reached for the children but missed. Will and Ono ran down the hill toward the bay.

Caris could see something happening ahead of them. Two groups of men were fighting.

"It's Will!" Abby yelled.

Will and another child were running from the men. They were running down the hill toward Caris.

"Will!" Caris cried out.

Will saw his mother.

Ono was not as fast and was falling behind. The girl tripped and went down. Will stopped and turned up the hill to help her.

Poipu had his chance. He seized Will by the front of his shirt and grabbed the girl kicking and screaming from the road.

Caris raced up the hill toward them and saw a man grab Will.

He had a long knife around the waist of his red skirt. She sprinted the last twenty yards.

"Let go of my son!" she demanded.

Poipu let go of Ono but grasped Will tighter. With his other hand, he pulled the long knife from his waistband.

When Caris had held the silver key on the beach road and made her secret wish, she had thought of her family's safety. She had been terrified during the hurricane that something would happen to her children. The only thing she wanted was the wish that popped into her mind—that she would always be able to protect her family and keep them safe.

She saw the knife. The man raised it above Will.

In her mind's eye, she had a vision of the knife flying out the man's hand, as if it had been knocked free by an invisible force. She looked again at the knife, and it flew from his hand, landing several feet away.

Poipu looked in surprise at the knife on the ground and scrambled toward it.

Caris had to stop him. He couldn't get to the knife. She envisioned him being hurled backward into the air, and when she made eye contact with Poipu, an unseen force hit him in the stomach. The invisible blow threw him several feet backward, causing him to land on his back.

He tried to stand.

Caris waved her hand motioning from left to right, and as if she were moving a toy, Poipu skidded across the dirt road onto the grass in the direction she motioned.

A number of the men who had been fighting saw what was happening and ran away in fear.

Poipu stayed on the ground, lying flat and pleading to Ku to forgive him. "The boy was not to be sacrificed," he called out. "Forgive me, Ku! Forgive me."

Caris reached for Will.

"Mom!" Will cried.

Caris had never held her son tighter than she did now. Abby ran to them, and Caris hugged them both not wanting to ever let go.

Keoni approached. He was certain that the beautiful woman who had defeated Poipu was a goddess. No mortal could have done what she had done.

"Please take the girl with you," he said. "She has no parents. No family." He placed Ono's small hand into Caris's hand.

William came forward up the hill.

"She was with you when you arrived at my house eight years ago," he said. "I didn't think it wise to tell. I didn't know where we'd meet her, and if I told you of the girl, my fear was that it could have impacted your actions."

Caris looked at Ono's innocent face. "What's your name?"

"Her name is Grace," Will answered.

On the ship, Caris unlocked the Schottenklein door and gave the key to William.

"I saw your wish," William said. "You used your wish to protect your son."

"Will I see you again?" Caris asked.

"As soon as you go through the doorway," William answered, "I'll see you then. When you open the door, set your mind to seeking your husband and Katie in 1864. I'm here now solely because of the information you give me when we meet then."

"Thank you," Caris said. "Thank you for everything."

She put her hand on the silver handle and opened the door. William's parlor in his house in Savannah was visible through the open doorway. Caris, Will, Abby, and Grace walked through. William remained on the ship and closed the door behind them.

CHAPTER 38

KATIE FINISHED EATING. EVAN WAS SAYING THEIR GOOD-byes to William and Mary Ellen in the kitchen when they heard the silver door in the next room open and close. There were people in the parlor.

Evan was the first to enter the parlor and see the most wonderful sight: Caris, Will, and Abby. There was a small girl, too, holding Caris's hand.

He opened his arms and moved toward his family, looking especially at Will. Caris had found him.

Katie came into the room from the kitchen.

"You're bleeding!" Caris pronounced when she saw her daughter's clothes.

"It's not my blood."

"It's from Dan Rose," Evan said. "He's at the hospital. He's been shot, and it's serious."

"Is he going to be okay?" Caris asked.

"I don't know. We'll check on him soon."

William and Mary Ellen entered the parlor. William was eight years younger than when Caris had seen him moments ago on the ship. Caris also recognized Mary Ellen as the aged woman she had met in Bluffton.

"It's December 1864, isn't it?" Caris asked.

"Yeah, how'd you know that?" Evan responded.

"It's a long story."

"I bet it is," Evan said, eying the little girl.

Over the next several minutes, Caris spoke privately with William about how she and the kids found the chest. William knew from Evan that they'd find it, but Caris made sure to let him know of the blue shutters and where the chest had come from. William kept insisting that Caris not tell him too much. She did, however, make sure that William knew when and where she would find Will.

Caris also spoke with Mary Ellen and made her promise that she'd convince Caris nearly a hundred and fifty years from now that all of this was real. She also told Mary Ellen of Natalie Larkin and that Mary Ellen would need to tell Natalie about the family finding the chest. Mary Ellen listened intently to everything Caris had to tell her.

Abby described to Evan and Katie how her mother had used magic to whoop up on the Hawaiian man who was going to hurt Will. Will told of appearing in the village and being taken to the temple where he met the little girl.

They all looked at her.

Caris and Evan knew that Grace would be part of their family. They had no idea how they were going to explain her to the authorities, but they'd do their best and were certain they'd adopt her.

Finally, they all gathered near the silver door in William's parlor—ready to return to Daufuskie Island. Ready to return to their own time.

"I'm thinking of the moment right after the helicopter came for Mr. Rose," Katie said.

"We can head to the hospital to check on him as soon as we get back."

"I'm taking a shower before we do anything," Caris said.

Katie opened the silver door and stepped through into the hallway of the lighthouse. Caris could see it was the hallway. She stepped through holding Will's hand. Abby held Grace by her small hand and came through after them.

Evan could see his family in the hallway of the lighthouse on the other side of the doorway. He turned to William and pulled off the thick cotton shirt from the stables.

"Keep it as a souvenir," William said.

"I want to thank you for everything," Evan replied.

"You are more than welcome. I'm sure it's not an adventure you'd want to repeat."

"No, probably not," Evan smiled and handed him the shirt.

He began stepping through the doorway when the front door of William's house flew open. Gregory Rawlins barged inside.

"You!" he yelled at Evan.

Evan was caught completely off guard. The last time he'd seen Rawlins, the big man was unconscious on the ground outside of the barn after Evan had bashed him in the face with the ax handle.

Gregory Rawlins came fast across the room. Evan tried to get through the door and shut it, but it was too late.

Rawlins knocked him through the doorway. The two of them collided into the opposite wall in the hallway of the lighthouse and hit the floor.

Caris and the kids screamed.

The weight of the two men banging into the wall and floor shook the lighthouse and caused the Schottenklein door to shut.

Evan began to stand.

"I've been waiting for this," Rawlins snarled.

He punched Evan twice in the face and body, sending Evan to the floor again. The impact caused the silver key to come out of Evan's pocket, and it landed on the hardwood floor of the hallway.

Colonel Maitland had reached the front of the lighthouse following after the girl he saw in the field. He thought she'd be here. She must have gone inside, he realized.

A warm, pleasant breeze drifted from the Calibogue Sound. This had been a truly amazing place. He thought about the two men he had seen in Savannah, the men he had followed into the brick house. They had probably come from this place and had gone through the silver door before him.

He thought of his own men searching the house in Savannah. He thought of his own time.

He climbed onto the porch of the lighthouse. The front door was unlocked. As he opened it, he heard a loud bang from upstairs and screams. The screams sounded like a woman and children. He rushed up the stairway.

Colonel Maitland came to the top of the stairs. He'd been in hand-to-hand combat numerous times over his career and immediately sensed there was a fight around the corner of the hallway.

Turning the corner, the colonel saw the man with the orange shirt on the ground. A much larger man was on top hitting him.

Colonel Maitland drew his sword, and before the larger man saw him, the colonel cracked the bottom of the sword's hilt into the right side of the big man's face. He fell forward onto the floor.

"Are you able to stand?" Colonel Maitland asked the man with the orange shirt.

Evan opened his eyes slightly. The British officer from Savannah was above him.

Colonel Maitland looked at the woman and children. Maybe they were the man's family.

He glanced at the bulky man on the ground. Colonel Maitland had struck him hard but was surprised that the blow to his face would knock out such a large man. The colonel was not aware, of course, that Gregory Rawlins had been recently knocked unconscious twice.

The silver door was a few feet on the other side of Rawlins, who wasn't moving. There was a silver key on the floor near his head.

Colonel Maitland was certain that the silver door was the same door he had come through into the lighthouse days earlier when he had been suffering from malaria.

Not knowing the degree of injury the man spread out on the floor actually had, or whether he was simply playing possum, Colonel Maitland pointed the tip of his sword at him and cautiously stepped over Rawlins.

Standing in front of the door, a thought occurred to Colonel Maitland as he sheathed his sword. Although it seemed impossible, he wondered whether the room in the brick house was on the other side of the silver door. He thought of his soldiers who had entered the house in Savannah. Would his men be on the other side of the door? He thought they might. Colonel Maitland was thinking that exact thought when he grasped the silver doorknob and pushed opened the door.

The blows that Evan received from Gregory Rawlins had put him on the verge of losing consciousness.

He lifted his head. Caris and the kids were coming toward him from his left. To his right, he could see the British officer who had pursued Dan and him into William's house in Savannah. He had one arm, and Evan was positive it was the same man. The man had stopped Gregory Rawlins from hitting him.

As the British officer was pushing open the silver door, Evan could see Rawlins raising himself onto all fours behind the man. He had not been knocked unconscious a third time.

"Watch out!" Evan called.

The officer drew his sword and turned around, right as Rawlins threw his fist. The punch landed squarely on Colonel Maitland's face. He wobbled back and dropped the sword.

Evan was on his feet moving forward to help the British officer before Rawlins could hit him again.

Rawlins picked up the sword, and as Evan approached, Rawlins jammed the sword into Evan's stomach.

Caris screamed in horror as the tip of the blade came through Evan's body and tore through the back of his T-shirt.

Evan's eyes went wide.

Rawlins had a grin of delight. He pulled the bloody sword from Evan.

Colonel Maitland regained his balance and landed a punch on the back of Rawlins's head. Rawlins turned swinging the sword fast on a downward angle. The blade sliced deep into the colonel's leg. Blood poured from the gash, soaking the white pants of his uniform.

Before Rawlins was able to swing the sword again, Colonel Maitland narrowed the gap between them by grabbing at Rawlins's coat with his one hand and pulling the two of them together. Rawlins lifted the colonel from the ground trying to smack the back of his head into the door.

Colonel Maitland's head hit the Schottenklein door with the full force of Rawlins's attack, violently swinging the door all of the way open. The two of them fell through into William Graffin's parlor.

On the other side of the open doorway, Caris could see into William's Graffin's house. She had expected it to be the same room that she and her family had just left in December 1864. But to Caris's utter surprise, a colonial-era British soldier was on the other side of the open door. He looked directly at her. The soldier's attention was quickly diverted to the two men who had crashed through the doorway and who were struggling on William's parlor floor.

"Colonel!" the soldier shouted.

Caris could see more British soldiers racing into the parlor. Two had their own swords out and stabbed the large man who had attacked her husband.

The soldier Caris had first seen looked at her again. He began to approach the open doorway. Another soldier saw her too.

Caris's only thought was to prevent a storm of men from coming through into the lighthouse. She knew nothing about them and didn't want them near her family. She needed to protect them. The kids were next to Evan crying hysterically.

She focused on the silver door, and with her mind, she caused it to slam closed. She saw the silver key on the floor near the door, and in an instant, she made it sail through the air and into the lock below the silver handle. The key turned under her control, locking the Schottenklein door.

She turned toward Evan, who was on the floor. One of the kids had lifted his shirt to his chest, exposing where the sword had entered. His hands were clutching his abdomen. Blood was everywhere.

He was telling them not to look as he struggled to breathe. Caris looked into his eyes. She could see his tears.

She placed her hand on the fatal wound. The bleeding stopped. The hole in his body miraculously closed as if it had never been there.

Caris thought of the wish she had made on the beach road. A wish made in love to protect her family and to always have the power to keep them safe.

CHAPTER 39

Two Months Later

THE AROMA OF COFFEE FILLED THE BEACH HOUSE AND stirred Caris from her sleep. She was on Daufuskie time and slept late into the morning.

She opened her eyes and took a deep breath. Although it was August and usually the warmest month of the year, a bedroom window was slightly open. The scent of fresh coffee was mixed with a rich bouquet of ocean breeze and salt air.

Evan was already awake and had made the pot of coffee. Her favorite coffee mug was next to the coffee maker waiting for her.

All of the kids were awake too. When Caris came into the living room, Abby, Grace, and Will were playing with the family's new puppy. They hadn't settled on a name yet, but Miracle was the leading choice. Abby and Will had been especially close over the last two months. Caris hadn't heard them argue once since their adventure at the beginning of the summer.

As for Grace, they planned to begin the adoption process in Atlanta once the summer ended. They still had no idea how they were going to explain her, but as far as Caris was concerned, she was already part of their family. She'd be protected. Caris knew it.

She went into the kitchen for her coffee. Katie was making cinnamon rolls for breakfast. Looking closer, Caris noticed that Katie was about a half inch above the kitchen floor. They'd given Katie rules about her flying, especially outside. So far, Katie had followed them. Caris didn't mind her defying gravity in the house. Evan didn't seem to mind either after all they'd been through.

She poured her coffee and went out the front door onto the porch. Evan was standing at the railing.

"Good morning, beautiful," he said.

"It's a nice morning," Caris responded. "I was curious if you've heard from Dan lately."

"No, it's still been two months since I saw him."

After the events at the lighthouse earlier in the summer, Evan had gone to the hospital to check on his friend. Dan would fully recover from the gunshot wound.

Evan told him everything that happened after Katie had flown him through the Schottenklein door to get him to the hospital. Their conversation eventually came around to the key and making a secret wish. Dan asked to see it.

When Evan visited Dan at the hospital the next day, he brought it with him. As far as Evan was concerned, it wasn't Evan's key. And if anyone had earned the right to make a wish, it was certainly Dan Rose. Evan brought him the key, and Dan made a secret wish. That had been two months ago.

A few days after that, when Evan had gone for a morning jog, Dan magically appeared next to him. Dan would not say his wish, but he did confide that he would be visiting places throughout history. Without giving details, he stressed he had designed his wish so he would always be an observer and could never interfere with history.

Dan had asked if Evan would like to know what had happened to Colonel Maitland. When Evan said he would, Dan explained that Colonel Maitland had secured the British lines at the Spring Hill redoubt and led the defense against the Americans and French. True to history, he had done his duty during the Siege of Savannah.

Also true to history, he had died after the battle. Malaria had not killed him. Instead, the deep gash in his leg delivered by Gregory Rawlins had become infected. Gangrene set in and killed him two weeks later.

As for Gregory Rawlins, the pages of history regarding him would remain forever blank. Evan had filled Dan in on what Caris had seen through the doorway when Colonel Maitland's men ended the wicked man's life with their swords in William Graffin's parlor.

In a big surprise, Dan had said that Kenny Shivers would indeed turn his life around in the years to come. Dan had laughed when he described to Evan that Kenny had been so convinced Evan had shot Dan that Kenny Shivers would eventually become a police officer.

"Don't worry," Dan had said, "I'm able to eventually convince him that you didn't shoot me. He'll return the wooden chest to you and Caris also."

Dan had visited Mary Ellen too. Despite her telling Caris her wish, she would continue to live a long, free life. She would eventually pass away at the ripe old age of 217.

Dan said he would stop by to visit Evan from time to time, and then he disappeared. Vanished into thin air to travel to whatever time period he wished to see.

Evan looked forward to seeing his friend again and hearing the firsthand accounts of history that Dan would tell. But for now, he would enjoy the last days of summer with his family.

Evan put his arm around Caris's waist on this fine August morning and clinked her coffee mug with his.

"You know," he said. "I haven't made a wish yet."

The silver key rested within his shorts pocket.

EPILOGUE

March 25, 1875

WILLIAM GRAFFIN ANCHORED HIS THREE-MASTED WOODEN ship in the Calibogue Sound and rowed to shore. He kept the lighthouse in view as he maneuvered the oars. He had a gift in the rowboat. It was a gift for the keeper of the lighthouse— a beautiful wooden door with a large area of silver within it.

The lighthouse keeper, Patrick Comer, suggested that a lighthouse was an odd place for such a beautiful door, but he accepted the gift graciously on William's one condition that the door must never be removed from the lighthouse.

William helped lug the door up the stairs and set it into place as the doorway for one of the upstairs bedrooms. After being a guest for a midafternoon meal, William made sure the Schottenklein door was locked.

Patrick Comer's daughter, a lovely young girl named Maggie, watched William curiously. He smiled at her. Neither of them had any idea that young Maggie would fall to her death from the lighthouse observation platform in the years to come.

William returned to the rowboat to deliver another gift. This gift was not for the lighthouse keeper.

He rowed along the backside of the island, passing the place where the Confederate soldier had shot at him and his friends more than ten years earlier.

He found Mary Ellen Hadley at her home. It would be a home she would enjoy for almost the next century and a half. The gift was not for her either. The gift was for a family that would one day own a beach house on the island. One day many, many years from now.

He handed Mary Ellen the wooden chest. Inside of the chest, the items included red silk, a glass jar, a silver key, and a note that William had copied that morning from another note he had carried with him since December 1864. They looked at the contents together and closed the rounded top.

"Put it in a safe place," he told Mary Ellen.

"Where?"

William thought of what Caris had said to him in his parlor more than a decade earlier. He had thought about it several times over the years.

"In your attic," he answered. "Nature will take care of the rest when the time comes."

ACKNOWLEDGMENTS

BACK WHEN I WAS FINISHING LAW SCHOOL IN 1995, I HAD A notion to write a novel. I had no idea what it would be about. As the years passed, ideas for a book came and went, but nothing really took root. And then one day, it hit me. I'd write a story with the main characters based on my own family. The perfect setting would be Daufuskie Island, which is truly a slice of Lowcountry heaven. The story had to have magic. A fun beach novel should have magic, after all.

When I started writing, our three children were Camille, Brigitte, and Tom. They inspired the characters of Katie, Abby, and Will. I worked on the novel over a couple of years in my free time, and along the way, we adopted Faith. Yep, she's Grace in the book. I'd like to give a huge thank-you to Camille, Brigitte, Tom, and Faith for letting me base the St. John children on each of you. I also need to acknowledge Brigitte's good sense of humor when she pointed out that the character based on her (Abby) was the troublemaker, whose wish started the whole mess in the story. For the record, Brigitte is not a troublemaker in real life. And Camille cannot fly.

I'd like to thank all of those who read my initial draft and who offered tremendously helpful comments and suggestions. Special thanks to Peggy Ashley for your editing insight. Thank you also to Allen Mendenhall, David Boy, and Lori Long.

Thank you to Mountain Arbor Press for agreeing to publish my novel and its professional staff who made the final editing and publishing process a walk in the park.

Haig Point is a real place, and thank you to HPCCA for allowing me to use it and the Haig Point lighthouse in my book. Thank you to Bloody Point and Freeport Marina for your approval too. I'd also like to thank Captain Skinny for letting me use his boat, the *Black Dagger,* to make the story more authentic. (If anyone is looking for some good family fun on Hilton Head Island, you cannot go wrong with a sail on the *Black Dagger.*)

I would have never been able to complete this project without the patience and support of my wonderful wife, Lara, to whom I especially owe a big thank you. Let's see what the next twenty years will bring.

And, of course, I thank God for putting the story there for me to work through and find. I had a lot of fun writing it.

ABOUT THE AUTHOR

JOHN LUEDER AND HIS FAMILY LIVE NEAR ATLANTA AND
spend time on Daufuskie Island whenever possible. In
addition to working on his next novel, John is an attorney;
the founding partner of the law firm of Lueder, Larkin &
Hunter, LLC; a travel and sailing enthusiast; and a diehard
fan of Canada's best band ever, Barenaked Ladies.